HUMANITY 2.0

HUMANITY

2.0

Edited by

Alex Shvartsman

an imprint of

ARC
MANOR
Rockville, Maryland

ISBN: 978-1-61242-309-8

www.PhoenixPick.com
Great Science Fiction & Fantasy
Free Ebook Every Month

Published by Phoenix Pick
an imprint of Arc Manor
P. O. Box 10339
Rockville, MD 20849-0339
www.ArcManor.com

CONTENTS

FOREWORD

_____Alex Shvartsman_____

"The stars are not for Man." —Sir Arthur C. Clarke, *Childhood's End*

"That is, not for biological humans 1.0." —Guilio Prisco

In his article for *KurzweilAI*, Guilio Prisco writes: "*Ultimately, I think space will not be colonized by squishy, frail and short-lived flesh-and-blood humans.... It will be up to our postbiological mind children, implemented as pure software based on human uploads and AI subsystems, to explore other stars and colonize the universe.*" Mr. Prisco is not a science fiction writer. He's a scientist, futurist and transhumanist who was, at one point, a senior manager in the European Space Agency. He's dead-serious about humanity exploring the stars sooner rather than later, and he's not alone.

In 2012, former astronaut Dr. Mae Jamison founded the 100 Year Starship project. Their stated mission is to make human interstellar travel capabilities a reality within a century. It may be a lofty goal, but they're funded by the likes of NASA and DARPA. Some of the world's smartest people are investing time, effort, and money into the possibility of interstellar travel in our—or perhaps our children's—lifetime, and no technology that may get our descendants *out there* is off the table. "*Eventually, they will travel between the stars as radiation and light beams,*" concludes Prisco.

When asked about the famous Clarke quote, Prisco is quick to point out that it was merely a narrative device used in *Childhood's End*.

Like most science fiction writers, Clarke was a vocal proponent of space travel. He wrote several pop-science books on the subject. And, of course, a great many stories.

Science and science fiction are ever in conversation. Writers look to the latest breakthroughs and emerging technologies to inspire their fiction, while scientists and engineers often turn to SF tales both to challenge themselves and to better understand how scientific innovation might affect society. Conscious of this symbiotic relationship, organizers regularly invite science fiction writers to speak at the 100 Year Starship Symposium. As of 2015, they instituted the Canopus Award for Interstellar Writing to encourage and recognize science fiction that examines interstellar travel. The inaugural winner in the short-form fiction category was "The Waves" by Ken Liu, the story which opens this anthology. (Full disclosure: my own "The Race for Arcadia" was one of the runners-up.)

"The Waves" and other stories collected in this book examine how interstellar flight might change humanity itself. Will we choose to upload our minds into a singularity? Enhance ourselves with alien DNA? Or will our bodies remain the same, but our culture and societal norms adapt to accommodate for effects of time dilation, or become subsumed by advanced alien cultures?

What will it mean to be human in such a future?

Ken Liu's story is a millennia-spanning saga that examines many different metamorphoses humanity might undergo, while holding a staunchly positive view of our future selves. Kenneth Schneyer's tale counters with a far more pessimistic outlook of human nature and its influence on the other species in the universe.

Our authors imagine different modes of interstellar travel: from cryo-ships in stories by Jody Lynn Nye and Caroline M. Yoachim, to the enormous generation vessels of Angus McIntyre and Alvaro Zinos-Amaro, to the instant-transfer portals of Nancy Fulda and David Walton. Whether uploaded, genetically re-engineered, or merged with an alien consciousness, the characters in these stories consistently retain at least some of their humanity—for better or for worse.

I selected two stories to serve as counter-points to the rest. In John Varley's "Picnic on Nearside" it is the aliens who come to us, and take over Earth; the remnants of humanity must adapt to life on the

Moon, outer planets and the asteroid belt. When faced with a difficult decision, the people in Robert Silverberg's "The Iron Star" make arguably the most human—but not humane—choices.

Finally, Mike Resnick brings a man forever changed by his journey to the stars back to Earth in the Hugo-nominated "The Homecoming," and Robert J. Sawyer's characters rediscover the stars in "Star Light, Star Bright."

Although their visions may differ wildly, these writers—as well as scientists and engineers from around the world—vividly imagine a future where our species will reach beyond Earth. And while space may not be hospitable to the flesh-and-blood *Homo sapiens* of today, to dream of reaching the stars is among the most human things we can do.

THE WAVES

Ken Liu

LONG AGO, just after heaven was separated from earth, Nü Wa wandered along the bank of the Yellow River, savoring the feel of the rich loess against the bottom of her feet.

All around her, flowers bloomed in all the colors of the rainbow, as pretty as the eastern edge of the sky, where Nü Wa had to patch a leak made by petty warring gods with a paste made of melted gemstones. Deer and buffalo dashed across the plains, and golden carp and silvery crocodiles frolicked in the water.

But she was all alone. There was no one to converse with her, no one to share all this beauty.

She sat down next to the water, and, scooping up a handful of mud, began to sculpt. Before long, she had created a miniature version of herself: a round head, a long torso, arms and legs and tiny hands and fingers that she carefully carved out with a sharp bamboo skewer.

She cupped the tiny, muddy figure in her hands, brought it up to her mouth, and breathed the breath of life into it. The figure gasped, wriggled in Nü Wa's hands, and began to babble.

Nü Wa laughed. Now she would be alone no longer. She sat the little figure down on the bank of the Yellow River, scooped up another handful of mud, and began to sculpt again.

Man was thus created from earth, and to earth he would return, always.

"What happened next?" a sleepy voice asked.

"I'll tell you tomorrow night," Maggie Chao said. "It's time to sleep now."

She tucked in Bobby, five, and Lydia, six, turned off the bedroom light, and closed the door behind her.

She stood still for a moment, listening, as if she could hear the flow of photons streaming past the smooth, spinning hull of the ship.

The great solar sail strained silently in the vacuum of space as the *Sea Foam* spiraled away from the sun, accelerating year after year until the sun had shifted into a dull red, a perpetual, diminishing sunset.

There's something you should see, João, Maggie's husband and the First Officer, whispered in her mind. They were able to speak to each other through a tiny optical-neural interface chip implanted in each of their brains. The chips stimulated genetically-modified neurons in the language-processing regions of the cortex with pulses of light, activating them in the same way that actual speech would have.

Maggie sometimes thought of the implant as a kind of miniature solar sail, where photons strained to generate thought.

João thought of the technology in much less romantic terms. Even a decade after the operation, he still didn't like the way they could be in each other's heads. He understood the advantages of the communication system, which allowed them to stay constantly in touch, but it felt clumsy and alienating, as though they were slowly turning into cyborgs; machines. He never used it unless it was urgent.

I'll be there, Maggie said, and quickly made her way up to the research deck, closer to the center of the ship. Here, the gravity simulated by the spinning hull was lighter, and the colonists joked that the location of the labs helped people think better because more oxygenated blood flowed to the brain.

Maggie Chao had been chosen for the mission because she was an expert on self-contained ecosystems and also because she was young and fertile. With the ship traveling at a low fraction of the speed of light, it would take close to four hundred years (by the ship's frame of reference) to reach 61 Virginis, even taking into account the modest time-dilation effects. That required planning for children and grandchildren so that, one day, the colonists' descendants might carry the memory of the three hundred original explorers onto the surface of an alien world.

She met João in the lab. He handed her a display pad without saying anything. He always gave her time to come to her own conclusions about something new without his editorial comment. That was one of the first things she liked about him when they started dating, years ago.

"Extraordinary," she said as she glanced at the abstract. "First time Earth has tried to contact us in a decade."

Many on Earth had thought the *Sea Foam* a folly, a propaganda effort from a government unable to solve real problems. How could sending a centuries-long mission to the stars be justified when there were still people dying of hunger and diseases on Earth? After launch, communication with Earth had been kept to a minimum and then cut. The new administration did not want to keep paying for those expensive ground-based antennas. Perhaps they preferred to forget about this ship of fools.

But now, they had reached out across the emptiness of space to say something.

As she read the rest of the message, her expression gradually shifted from excitement to disbelief.

"They believe the gift of immortality should be shared by all of humanity," João said. "Even the farthest wanderers."

The transmission described a new medical procedure. A small, modified virus—a molecular nano-computer, for those who liked to think in those terms—replicated itself in somatic cells and roamed up and down the double helices of DNA strands, repairing damage, suppressing certain segments and overexpressing others, and the net effect was to halt cellular senescence and stop aging.

Humans would no longer have to die.

Maggie looked into João's eyes. "Can we replicate the procedure here?" *We will live to walk on another world, to breathe unrecycled air.*

"Yes," he said. "It will take some time, but I'm sure we can." Then he hesitated. "But the children..."

Bobby and Lydia were not the result of chance but the interplay of a set of careful algorithms involving population planning, embryo selection, genetic health, life expectancy, and rates of resource renewal and consumption.

Every gram of matter aboard the *Sea Foam* was accounted for. There was enough to support a stable population, but little room for error. The children's births had to be timed so that they would have enough time to learn what they needed to learn from their parents, and then take their place as their elders died a peaceful death, cared for by the machines.

"...would be the last children to be born until we land," Maggie finished João's thought. The *Sea Foam* had been designed for a precise population mix of adults and children. Supplies, energy, and thousands of other parameters were all tied to that mix. There was some margin of safety, but the ship could not support a population composed entirely of vigorous, immortal adults at the height of their caloric needs.

"We could either die and let our children grow," João said, "or we could live forever and keep them always as children."

Maggie imagined it: the virus could be used to stop the process of growth and maturation in the very young. The children would stay children for centuries, childless themselves.

Something finally clicked in Maggie's mind.

"That's why Earth is suddenly interested in us again," she said. "Earth is just a very big ship. If no one is going to die, they'll run out of room eventually, too. Now there is no other problem on Earth more pressing. They'll have to follow us and move into space."

You wonder why there are so many stories about how people came to be? It's because all true stories have many tellings.

Tonight, let me tell you another one.

There was a time when the world was ruled by the Titans, who lived on Mount Othrys. The greatest and bravest of the Titans was Cronus, who once led them in a rebellion against Uranus, his father and a tyrant. After Cronus killed Uranus, he became the king of the gods.

But as time went on, Cronus himself became a tyrant. Perhaps out of fear that what he had done to his own father would happen to him, Cronus swallowed all his children as soon as they were born.

Rhea, the wife of Cronus, gave birth to a new son, Zeus. To save the boy, she wrapped a stone in a blanket like a baby and fooled Cronus into swallowing that. The real baby Zeus she sent away to Crete, where he grew up drinking goat milk.

Don't make that face. I hear goat milk is quite tasty.

When Zeus was finally ready to face his father, Rhea fed Cronus a bitter wine that caused him to vomit up the children he had swallowed; Zeus's brothers and sisters. For ten years, Zeus led the Olympians—for that was the name by which Zeus and his siblings would come to be known—in a bloody war against his father and the Titans. In the end, the new gods won against the old, and Cronus and the Titans were cast into lightless Tartarus.

The Olympians went on to have children of their own, for that was the way of the world. Zeus himself had many children, some mortal, some not. One of his favorites was Athena, the goddess who was born from his head, from his thoughts alone. There are many stories about them as well, which I will tell you another time.

But some of the Titans who did not fight by the side of Cronus were spared. One of these, Prometheus, molded a race of beings out of clay, and it is said that he then leaned down to whisper to them the words of wisdom that gave them life.

We don't know what he taught the new creatures, us. But this was a god who had lived to see sons rise up against fathers, each new generation replacing the old, remaking the world afresh each time. We can guess what he might have said.

Rebel. Change is the only constant.

"Death is the easy choice," Maggie said.

"It is the right choice," João said.

Maggie wanted to keep the argument in their heads, but João refused. He wanted to speak with lips, tongue, bursts of air, the old way.

Every gram of unnecessary mass had been shaved off the *Sea Foam*'s construction. The walls were thin and the rooms closely packed. Maggie and João's voices echoed through the decks and halls.

All over the ship, other families, who were having the same argument in their heads, stopped to listen.

"The old must die to make way for the new," João said. "You knew that we would not live to see the *Sea Foam* land when you signed up for this. Our children's children, generations down the line, are meant to inherit the new world."

"We can land on the new world ourselves. We don't have to leave all the hard work to our unborn descendants."

"We need to pass on a viable human culture for the new colony. We have no idea what long-term consequences this treatment will have on our mental health—"

"Then let's do the job we signed up for: exploration. Let's figure it out—"

"—if we give in to this temptation, we'll land as a bunch of four-hundred-year-olds who were afraid to die and whose ideas were ossified from old Earth. How can we teach our children the value of sacrifice, of the meaning of heroism, of beginning afresh? We'll barely be human."

"We stopped being human the moment we agreed to this mission!" Maggie paused to get her voice under control. "Face it, the birth allocation algorithms don't care about us, or our children. We're nothing more than vessels for the delivery of a planned, optimal mix of genes to our destination. Do you really want generations to grow and die in here, knowing nothing but this narrow metal tube? I worry about *their* mental health."

"Death is essential to the growth of our species." His voice was filled with faith, and she heard in it his hope that it was enough for both of them.

"It's a myth that we must die to retain our humanity." Maggie looked at her husband, her heart in pain. There was a divide between them, as inexorable as the dilation of time.

She spoke to him now inside his head. She imagined her thoughts, now transformed into photons, pushing against his brain, trying to illuminate the gap. *We stop being human at the moment we give in to death.*

João looked back at her. He said nothing, either in her mind or aloud, which was his way of saying all that he needed to say.

They stayed like that for a long time.

God first created mankind to be immortal, much like the angels.

Before Adam and Eve chose to eat from the Tree of the Knowledge of Good and Evil, they did not grow old and they never became sick. During the day, they cultivated the Garden, and at night, they enjoyed each other's company.

Yes, I suppose the Garden was a bit like the hydroponics deck.

Sometimes the angels visited them, and—according to Milton, who was born too late to get into the regular Bible—they conversed and speculated about everything: Did the Earth revolve around the Sun or was it the other way around? Was there life on other planets? Did angels also have sex?

Oh no, I'm not joking. You can look it up in the computer.

So Adam and Eve were forever young and perpetually curious. They did not need death to give their life purpose, to be motivated to learn, to work, to love, to give existence meaning.

If that story is true, then we were never meant to die. And the knowledge of good and evil was really the knowledge of regret.

"You know some very strange stories, Gran-Gran," six-year old Sara said.

"They're old stories," Maggie said. "When I was a little girl, my grandmother told me many stories and I did a lot of reading."

"Do you want me to live forever like you, and not grow old and die someday like my mother?"

"I can't tell you what to do, sweetheart. You'll have to figure that out when you're older."

"Like the knowledge of good and evil?"

"Something like that."

She leaned down and kissed her great-great-great-great—she had long lost count—granddaughter, as gently as she could. Like all children born in the low gravity of the *Sea Foam*, her bones were thin and delicate, like a bird's. Maggie turned off the nightlight and left.

Though she would pass her four hundredth birthday in another month, Maggie didn't look a day older than thirty-five. The recipe for the fountain of youth, Earth's last gift to the colonists before they lost all communications, worked well.

She stopped and gasped. A small boy, about ten years in age, waited in front of the door to her room.

Bobby, she said. Except for the very young, who did not yet have the implants, all the colonists now conversed through thoughts rather than speech. It was faster and more private.

The boy looked at her, saying nothing and thinking nothing at her. She was struck by how like his father he was. He had the same expressions, the same mannerisms, even the same ways to speak by not speaking.

She sighed, opened the door, and walked in after him.

One more month, he said, sitting on the edge of the couch so that his feet didn't dangle.

Everybody on the ship was counting down the days. In one more month they'd be in orbit around the fourth planet of 61 Virginis; their destination, a new Earth.

After we land, will you change your mind about—she hesitated, but went on after a moment—*your appearance?*

Bobby shook his head, and a hint of boyish petulance crossed his face. *Mom, I've made my decision a long time ago. Let it go. I like the way I am.*

In the end, the men and women of the *Sea Foam* had decided to leave the choice of eternal youth to each individual.

The cold mathematics of the ship's enclosed ecosystem meant that when someone chose immortality, a child would have to remain a child until someone else on the ship decided to grow old and die, opening up a new slot for an adult.

João chose to age and die. Maggie chose to stay young. They sat together as a family and it felt a bit like a divorce.

"One of you will get to grow up," João said.

"Which one?" Lydia asked.

"We think you should decide," João said, glancing at Maggie, who nodded reluctantly.

Maggie had thought it was unfair and cruel of her husband to put such a choice before their children. How could children decide if they wanted to grow up when they had no real idea what that meant?

"It's no more unfair than you and I deciding whether we want to be immortal," João had said. "We have no real idea what that means either. It is terrible to put such a choice before them, but to decide *for* them would be even more cruel." Maggie had to agree that he had a point.

It seemed like they were asking the children to take sides. But maybe that was the point.

Lydia and Bobby looked at each other, and they seemed to reach a silent understanding. Lydia got up, walked to João, and hugged him. At the same time, Bobby came and hugged Maggie.

"Dad," Lydia said, "when my time comes, I will choose the same as you." João tightened his arms around her, and nodded.

Then Lydia and Bobby switched places and hugged their parents again, pretending that everything was fine.

For those who refused the treatment, life went on as planned. As João grew old, Lydia grew up: first an awkward teenager, then a beautiful young woman. She went into engineering, as predicted by her aptitude tests, and decided that she *did* like Catherine, the shy young doctor that the computers suggested would be a good mate for her.

"Will you grow old and die with me?" Lydia asked the blushing Catherine one day.

They married and had two daughters of their own—to replace them, when their time came.

"Do you ever regret choosing this path?" João asked her one time. He was very old and ill by then, and in another two weeks the computers would administer the drugs to allow him to fall asleep and not wake up.

"No," Lydia said, holding his hand with both of hers. "I'm not afraid to step out of the way when something new comes to take my place."

But who's to say that we aren't the 'something new'? Maggie thought.

In a way, her side was winning the argument. Over the years, more and more colonists had decided to join the ranks of the immortals. But Lydia's descendants had always stubbornly refused. Sara was the last untreated child on the ship. Maggie knew she would miss the nightly story times when she grew up.

Bobby was frozen at the physical age of ten. He and the other perpetual children integrated only uneasily into the life of the colonists. They had decades—sometimes centuries—of experience, but retained juvenile bodies and brains. They possessed adult knowledge, but kept the emotional range and mental flexibility of children. They could be both old and young in the same moment.

There was a great deal of tension and conflict about what roles they should play on the ship, and, occasionally, parents who once thought they wanted to live forever would give up their spots when their children demanded it of them.

But Bobby never asked to grow up.

My brain has the plasticity of a ten-year-old's. Why would I want to give that up? Bobby said.

Maggie had to admit that she always felt more comfortable with Lydia and her descendants. Even though they had all chosen to die, as João did, which could be seen as a kind of rebuke of her decision, she found herself better able to understand their lives and play a role in them.

With Bobby, on the other hand, she couldn't imagine what went on in his head. She sometimes found him a little creepy, which she agreed was a bit hypocritical, considering he only made the same choice she did.

But you won't experience what it's like to be grown, she said. *To love as a man and not a boy.*

He shrugged, unable to miss what he never had. *I can pick up new languages quickly. It's easy for me to absorb a new worldview. I'll always like new things.*

Bobby switched to speech, and his boyish voice rose as it filled with excitement and longing. "If we meet new life and new civilization down there, we'll need people like me, the forever children, to learn about them and understand them without fear."

It had been a long time since Maggie had really listened to her son. She was moved. She nodded, accepting his choice.

Bobby's face opened in a beautiful smile, the smile of a ten-year-old boy who had seen more than almost every human who had ever lived.

"Mom, I'll get that chance. I came to tell you that we've received the results of the first close-up scans of 61 Virginis e. It's inhabited."

Under the *Sea Foam*, the planet spun slowly. Its surface was covered by a grid of hexagonal and pentagonal patches, each a thousand miles across. About half of the patches were black as obsidian, while the rest were a grainy tan. 61 Virginis e reminded Maggie of a soccer ball.

Maggie stared at the three aliens standing in front of her in the shuttle bay, each about six feet tall. The metallic bodies, barrel-shaped and segmented, rested on four stick-thin, multi-jointed legs.

When the vehicles first approached the *Sea Foam*, the colonists had thought they were tiny scout ships until scans confirmed the absence of any organic matter. Then the colonists had thought they were autonomous probes until they came right up to the ship's camera, displayed their hands, and lightly tapped the lens.

Yes, *hands*. Midway up each of the metallic bodies, two long, sinuous arms emerged and terminated in soft, supple hands made of a fine alloy mesh. Maggie looked down at her own hands. The alien hands looked just like hers: four slender fingers, an opposable thumb, flexible joints.

On the whole, the aliens reminded Maggie of robotic centaurs.

At the very top of each alien body was a spherical protuberance studded with clusters of glass lenses, like compound eyes. Other than the eyes, this "head" was also covered by a dense array of pins attached to actuators that moved in synchrony like the tentacles of a sea anemone.

The pins shimmered as though a wave moved through them. Gradually, they took on the appearance of pixelated eyebrows, lips, eyelids—a face, a human face.

The alien began to speak. It sounded like English but Maggie couldn't make it out. The phonemes, like the shifting patterns of the pins, seemed elusive, just beyond coherence.

It is *English*, Bobby said to Maggie, *after centuries of pronunciation drift. He's saying 'Welcome back to humanity.'*

The fine pins on the alien face shifted, unveiling a smile. Bobby continued to translate. *We left Earth long after your departure, but we were faster, and passed you in transit centuries ago. We've been waiting for you.*

Maggie felt the world shift around her. She looked around, and many of the older colonists, the immortals, looked stunned.

But Bobby, the eternal child, stepped forward. "Thank you," he said aloud, and smiled back.

Let me tell you a story, Sara. We humans have always relied on stories to keep the fear of the unknown at bay.

I've told you how the Mayan gods created people out of maize, but did you know that before that, there were several other attempts at creation?

First came the animals: brave jaguar and beautiful macaw, flat fish and long serpent, the great whale and the lazy sloth, the iridescent iguana and the nimble bat. (We can look up pictures for all of these on the computer later.) But the animals only squawked and growled, and could not speak their creators' names.

So the gods kneaded a race of beings out of mud. But the mud men could not hold their shape. Their faces drooped, softened by water, yearning to rejoin the earth whence they were taken. They could not speak but only gurgled incoherently. They grew lopsided and were unable to procreate, to perpetuate their own existence.

The gods' next effort is the one of most interest to us. They created a race of wooden manikins, like dolls. The articulated joints allowed their limbs to move freely. The carved faces allowed their lips to flap and eyes to open. The stringless puppets lived in houses and villages, and went busily about their lives.

But the gods found that the wooden men had neither souls nor minds, and so they could not praise their makers properly. They sent a great flood to destroy the wooden men, and asked the animals of the jungle to attack them. When the anger of the gods was over, the wooden men had become monkeys.

And only then did the gods turn to maize.

Many have wondered if the wooden men were really content to lose to the children of the maize. Perhaps they're still waiting in the shadows for an opportunity to come back, for creation to reverse its course.

The black hexagonal patches were solar panels, Atax, the leader of the three envoys from 61 Virginis e, explained. Together, they provided the power needed to support human habitation on the planet. The tan patches were cities, giant computing arrays where trillions of humans lived as virtual patterns of computation.

When Atax and the others colonists had first arrived, 61 Viriginis e was not particularly hospitable to life from Earth. It was too hot, the air was too poisonous, and the existing alien life—, mostly primitive microbes, was quite deadly.

But Atax and the others who had stepped onto the surface were not human, not in the sense Maggie would have understood the term. They were composed of more metal than water, and they were no longer trapped by the limits of organic chemistry. The colonists quickly constructed forges and foundries, and their descendants soon spread out across the globe.

Most of the time they chose to merge into the Singularity, the overall World-Mind that was both artificial and organic, where eons passed in a second as thought was processed at the speed of quantum computation. In the world of bits and qubits, they lived as gods.

But sometimes, when they felt the ancestral longing for physicality, they could choose to become individuals and be embodied in machines, as Atax and his companions were. Here, they lived in the slow-time, the time of atoms and stars.

There was no more line between the ghost and the machine.

"This is what humanity looks like now," Atax said, spinning around slowly to display his metal body for the benefit of the colonists on the *Sea Foam*. "Our bodies are made of steel and titanium, and our brains graphene and silicon. We are practically indestructible. Look, we can even move through space without the need for ships, suits, layers of protection. We have left corruptible flesh behind."

Atax and the others gazed intently at the ancient humans around them. Maggie stared back into their dark lenses, trying to fathom how the machines felt. Curiosity? Nostalgia? Pity?

Maggie shuddered at the shifting, metallic faces, a crude imitation of flesh and blood. She looked over at Bobby, who appeared ecstatic.

"You may join us, if you wish, or continue as you are. It is of course difficult to decide when you have no experience of our mode of existence. Yet you must choose. We cannot choose for you."

Something new, Maggie thought.

Even eternal youth and eternal life did not appear so wonderful compared to the freedom of being a machine, a thinking machine endowed with the austere beauty of crystalline matrices instead of the messy imperfections of living cells.

At last, humanity has advanced beyond evolution into the realm of intelligent design.

"I'm not afraid," Sara said.

She had asked to stay behind for a few minutes with Maggie after all the others had left. Maggie gave her a long hug, and the little girl squeezed her back.

"Do you think Gran-Gran João would have been disappointed in me?" Sara asked. "I'm not making the choice he would have made."

"I know he would have wanted you to decide for yourself," Maggie said. "People change, as a species and as individuals. We don't know what he would have chosen if he had been offered your choice. But no matter what, never let the past pick your life for you."

She kissed Sara on the cheek and let go. A machine came to take Sara away by the hand so that she could be transformed.

She's the last of the untreated children, Maggie thought. *And now she'll be the first to become a machine.*

Though Maggie refused to watch the transformation of the others, at Bobby's request, she watched as her son was replaced piece by piece.

"You'll never have children," she said.

"On the contrary," he said, as he flexed his new metal hands, so much larger and stronger than his old hands, the hands of a child, "I will have countless children, born of my mind." His voice was a pleasant electronic hum, like a patient teaching program's. "They'll inherit from my thoughts as surely as I have inherited your genes. And some day, if they wish, I will construct bodies for them, as beautiful and functional as the ones I'm being fitted with."

He reached out to touch her arm, and the cold metal fingertips slid smoothly over her skin, gliding on nanostructures that flexed like living tissue. She gasped.

Bobby smiled as his face, a fine mesh of thousands of pins, rippled in amusement.

She recoiled from him involuntarily.

Bobby's rippling face turned serious, froze, and then showed no expression at all.

She understood the unspoken accusation. What right did she have to feel revulsion? She treated her body as a machine too, just a machine of lipids and proteins, of cells and muscles. Her mind was maintained in a shell too, a shell of flesh that had long outlasted its designed-for life. She was as "unnatural" as he.

Still, she cried as she watched her son disappear into a frame of animated metal.

He can't cry any more, she kept on thinking, as if that was the only thing that divided her from him.

Bobby was right. Those who were frozen as children were quicker to decide to upload. Their minds were flexible, and to them, to change from flesh to metal was merely a hardware upgrade.

The older immortals, on the other hand, lingered, unwilling to leave their past behind, their last vestiges of humanity. But one by one, they succumbed as well.

For years, Maggie remained the only organic human on 61 Virginis e, and perhaps the entire universe. The machines built a special house for her, one insulated from the heat and poison and ceaseless noise of the planet, and Maggie occupied herself by browsing through the *Sea Foam*'s archives, the records of humanity's long, dead past. The machines left her pretty much alone.

One day, a small machine, about two feet tall, came into her house and approached her hesitantly. It reminded her of a puppy.

"Who are you?" Maggie asked.

"I'm your grandchild," the little machine said.

"So Bobby has finally decided to have a child," Maggie said. "It took him long enough."

"I'm the 5,032,322th child of my parent."

Maggie felt dizzy. Soon after his transformation into a machine, Bobby had decided to go all the way and join the Singularity. They had not spoken to each other for a long time.

"What's your name?"

"I don't have a name in the sense you think of it. But why don't you call me Athena?"

"Why?"

"It's a name from a story my parent used to tell me when I was little."

Maggie looked at the little machine, and her expression softened. "How old are you?"

"That's a hard question to answer," Athena said. "We're born virtual and each second of our existence as part of the Singularity is composed of trillions of computation cycles. In that state, I have more thoughts in a second than you have had in your entire life."

Maggie looked at her granddaughter, a miniature mechanical centaur, freshly made and gleaming, and also a being much older and wiser than she by most measures.

"So why have you put on this disguise to make me think of you as a child?"

"Because I want to hear your stories," Athena said. "The ancient stories."

There are still young people, Maggie thought, *still something new. Why can't the old become new again?*

And so Maggie decided to upload as well, to rejoin her family.

In the beginning, the world was a great void crisscrossed by icy rivers full of venom. The venom congealed, dripped, and formed into Ymir, the first giant, and Auðumbla, a great ice cow.

Ymir fed on Auðumbla's milk and grew strong.

Of course you have never seen a cow. Well, it is a creature that gives milk, which you would have drunk if you were still...

I suppose it is a bit like how you absorbed electricity, at first in trickles, when you were still young, and then in greater measure as you grew older, to give you strength.

Ymir grew and grew until finally, three gods, the brothers Vili, and Vé, and Odin, slew him. Out of his carcass the gods created the world: his blood became the warm, salty sea, his flesh the rich, fertile earth, his bones the hard, plow-breaking hills, and his hair, the swaying, dark forests. Out of his wide brows the gods carved Midgard, the realm in which humans lived.

After the death of Ymir, the three brother gods walked along a beach. At the end of the beach, they came upon two trees leaning against each other. The gods fashioned two human figures out of their wood. One of the brother gods breathed life into the wooden figures, another endowed them with intelligence, and the third gave them sense and speech. And this was how Ask and Embla, the first man and the first woman, came to be.

You are skeptical that men and women were once made from trees? But you're made of metal. Who's to say trees wouldn't do just as well?

Now let me tell you the story behind the names. "Ask" comes from *ash*, a hard tree that is used to make a drill for fire. "Embla" comes from *vine*, a softer sort of wood that is easy to set on fire. The motion of twirling a fire drill until the kindling is inflamed reminded the people who told this story of an analogy with sex, and that may be the real story they wanted to tell.

Once your ancestors would have been scandalized that I speak to you of sex so frankly. The word is still a mystery to you, but without the allure that it once held. Before we found how to live forever, sex and children were the closest we came to immortality.

Like a thriving hive, the Singularity began to send a constant stream of colonists away from 61 Virginis e.

One day, Athena came to Maggie and told her that she was ready to be embodied and lead her own colony.

At the thought of not seeing Athena again, Maggie felt an emptiness. *So it was possible to love again, even as a machine.*

Why don't I come with you? she asked. *It will be good for your children to have some connection with the past.*

And Athena's joy at her request was electric and contagious.

Sara came to say goodbye to her, but Bobby did not show up. He had never forgiven her for her rejection of him the moment he became a machine.

Even the immortals have regrets, she thought.

And so a million consciousnesses embodied themselves in metal shells shaped like robot centaurs, and like a swarm of bees leaving to found a new hive, they lifted into the air, tucked their limbs together so that they were shaped like graceful teardrops, and launched themselves straight up.

Up and up they went, through the acrid air, through the crimson sky, out of the gravity well of the heavy planet, and steering by the shifting flow of the solar wind and the dizzying spin of the galaxy, they set out across the sea of stars.

Light year after light year, they crossed the void between the stars. They passed the planets that had already been settled by earlier colonies, worlds now thriving with their own hexagonal arrays of solar panels and their own humming Singularities.

Onwards, they flew, searching for the perfect planet, the new world that would be their new home.

While they flew, they huddled together against the cold emptiness that was space. Intelligence, complexity, life, computation—everything seemed so small and insignificant against the great and eternal void. They felt the longing of distant black holes and the majestic glow of exploding novas. And they pulled closer to each other, seeking comfort in their common humanity.

As they flew on, half dreaming, half awake, Maggie told the colonists stories, weaving her radio waves among the constellation of colonists like strands of spider silk.

There are many stories of the Dreamtime, most secret and sacred. But a few have been told to outsiders, and this is one of them.

In the beginning there was the sky and the earth, and the earth was as flat and featureless as the gleaming titanium alloy surface of our bodies.

But under the earth, the spirits lived and dreamed.

And time began to flow, and the spirits woke from their slumber.

They broke through the surface, where they took on the forms of animals: Emu, Koala, Platypus, Dingo, Kangaroo, Shark.... Some even took the shapes of humans. Their forms were not fixed, but could be changed at will.

They roamed over the earth and shaped it, stamping out valleys and pushing up hills, scraping the ground to make deserts, digging through it to make rivers.

And they gave birth to children, children who could not change forms: animals, plants, humans. These children were born from the Dreamtime but not of it.

When the spirits were tired, they sank back into the earth whence they came. And the children were left behind with only vague memories of the Dreamtime, the time before there was time.

But who is to say that they will not return to that state, to a time when they could change form at will, to a time where time had no meaning?

And they woke from her words into another dream.

One moment, they were suspended in the void of space, still light years from their destination. The next, they were surrounded by shimmering light.

No, not exactly *light*. Though the lenses mounted on their chassis could see far beyond the spectrum visible to primitive human eyes, this energy field around them vibrated at frequencies far above and below even their limits.

The energy field slowed down to match the subluminal flight of Maggie and the other colonists.

Not too far now.

The thought pushed against their consciousness like a wave, as though all their logic gates were vibrating in sympathy. The thought felt both alien and familiar.

Maggie looked at Athena, who was flying next to her.

Did you hear that? They said at the same time. Their thought strands tapped each other lightly, a caress with radio waves.

Maggie reached out into space with a thought strand, *You're human?*

29

A pause that lasted a billionth of a second, which seemed like an eternity at the speed they were moving.

We haven't thought of ourselves in that way in a long time.

And Maggie felt a wave of thoughts, images, feelings push into her from every direction. It was overwhelming.

In a nanosecond she experienced the joy of floating along the surface of a gas giant, part of a storm that could swallow Earth. She learned what it would be like to swim through the chromosphere of a star, riding white-hot plumes and flares that rose hundreds of thousands of miles. She felt the loneliness of making the entire universe your playground, yet having no home.

We came after you, and we passed you.

Welcome, ancient ones. Not too far now.

There was a time when we knew many stories of the creation of the world. Each continent was large and there were many peoples, each told their own story.

Then many peoples disappeared, and their stories forgotten.

This is one that survived. Twisted, mangled, retold to fit what strangers want to hear, there is nonetheless some truth left in it.

In the beginning the world was void and without light, and the spirits lived in the darkness.

The Sun woke up first, and he caused the water vapors to rise into the sky and baked the land dry. The other spirits—Man, Leopard, Crane, Lion, Zebra, Wildebeest, and even Hippopotamus—rose up next. They wandered across the plains, talking excitedly with each other.

But then the Sun set, and the animals and Man sat in darkness, too afraid to move. Only when morning came again did everyone start going again.

But Man was not content to wait every night. One night, Man invented fire to have his own sun, heat and light which obeyed his will, and which divided him from the animals that night and forever after.

So Man was always yearning for the light, the light that gives him life and the light to which he will return.

And at night, around the fire, they told each other the true stories, again and again.

Maggie chose to become part of the light.

She shed her chassis, her home and her body for such a long time. Had it been centuries? Millennia? Eons? Such measures of time no longer had any meaning.

Patterns of energy now, Maggie and the others learned to coalesce, stretch, shimmer, and radiate. She learned how to suspend herself between stars, her consciousness a ribbon across both time and space.

She careened from one edge of the galaxy to the other.

One time, she passed right through the pattern that was now Athena. Maggie felt the child as a light tingling, like laughter.

Isn't this lovely, Gran-gran? Come visit Sara and me sometime!

But it was too late for Maggie to respond. Athena was already too far away.

I miss my chassis.

That was Bobby, whom she met hovering next to a black hole.

For a few thousand years, they gazed at the black hole together from beyond the event horizon.

This is very lovely, he said. *But sometimes I think I prefer my old shell.*

You're getting old, she said. *Just like me.*

They pressed against each other, and that region of the universe lit up briefly like an ion storm laughing.

And they said goodbye to each other.

This is a nice planet, Maggie thought.

It was a small planet, rather rocky, mostly covered by water.

She landed on a large island, near the mouth of a river.

The sun hovered overhead, warm enough that she could see steam rising from the muddy riverbanks. Lightly, she glided over the alluvial plains.

The mud was too tempting. She stopped, condensed herself until her energy patterns were strong enough. Churning the water, she scooped a mound of the rich, fertile mud onto the bank. Then she sculpted the mound until it resembled a man: arms akimbo, legs splayed, a round head with vague indentations and protrusions for eyes, nose, mouth.

She looked at the sculpture of João for a while, caressed it, and left it to dry in the sun.

Looking about herself, she saw blades of grass covered with bright silicon beads and black flowers that tried to absorb every bit of sunlight. She saw silver shapes darting through the brown water and golden shadows gliding through the indigo sky. She saw great scale-covered bodies lumbering and bellowing in the distance, and close by, a great geyser erupted near the river, and rainbows appeared in the warm mist.

She was all alone. There was no one to converse with her, no one to share all this beauty.

She heard a nervous rustling and looked for the source of the sound. A little ways from the river, tiny creatures with eyes studded all over their heads like diamonds peered out of the dense forests, made of trees with triangular trunks and pentagonal leaves.

Closer and closer, she drifted to those creatures. Effortlessly, she reached inside them, and took ahold of the long chains of a particular molecule, their instructions for the next generation. She made a small tweak, and then let go.

The creatures yelped, and skittered away at the strange sensation of having their insides adjusted.

She had done nothing drastic, just a small adjustment, a nudge in the right direction. The change would continue to mutate and the mutations would accumulate, long after she left. In another few hundred generations, the changes would be enough to cause a spark, a spark that would feed itself until the creatures would start to think of keeping a piece of the sun alive at night, of naming things, of telling stories to each other about how everything came to be. They would be able to choose.

Something new in the universe. Someone new to the family.

But for now, it was time to return to the stars.

Maggie began to rise from the island. Below her, the sea sent wave after wave to crash against the shore, each wave catching and surpassing the one before it, reaching a little further up the beach. Bits of sea foam floated up and rode the wind to parts unknown.

JUSTICE AND SHADOW

_____Angus McIntyre_____

SHADOW WAS IN THE HOTROOM sweating out cancers when the signal came in. An encysted tumor, shiny and red as a pomegranate seed, gleamed for a moment against the skin of her arm before she brushed it away. Where the tumor had emerged, the edges of the wound were already beginning to close up. In a minute the black satin of her skin was once again whole and unblemished.

She had been meditating, cut off from the Weave, but the signal overrode her preferences and plunged her back abruptly into shared dataspace. Information flooded in as sounds and sensations: the chatter of the other triples working the same section of the sail, the flutter of telemetry from *Ortheia* and her own bodyware. There were whispers of message traffic from members of other clades—linesmen and spindoctors and thrusters—and even the distant murmur of the passengers; grubs and ghosts in their shielded bubbles. And above it all, imperious and urgent, the voice of the Chief Sailmaker calling assembly.

The module that held the Chief Sailmaker and her court was a steel teardrop dangling from the web of cables that trailed from the rim of *Ortheia*'s vast solar sail. The module, with its birthing dens and nurseries, machine shops and meeting halls, lay almost sixty kilometers from the cramped hotroom where Shadow floated. For Shadow to answer the call in person would have taken more than a day's travel, inching along the rim lines to the closest anchor point and then traversing the cable web node by node until she came to the right module.

The ship's Weave made that unnecessary. When Shadow joined the virtual assembly, the Chief Sailmaker was already seated lotus fashion on her raised dais, her broad face serene and impassive. Her avatar was larger than life-size, so that she dwarfed the consorts gathered on either side of her, her head almost touching the vaulted ceiling of the hall. The avatar's stylized design accentuated the maternal grace of her features, while behind her a live image of the vast disc of the sail surrounded her body like an aureole.

At the sight of the great mother of them all, in all her wisdom and fecundity, Shadow always felt a tightening in her throat. She bowed her head and let the Sailmaker's beneficent gaze sweep over her.

When she raised her head again, she saw that the hall was not at anything close to capacity. Barely a dozen triples were present. Shadow, with her triplemates Talent and Frost, found herself close to the front. She felt abruptly apprehensive, uncertain whether she had been summoned for praise or rebuke.

The Sailmaker began without preamble. "Glimmer, Arrow, Justice," she said. She looked around the hall again. "Who has spoken with them recently?"

Shadow's heart skipped at the mention of Justice. The other names meant nothing to her. She guessed that they must be the members of Justice's new triple.

The Sailmaker turned her head slowly. This time there was no doubt that she was looking at Shadow. Shadow flinched under her stare, then shook her head. Justice had cut all contact when she had left the triple. The messages Shadow had sent—pleading, reasoning, questioning—had gone unanswered.

"Glimmer's triple worked near us a ship-month ago," said a sailmaker named Prospect. Shadow thought back. About a ship-month ago, her own triple had passed close to Prospect's as they worked on a section of dust-damaged sail, close enough to exchange line-of-sight signals. Had Justice been there too, almost within reach, hidden only by the curve of the sail?

34

"You have not spoken to Glimmer since?" the Sailmaker asked.

"No," said Prospect.

"Anyone?"

No one spoke and Shadow felt abruptly anxious. Could something have happened? But surely she would have heard if there had been an accident.

"Sailmaker--" Prospect began.

The Sailmaker raised one delicate hand. "Glimmer's triple has left the sail," she said. A buzz of surprise rippled through the Weave.

To be a sailmaker was to live always on and around the sail. Sailmakers might occasionally visit one of the closer hab modules for rest or recreation, but that was as far as most ever went. Only a rare few ever traveled farther than that and never for long. To leave the sail permanently was unimaginable. It was a departure less final than death, perhaps, but not by much.

"They have left the sail," the Sailmaker repeated. "I am sending a triple to bring them back. Volunteers?"

Shadow was the first to step forward. After a moment's hesitation, Talent and Frost did the same.

The Sailmaker nodded slowly. "Yes," she said. "Shadow. You will be my emissary."

The hall shrank. The other triples disappeared, leaving Shadow's triple alone with the Sailmaker and her consorts.

"Hear me now," the Sailmaker said.

The three suns of the Cluster gleamed on the silver ocean of the sail as Shadow readied the spiders for travel. *Ortheia*'s destination, the white star Secundus, lay ahead of them, hidden now behind the dishes of a sensor array. Over Shadow's left shoulder, one tiny point of light was not a star but the stretched sail of *Ortheia*'s sister ship *Hikane*, tacking towards Mehmet's Star and its family of planets. *Ortheia* would call there too, but not for almost two decades. Shadow expected to be alive to see it, but it might be her last planetfall. Even with bodies designed for space—flesh that expelled cancers instead of hoarding them inside, bone that kept its density in microgravity, heart and lungs optimized for weightlessness—crewmembers died young. When Shadow next went home, it would be as a mute ghost in the Sailmaker's archives.

Frost emerged from the airlock, carrying a pack of feed-tubes and power cells. Tiny blue-white lights sparkled on the shoulders of her skinsuit, imitating the sky around them. Shadow looked up from her work for a moment and rested her eyes on the sky: a blazing jewel-box of stars so close to one another that ships could sail between them in less than a lifetime, skeins of dust and gas as rich as silk and insubstantial as dreams, the distant haze of the Milky Way. A song rose unbidden in her mind and she opened her mouth and sockets to sing before she remembered that she had written the song for Justice. She drove the song from her mind and bent to her task again.

"Ready?" asked Frost.

"Almost," said Shadow. She had had to rouse one of the spiders from hibernation. The mechanimal was still sluggish, its movements awkward and hesitant. She guided its clawed feet to the cable track and waited for it to tighten its grip on the wire.

"Justice was in your triple before," said Frost.

"Yes," said Shadow.

"If—" Frost began, then stopped. Shadow guessed what she was thinking: does Shadow want her back? And if she does return, which of us will have to go? Will it be Talent? Or me?

"I am going because the Sailmaker wishes it," Shadow said. "No other reason."

"Ah," said Frost.

The spider shivered and flexed its legs. Shadow placed her hand under its belly, feeling the pulse of its life through the thin ceramic plates of its carapace.

"Let's go," Shadow said.

At the anchor point where the cable joined the sail, they stopped to connect to a diagnostic node. The node was not accessible to sailmakers through the global Weave—an old jurisdictional dispute with the linesmen, who claimed everything that touched the trailing cables as theirs—but it grudgingly shared what it knew when interrogated directly.

In the node's records, Shadow found what she was looking for. The recording showed a small group of humans and mechanimals—Shadow counted three sailmakers and four spiders—threading their way between the branching radiator fins that crowned the anchor point.

"Is that them?" Talent said.

Shadow studied the recording, trying to recognize Justice from the patterns on her skinsuit. She could not decide if it was her or not. Justice might have changed the patterns after she left Shadow's triple. To change your triple was to change your own identity and everything that went with it.

"What do they have there?" asked Frost.

Something grayish-white was balanced upright on the back of the last spider. One of the sailmakers—Justice?—floated alongside as if watching over it. Whatever it was, it was taller and bulkier than the sailmaker; humanoid in shape but oddly rigid.

"Show us other views," Shadow told the node.

"No other recordings are available."

"Replay the recording we have already seen," Shadow ordered.

"The recording is no longer available."

"Are you denying us access?" Talent said. "Because—"

"The recording is no longer available," the node said.

From the anchor point, they started to descend the cable. The cable was as thick as Shadow's waist, a taut bowstring stretched among the stars. Smaller satellite cables ran parallel to it—power lines and guide wires and others whose function Shadow could not guess at.

The spiders transferred their grip from the rim lines that surrounded the sail to the guide wires without hesitation, their claws deftly finding the grip points on the wires, their legs adjusting smoothly to the new mode of locomotion. Moving in unison, they began to pull themselves out into the void.

Their riders were less comfortable with the transition. Sailmakers' lives were bounded by the sail; at any moment they had only to turn their heads to see it filling a third or more of the sky. They spent their working days clipped onto the arcing lines that stiffened the sail, the silvered canvas spread like a floor below them. And if

37

the sail itself was hardly more substantial than the vacuum that surrounded it—soap-bubble thin, so fragile that even a breath could damage it—its sheer scale still created an impression of solidity. Now it was at their backs and they were moving out into nothing, creeping along a cable that seemed to shrink ahead of them to the dimensions of a thread.

For the first time, Shadow fully understood that there was more to *Ortheia* than the sail. The sail was the ship's most visible structure, giving it life and motion. Yet as the spiders crept along the cable, Shadow was reminded that the cables trailing behind the sail constituted a huge and complex machine in their own right. They formed a dynamic mesh that stretched and shrank as needed, its delicate balance maintained by tensioning nodes studded along the great cables, watched over by an army of linesmen almost as numerous and industrious as the sailmakers.

In the end, Shadow thought, it was a question of perspective. If you asked a sailmaker what *Ortheia* was, you would get one answer. If you asked a linesman or a spindoctor, you would get another. And if you asked a passenger, they would probably tell you that the only things that counted were the modular lifesystems that *Ortheia* towed behind her: fragile bubbles of light and air suspended in the blackness, their shielded interiors home to human organisms too delicate to survive in space without protection.

The first module they came to was a machine pod, its cavernous interior filled with giant machines turning out the materials needed to keep the sailship in working order: womb-like bioreactors brewing compound to patch the sail, organic extruders spinning out kilometer after kilometer of fresh cable. If there were human crew aboard, they kept to themselves and did not respond to the greetings that Shadow's triple sent them. They rested for a little while and then moved on.

A half-klick down the cable, they met their first linesman. It was working on a transverse cable, stripping out worn sections and replacing them with fresh line. When Shadow first saw it, it was no bigger than an insect, a mote moving against the blackness. Close up, however, the linesman's true size became apparent. Larger than a consort, it was almost as tall as the Sailmaker herself. Its patched skinsuit was crusted with a shaggy layer of organic detritus, and the barrel-like helmet that hid its face was scorched and battered.

In the local Weave, the linesman presented not as a neuter giant but as a baseline human of modest size with features that Shadow recognized as masculine and, by historic convention, attractive.

The linesman's avatar assumed a posture that indicated conventional politeness flavored with just a touch of impatience. "More sailmakers," it said. "What brings you here?"

"Others came this way?" Talent asked.

"Another three," the linesman said. "Friends of yours?"

"Perhaps," said Shadow.

"Three," the linesman repeated. "And their mounts. And—" It left the sentence hanging.

"And what?" Frost said.

"You were unaware?" the linesman said. Its avatar took on an expression of amusement. "They had a grub with them."

Shadow's triple were silent. "A grub?" said Shadow at last.

"To all appearances. Wrapped in a spacesuit out of the history archives, like a tiny worldlet on the move, full of air and water and heat to keep the fragile creature alive." The avatar clicked its tongue, smile deepening. "And a frightened pale little face peering out of its bubble."

"It makes no sense," said Frost.

"The Sailmaker said nothing of this," said Talent.

Shadow shook her head slowly. She could think of no reason why Glimmer's triple would have escorted a grub down the cable. For that matter, she could think of no reason why a grub should leave the safety of a passenger module and venture out into space with no more than a spacesuit between it and a hostile universe.

Even in the commonality of the Weave contact between crew and passengers was infrequent. Each was aware of the other's presence, of course, and in a virtual space where anyone could be anything, there was no reason not to interact. Yet usually crew and passengers kept to themselves. It came down to a gulf of experience and interest. A planet dweller could no more hope to understand the life of a sailmaker, bound in service to the ship and her companions, than a sailmaker could immerse herself in whatever trivia preoccupied an entity bred to live on the surface of a planet. And while the passengers might exhibit fully as many engineered adaptations as any of *Ortheia*'s crew, the crew regarded them with a certain degree of disdain. The universe held two kinds of beings: the space-adapted, and grubs.

It troubled Shadow that a grub should venture out into space. It was against the order of things as she understood it. And she had a premonition that whatever the reason for the grub's excursion, no good was likely to come of it.

Branch, and branch again. Ten kilometers down-cable, they came to a life module whose exterior was heavily decorated with intricate arabesques, the sharp lines of the design just a little softened by the impact of years of cosmic dust. The oldest modules were centuries old, as old as the ship itself. The populations they sheltered had long since diverged from whatever societies had given birth to them, becoming microcosms to themselves, growing insular and suspicious. Shadow's triple surveyed the bullet-shaped module with its slowly-spinning core and sent out the requisite greetings and requests for safe passage. Receiving no reply, they passed on.

At the next node they left the cable that they had been following and ascended a transverse line, the spiders hauling them claw over claw toward a nodal point where another module hung. This one was spherical, glowing against the darkness like a bead of quicksilver. Around its equator, a cluster of shuttlecraft slept behind armored baffles, waiting for the day they would see service again.

Shadow and her companions skirted that module too, and turned onto another trunk cable. They were heading inexorably toward the tail of the string of beads that *Ortheia* dragged in her wake, away from everything they knew. Behind them, the sail was a dark void embraced by a slender crescent of silver. Already it seemed like an abstraction. When Shadow closed her eyes, she saw not the familiar silver sea but a universe of wires, dots of light linked by glimmering threads. She tightened her grip on the spider's harness, afraid that if she relaxed her hold she might fall through the gaps in the mesh.

The Weave connection opened up suddenly when they were still half a kilometer from their final destination. Already they were close enough to see details on the dust-polished hull of the ancient module: radiators and antennae, doors and vents, all the colossal architecture that spoke of the self-contained world within. Then, without warning, it flickered and vanished. They stood in a broad hall, the walls decorated with abstract patterns that evoked knots and cables, trailing wires leaping from gallery to gallery in dizzying profusion.

The Linemaster looked much as Shadow had imagined him, tall and gaunt, with a linesman's features stylized and exaggerated and made huge. He sat amid a cats-cradle of rope that cast a chiaroscuro of light and dark over his body.

"No farther," he said, his basso voice like thrumming wires. The three sailmakers stared at him uncomprehendingly.

"We've come this far and he wants us to turn back?" Frost whispered to Shadow.

"We are here on behalf of the Sailmaker," said Shadow aloud. "Perhaps—"

"The situation has changed," said the Linemaster. The next moment he was no longer alone. The virtual space stretched to accommodate three other huge figures. On his left sat the Sailmaker; on his right, the Engineer. The third figure, Shadow realized with a shock, was the Captain itself. She bowed her head.

"The decision has been made, Shadow," said the Sailmaker, her face set and resentful.

Somewhere inside the module ahead, if the Sailmaker had told the truth, was Justice. Yet now the ship's officers had assembled to order Shadow to go no farther.

Frustration overrode caution. "I don't understand," she said. "What is in that module?"

"Hell," said the Engineer. "Hell is in there."

The Linemaster shot him a look of irritation. "That module is under embargo," he said. "The scholar and his companions should never have entered."

"Shadow," the Sailmaker said. "Your mission is over. Come home."

"What about Justice?" Shadow asked, suddenly stubborn. "Glimmer? Arrow?"

"You cannot help your friends now," said the Captain.

Shadow looked around. Talent and Frost stood open-mouthed, as if horrified by her insubordination. She could feel them shrinking away from her.

Shadow shook her head. "No."

"No?" said the captain.

"No," Shadow said.

"I cannot stop you," said the Sailmaker.

The other officers were gone, the shared space reduced to a featureless bubble that held only Shadow and the Sailmaker.

"No," said Shadow.

"Bring back Justice and the others if you can. Leave Samar."

"Samar? Who is Samar?"

"I have given you a code. To protect you when you are inside."

The shared space blinked and vanished.

The interior of the module was dark and still, the lifesystem expending barely enough energy to keep the air circulating and prevent liquids from freezing out. Sampling the air with the sensors in her skinsuit, Shadow tasted dust and decay, burned chemicals and spoiled organics.

She fought against the urge to turn back, wishing that Frost and Talent were still there to help her through this realm of the dead. Even the local Weave was silent. Only ghosts moved through the virtual overlay, electronic echoes of beings that had once lived here. Whatever protocols they used were long obsolete; when Shadow tried to engage with them, they gave no sign of registering her presence. After a few fruitless attempts, she gave up trying to communicate and moved on.

A hundred meters beyond the main airlock, Shadow entered an open gallery lined with dead trees, their grey trunks furred with dust. Withered leaves still clung to their slender branches. Above her, a suited body floated in mid-air, arms outstretched, revolving slowly around its own center of mass. A constellation of tiny spheres of blood and ragged metallic fragments orbited the drifting corpse, glittering in the beam of Shadow's helmet light.

Even after she had peered through the broken faceplate to find the face of a stranger, even after she had recognized the arrow-head pattern picked out in lights on the back of her suit, Shadow could not let go of the idea that it was Justice who hung there, torn and broken. She hovered beside Arrow's body as if searching for some clue that would confirm her worst fears.

With explosive suddenness, something lunged out of the shadows below. She caught a glimpse of a scorpion body with jointed metal legs, a triad of armored turrets swiveling to target her. Convulsively, she pushed the body away, sending herself flying in the opposite direction. The branches of a dead tree caught her and held her fast.

Targeting lights glowing like eyes, the machine stalked toward her. Shadow could feel it in the Weave as well, its malign presence filling the data space. Her bodyware convulsed as the war machine probed it for vulnerabilities.

It stopped just below her, weapons trained. She froze, waiting to die, but to her surprise the burst of gunfire never came.

"Code accepted," said the machine. It stepped backward, playing out its movements in reverse with exaggerated precision, and tucked itself into its lair again.

Shadow found the rest of Glimmer's group at the end of a long hallway lined with narrow niches. One of the sailmakers lay on the floor, staring at the ceiling with sightless eyes. The second sat against a wall, her head bowed. The dying grub in its bulky spacesuit was propped up beside her. Shadow saw that they were holding hands, the sailmaker's slender fingers resting lightly in the palm of the suit's heavy gauntlet.

The sailmaker looked up as Shadow approached and Shadow knew her at once. She recognized the pattern on the skinsuit, the same one that Justice had always worn. Her heart leapt. She looked for injuries and found none.

"Justice," she said. "It's me."

Justice stared at her hollow-eyed, her face empty of expression.

It was the grub that spoke first. Even through the Weave, its voice sounded tired and old. When Shadow turned toward it, she saw that its armored suit was scarred with bullet impacts. Puddles of sealant leaking from inside had stained the white plastic. Only the thin mist that formed and faded on the clear bubble of the visor showed that the grub still breathed.

"Which one are you?" the grub asked.

"My name is Shadow."

The grub nodded. "Ah, yes," it said. "She talked about you."

Even for a grub, he was strikingly ugly. He had blue eyes set in a narrow, pale face, a thin blade of a nose, a jaw fringed with white hair. Where the patch cords from his suit entered the skin of his throat and temples, the skin was red and angry-looking.

"And you are?" asked Shadow.

The grub coughed. "Samar Ussinik. So, are you here to help me, or to finish me off?"

"I don't know," Shadow said.

"You're wasting your time either way."

Shadow looked at Justice again, then back to the grub. "What is this place?" she asked.

"You might call it a library. A very old one."

"They told me it was hell," Shadow said.

Ussinik stiffened, then relaxed. "Yes," he said. "They would think that."

Shadow reached out and gripped the shoulders of the grub's suit, trying to feel the living creature through the layers of armor. "No more riddles," she said. "Tell me what this is about."

Ussinik opened his mouth, but it was Justice who spoke. "Leave us," she said.

Shadow shook his head. "No. You're coming back with me."

Justice turned her head away. "I can't go back. I killed Glimmer."

Shadow stared, unable to understand. Sailmakers did not kill one another. Murder was something that grubs did. Gentle Justice could not be a killer.

Ussinik coughed again. "She saved my life," he said. "When her companion turned that robot on us."

Maybe it was hell after all, Shadow thought. Questions and answers that made no sense. War machines. People killing each other.

"The Sailmaker gave us the code for entry," Ussinik said. "The code to shut down that machine. Then she must have changed her mind. Wanted to bury the evidence."

"What are you?" Shadow asked. "What did you come here for?"

The man closed his eyes, pain showing on his face. "Knowledge," he said. "My whole life—" Another cough. "This is a very old place," he said. "It holds things that have been forgotten. Put away. It holds… possibilities. I wanted—" Another spasm of pain jolted him. "—shake things up."

"But why?"

"Stagnation. You sailmakers, linesmen, all the rest. Overspecialized. Social insects, blindly obedient to your kings and queens. And the petty little creatures in their pods, calling themselves true humans. Baselines. Just as inward-looking, inbred—" His pallid face contorted. "Humanity was never meant to be like this." He nodded toward Justice. "She understood."

Shadow did not. She shook her head. "I can help you," she said.

"I doubt it," the scholar said. "But there is something that you can do for me."

Shadow looked at Justice, and saw her nod.

"When I die," Ussinik said, "Take the data store from my suit. It holds everything I have learned. Take it back to my people." He closed his eyes for a moment. "In person. Not through the Weave. This is not for the Sailmaker. There is nothing…nothing she can use. Nothing she deserves to have."

"I understand," said Shadow.

"Not the sailmaker's idea," said Justice. "Mine. It was my idea to come here." She sounded intensely weary, as if something inside her had broken.

"But why?" Shadow asked.

"Because I was in love with him," Justice said.

Shadow remembered how she had found them, their hands linked. "And us?" she said.

Justice shrugged. "You never answered my messages," she said.

"I sent you messages too," Shadow said.

"They never reached me."

They were both silent then. The Sailmaker again, Shadow thought. Useless to ask why she acted as she did. Kings and queens do not explain themselves to their subjects.

There was a hiss as the pressure in the airlock equalized. Through the window set in the inner door, Shadow saw the red eyes of the robot glowing in the darkness beyond.

She glanced at the spacesuit. The human inside was silent, eyes closed and head bowed, but Shadow thought he was still alive.

"Do you love him more than me?" she asked.

"It's not about more or less," said Justice. "I loved you because of the way your songs made me feel. But Samar knew so much. He could make me understand things. When you sang to me, I asked myself questions. When he spoke to me, I heard the answers."

Shadow thought about the invisible threads that tied them all together, sailmakers and linesmen and grubs and all the rest. In the Weave, anyone could be anything they wanted. A linesman could look like a baseline, or a baseline like a linesman. Age and youth were erased. A grub could reach out to comfort a grieving sailmaker with poetry and history and science. Anything was possible and nothing was forbidden.

She imagined the slow courtship unfolding. A chance encounter in the Weave—or had it been chance?—and the exchange of ideas and confidences. At some point, Samar must have spoken of his obsession, the treasure house of knowledge locked away in the abandoned module. Was that when the Sailmaker, seeing and hearing everything, recognized an opportunity?

"It doesn't matter," said Justice. "He's dying now. Just leave us, Shadow."

Shadow touched the control for the outer door. "I'm not leaving either of you," she said. She tried to meet Justice's eyes, but Justice only looked away.

"Don't look at me," Justice said. "I'll go with you. Just don't look at me."

On the platform outside, they found a single spider tethered to a railing. Obedient to the orders of the Captain, Talent and Frost had gone back, but they had left Shadow a parting gift.

Working in silence, Shadow and Justice managed to lift the scholar onto the creature's back. "We will get help for him," Shadow said. "And then we can all begin again." She flinched inwardly at the false optimism in her own voice. I disobeyed the Sailmaker, she thought. And Justice has Glimmer's blood on her hands.

She glanced back again and saw Justice standing by the railing, her head bowed as if in deep thought. Shadow turned back to her task, methodically checking and tightening the straps that held the spacesuit to the spider's back.

When she looked back again, the platform was empty and Justice was gone.

Shadow stood on the cable, looking up at the stars. She wondered whether one of the bright dots above her was Justice and whether she was looking down, searching for Shadow in the mesh of *Ortheia's* cable web.

"Very hard to see anyone from up there," Shadow said. "It's a question of scale."

She was tiny compared to the ship, but the ship was a gossamer thing too, a frail dust mote flung between the stars. The universe was too large and indifferent to acknowledge even the grandest human story, the richest love or the most violent hate.

"Did you love her?" Shadow asked the scholar.

"Who?"

"Justice."

"Oh. Yes. Yes, of course. That is to say…" His voice was very weak now.

Shadow looked at the distant disk of the sail and thought about the long climb that lay ahead of her.

"You won't forget…what we talked about?" said Ussinik.

Shadow looked at the pale face inside the helmet, like a bleached skull in the starlight.

"No," she said. "I won't forget."

NEXUS

_____*Nancy Fulda*_____

TYRA TUGGED HER JACKET TIGHTER as she approached the JumpPort. "Stay still," she whispered to the squirming ball of fur against her stomach. "Do you *want* them to take you away?"

Sapphire-bright eyes peered back at her. "Mreowff?"

"Just a little longer. I promise." She stroked Zek's ears and pushed his head back inside the jacket. He made a sound somewhere between a purr and a hiss.

The outer wall of the JumpPort was intimidating: six meters of ceramic slicing across an amber sky. The surface thrummed beneath her fingers. Transport drones buzzed near the main entrance, delivering and retrieving passengers, but here beside the freight doors the air was still. Nothing but Zek, Tyra, and a couple of lonely brush beetles. A heavy grain transport had just left, leaving furrows in the dirt. Swirls of dust marked the path it had taken.

Tyra took a deep breath. She had to stand on tip-toes to reach the control console—she was only ten, and small for her age—but when her fingers reached the button the freight doors slid open with a sound like thunder. Tyra jumped backward. She glanced around to be sure she was alone, then slipped inside the building and closed the doors from the inside. They rumbled, but no one came to see what caused the noise.

Huh. So Tobin had been telling the truth after all. She hadn't quite believed him, when he'd told her how easy it was to get into the Port. These doors were supposed to be kept locked; but she figured transport workers could be as lazy as anyone else.

The freight bay was dim inside, full of machinery and dusty bales of produce. Loud clangs and thumps echoed through the walls. Tyra picked her way across the empty space, ears pricked for approaching footsteps. *The workers stick with the transports, mostly,* Tobin had told her. *The back hallways should be empty, but if you do run into someone, just pretend to be lost. They'll take you straight to the main information desk.*

Tyra practiced it out in her mind. The information worker would ask for Tyra's name. Tyra would lie and pretend to be someone else. A moment later she'd act like she saw her parents across the room. *Say thank you and smile like the most adorable kid in the world,* Tobin had advised. *Then run your legs off. They'll never find you in the crowd.*

Tyra sighed. Her older brother made it sound so easy. He'd been hopping planets for years now, and the signs were beginning to show. Thin hair, patchy skin. Every time he showed up at the Children's Refuge, the matron had a fit. But he was a grown-up now, on paper at least. They couldn't send him to the hospital unless he let them, and they couldn't stop him from jumping. Not when he knew how to sneak in and out of every Port between here and Sergus.

She wished he was here, instead of off seeing fancy planets.

"Mreowff?" Zek poked his head out of Tyra's jacket, a sleek bundle of lavender spots and deep blue fur. He hopped onto her shoulder and stretched, teeth gaping in a yawn.

"Zek!" Tyra hissed. "What are you doing?"

Zek cocked his head as if to say, *What's your problem? There's no one here.* Then he jumped to the floor and began sniffing along the machinery.

Tyra followed, heart thumping. She should have waited for Tobin. She'd *planned* on waiting for Tobin, even though there was no telling when he'd show up again, or if he even would. But then the Matron caught sight of Zek slinking through the halls after curfew, and shrieked like a banshee for a full ninety seconds. The next morning a bunch of men showed up wearing uniforms with scary equipment hanging from their belts, talking back and forth in their headsets.

All because of Zek.

Tyra's throat clogged, and she hurried to scoop him back onto her shoulder. She *couldn't* lose Zek, she just couldn't. Not after she'd kept him secret for so many years.

She followed the corridors toward the Jump platforms. It wasn't hard to find the way: Her skin prickled as she got closer, and the floor vibrated beneath her feet. By the time she found an open robot hatch leading to the public waiting areas, she felt like a battery charged past capacity. Zek's fur crackled when she stroked it.

The robot hatch wasn't very big. Tyra had to crawl through on hands and knees, pausing now and then to wipe grit from her palms. It smelled like oil and overheated gears, and she was glad when she finally pushed open the flap on the far end. She got her first real look at Pelecia's travel hub.

The room was amazing. Delicate arches spanned the ceiling, supporting skylights and filigree panels. Colored glass cast a warm glow across the shifting tapestry of travelers. Transports and message drones hummed through the air overhead. Street vendors lined the waiting areas, hawking overpriced mementos. And at the center of the highest arch, like a giant kraken dragged from an electrical sea, hung the mechanical monstrosity of the Nexus. Hydraulic arms hissed and shifted, keeping each glowing platform aligned with that *other* space, the place where all the distances were different.

Tyra's chest felt heavy. She'd heard of the Nexus, of course. She'd even seen it in holovids. But it had a *weight* in real life, a magnitude she'd never anticipated. Pulses of energy thrummed from the central generators, fighting for dominance with her heartbeat. No wonder people weren't allowed to spend more than two years working near the thing.

"I'd get up off the floor if I were you."

Tyra jumped. She hadn't noticed the man sitting beside her. "You're on the floor, too."

"Yes, but I didn't just drag my pet and backpack through a robot hatch." He squinted. "That *is* a pet, isn't it, and not some parasite that latched onto your shoulder?"

51

Zek hissed and fluffed up his fur. Tyra stuffed him back inside her jacket. Then she climbed off the floor and batted the dust from her knees.

"This is a ritzy sort of place, you know?" The stranger continued. "They don't look too kindly on trespassers."

"Who says I'm trespassing?"

"The first desk clerk you can't produce a passport for, that's who." The man scratched a thin patch on his hair. He wasn't so old as Tyra had thought at first. Pale skin, baggy eyes, but the muscles on his exposed arms told a different story. "You ever Jumped before?"

"Does it matter?"

"Suppose not." He laid his head against the wall and sucked quick, shallow breaths. Tyra watched, fascinated. How many worlds had he been to? Fifteen? Thirty? He must have started late, if he was still alive by now.

Passengers threaded past them, a shifting sea of bodies twice Tyra's size, toting handbags and trailed by self-powered suitcases. Humans, mostly, but a couple of orange-shelled Antegrals poked here and there out of the crowd. They stood five deep in lines to show their passports, then shuffled toward dynamic ramps leading to the ever-moving portals of the Nexus. "So many people," Tyra murmured, daunted. Some of the lines ran twice around the inside of the building.

"Big week for travelers," the man said, shrugging. He jerked his head toward the longest pair of lines. "They're headed for Old Earth Mecca, mostly. Pelecia's one of the only worlds with a link to the First Planet."

"Have you been there?" Tyra asked.

"Old Earth?" The man laughed. "Kid, why would I want to go *there?* We brought it all with us, everything that place had to teach."

"But—"

"It's the other direction you ought to be heading, little stowaway. Out where it's all different." He pulled a little bottle from his pocket, downed the contents between wheezing breaths. "They change us, you know. Every world we visit. We're not even all the same species anymore."

"*Homo sapiens sapiens,*" Tyra said automatically, repeating what she'd heard at school. "Of course we are."

"You only say that because you've never Jumped."

Tyra pressed her lips together. The man's talk made her nervous. He was creepy-weird-crazy, like Tobin, jumping and jumping and not caring what it did to him.

Or to the people who loved him.

"Come on, admit it," the man said, pointing. His arm trembled slightly. "You've never Jumped, have you?"

Tyra hesitated, then shook her head. "My parents didn't think it was right, using up a child's Jumps just to keep the family together."

"Found work off-planet, did they? Left you at the Refuge?"

"They're coming back," Tyra said defensively.

"Sure they are."

Tyra opened her mouth to protest, but a strangled shriek cut through her thoughts. A nearby woman had dropped her handbag, knuckles pressed to her mouth in horror. "Nexus and Heavens, what is that *thing?*"

She pointed straight at Tyra.

Tyra glanced down. Zek had crawled out of her jacket again, silky fur brushing her neck. She grabbed at him, but the woman with the handback was faster. A vicious slap sent Zek flying, bouncing off the back of another traveler.

"Stop it!" Tyra shouted. "Stop it, stop it!" She darted forward, scooping up her hissing companion just before a disgusted traveler could squash him beneath his boot.

"It bit her!" a different woman shouted. "It tried to bite her! Someone call security."

Tyra pushed past the growing chaos, Zek squirming beneath her fingers. Why did everyone hate him so?

Crowds folded around her, and within moments she'd reached a new group of people. Tobin was right about that, too. *If you're small enough*, he said, *people just ignore you. I guess they figure you're someone else's problem.* The hysterical woman was still shouting, but her voice faded with distance.

Tyra squirmed toward the nearest ramp, ducking beneath the dangling whiskers of a Djorn. She had to get off this planet. She'd known it for a long time, even though she couldn't explain the reasons. It was like a ball of need inside her, pushing her forward.

But where? She couldn't go to her parents. They'd take Zek away from her, and probably send her back to the Refuge. She couldn't go to Tobin, either. She didn't know where he was, and even if she did, she didn't want to live like he did. She didn't want to see all the planets. She just wanted *away*; someplace safe, someplace different.

A pair of security guards pushed through the crowd. Tyra ducked away before they could spot her. There was no time to pick a planet, no time to find the best way to sneak near the gate. She'd just have to run fast enough, and duck past the barriers before anyone stopped her. They wouldn't follow her, not through the gate. No one was going to waste their Jumps on one silly, runaway child.

She reached a ramp and sprinted upward, threading past boots and claws and suitcases. The Nexus rotated above her, glowing portals swinging into position. The shifting ramp made her dizzy.

Four or five Jumps in a lifetime, sometimes as many as seven. That was all anybody got. After that, the tissues in your body started breaking down. You became like Tobin—a walking dead man, rushing to see as many planets as you could before the end.

Four or five Jumps in a lifetime.

So how many Jumps did Tyra have to make? How many portals did she have to cross before they didn't dare send her back?

The barrier was up ahead. Tyra could see the ticket clerk, checking passports and waving travelers toward the portal. The lights seemed to flicker every time someone stepped through it. She dodged past the guardrails, her eyes locked on the blinding ripple of light. If she just ran fast enough…

Strong fingers bit into her shoulder. "Hold up, there, Missy. Where are your parents?"

Tyra struggled. It wasn't fair. The big man wasn't even a security guard, just one of the passengers near the front of the transport line. Tears pricked at her eyes. They'd take her back to the Refuge now, and they'd put her under close supervision, and she'd never have a chance to sneak off-planet again. Worse, the matron would call the exterminators, and Zek would be gone forever.

"Let go!" Tyra shouted, but the big man held firm.

A crowd began to gather, passengers further down the line pressing forward to see the cause of the ruckus. Tyra's head was pounding, breath coming hard in her lungs. She couldn't get enough air somehow, and the low, pulsing thrum of the Nexus drowned out everyone's voices.

Then Zek was there, darting from her jacket and digging his teeth into the big man's hand. The man recoiled, and the pain in Tyra's shoulder lessened.

Tyra pulled free. She bumped into a suitcase, knocking it over. Someone shouted. A group of security guards appeared in her vision, but they were too far away. The portal was inches in front of her. If she ran…if she just ran fast enough…

She passed through.

On the other side, everything was different.

The air was different, the heat was different, the weight was different, the shape of the Nexus was different. Tyra's lungs gagged on thick, humid air, a taste like sour copper clogging her throat. She stumbled, knees buckling, and hit the ground far harder than she expected. When she tried to get up, nothing worked as it ought to. Her arms felt too heavy, and her head was spinning.

"Take it easy," someone said, reaching to steady her elbow. "It takes a while to adapt to the air on this side."

Tyra tried to pull away, but she stumbled again, this time knocking into a multi-legged Sanchid waiting for its turn through the portal. It *clucked* at her and scuttled aside.

She whirled around, heart pounding. She had to get away, she had to…

Something changed.

Everything felt *right* somehow. Tyra couldn't explain it. She ought to be running. They'd send a message drone through the portal any minute now, telling this crisply-dressed security guard that Tyra was an illegal Jumper. They'd take Zek away. They might even kill him…. But she let the guard help her to her feet instead.

Zek chirruped, crawling onto Tyra's shoulder. He fluffed his fur, cocking his head toward the uniformed woman. She smiled faintly, as though an unspoken question had been answered.

"You…you're not afraid of him?" Tyra blurted.

"This little guy?" the uniformed woman stroked Zek's forehead. "Naw. I doubt you understand what you're actually carrying, though. Let me hold him, please."

Tyra clutched Zek reflexively. "He's mine."

The guard's smile had faded. "That creature is contraband on every planet from here to Terecheb. What's your name?"

Around them, traffic resumed at the gate. Passengers filed through the portal in ordered rows, alternating directions. Many of them glanced at Zek and recoiled, but the sight of the security guard seemed to reassure them.

"Your name?" The woman prompted.

Tyra hesitated. There wasn't much point in lying, not now. "Tyra."

"And where'd you find this little guy, Tyra?"

"I didn't find him anywhere. Zek found *me*. Years and years ago."

Tyra didn't mention the rest of the story—how she'd cried herself to sleep for five nights in a row, because Tobin was dying and her parents had messaged that they were staying away for *another* year. How Zek had shown up outside her window. How the other children had screamed when they saw him.

"Is that when you decided to run away?"

Tyra's thoughts pulled up short. "What?"

"After Zek showed up. Is that when you decided to run away?"

"I don't know. Maybe. I just…the Refuge just gets worse and worse. The Matron's always griping about money, but most of the parents don't send her any, and some of the other kids are bullies…. Please don't send me back!"

"That remains to be seen," the guard said in a flat tone. "Now. I promise, if you still want Zek back in a minute, you can have him. But you *will* let me hold him." She held out an insistent hand. Reluctantly, Tyra detached Zek's claws from her shoulder. He whimpered and tried to crawl off the woman's palm.

And then he started changing.

The fur melted, the eyes shrunk to baggy slits. His snout grew longer, his teeth larger. Soon, instead of the fluffy, wide-eyed companion Tyra had grown accustomed to, she was staring at a hunchbacked deformity, coated with drool and a smattered patch of scales.

"What are you doing to him?"

The guard tapped a device on her belt. "Psychic inhibitor. I'm not doing anything to him, honey. Your friend here is an Andellian swampcat. They're telepathic—protect themselves from predators by appearing to be allies. It's an incredibly effective survival strategy."

"But that's not right. Zek has fur! He even sheds it. Makes a mess on my pillow."

"What you saw," the guard said gently, "was an illusion created by your mind and his. He became what you wanted him to be, so that you would protect him." She held up the hairless, lumpy creature. "*This* is what Zek really looks like. This is what other people see."

"But..." Tyra's chest had gone cold. It couldn't be. Zek was her friend. He wouldn't deceive her.

"Tyra, swampcats are *extremely* persuasive. When they find a human who's sensitive to their abilities—and there aren't many—they latch on like leeches. Grown men have been known to abandon their families, squander their resources, even murder acquaintances, if they thought it would protect their little allies. That's why swampcats are forbidden on most worlds."

Tyra pressed her lips together. "I don't care. I love him!"

"I don't doubt that you do." The guard raised an eyebrow. "The question is, now that he's over here with me, do you still want to leave the Refuge?"

Tyra considered. The burning desire, the inescapable *need* had vanished, but..."Yes," she said soberly. "I don't want to live at the Refuge anymore. And I don't care if Zek's ugly and scaly. He's the only one who's always been there for me. Please? Give him back?"

The guard smiled and released Zek. He bounded gleefully back onto Tyra's shoulder, deep blue fur sprouting as he came. "Mreowf?" he inquired, rubbing her cheek. "Mreowf?"

"We had to be sure," the guard said. "Bonding with a swampcat is no idle matter. If it's not voluntary on both sides, the human partner becomes unstable."

Tyra held Zek closer. "I don't understand."

"It's...well, it's a little bit like a marriage. If the partners love each other and work together, it can be a marvelous thing. But if one dominates the other, the result is pain and misery. I had to find out whether Zek was dominating you, or whether your feelings for him were real. It appears they are real."

"So…you won't take Zek away?"

"No. Swampcats are native to Bevlin. They often bring their foundlings here. I doubt it was an accident that you chose this particular portal to enter."

"That's why you weren't afraid of Zek," Tyra said. "Because people here are used to swampcats."

"They're dangerous critters, make no mistake. But when the bond develops healthily, something magnificent happens. The swampcat's influence activates neural pathways that normally remain dormant, creates possibilities that never before existed for the human race. All of the Port guards here know to watch for them."

Tyra stroked Zek's fur, staring deep into bright blue eyes. "So this is your home, huh? How did you end up all the way over on Pelecia?"

Zek mreowfed contentedly. An image of Tobin flashed into Tyra's mind. Tobin, shouldering a backpack and stepping through a portal.

"You got trapped in Tobin's backpack?"

Zek managed to look bashful.

"There's a research institute two cities over," The guard continued. "Our government is studying the bond between humans and swampcats, and they've granted asylum to anyone the swampcats bring. You can stay here, if you wish. As long as your parents agree to it."

Tyra hugged Zek tighter. "They will, they will. I'm sure of it!" If they were willing to leave her in a Refuge on Pelecia, surely they wouldn't object to an Institute on Bevlin. It sounded scientific and educated. Her parents liked things like that.

"You don't have to decide right away," the guard said. "You have to understand, Tyra. The bond with a swampcat changes people. If you stay with us—if you stay with *Zek*—you'll be different from your parents, different from everyone you've already known."

"I'm already different," Tyra said soberly. "Please. I just want to be with Zek."

The guard smiled and held out her hand. "I thought you might say that. Come on, then. Let's fill out your paperwork. There's a *lot* of it."

Tyra felt dizzy. She could stay? They could *both* stay? It seemed too good to be true. But Zek purred and rubbed his nose against her shoulder, and the Nexus thrummed quietly overhead, and the strange-smelling air of this planet no longer seemed quite so alien. With a warm feeling of confidence in her gut, Tyra took the woman's hand and walked with her down the rampway.

Behind them, a message drone flicked through the portal, peeping urgently. No one seemed in a hurry to listen to it.

A LACK OF CONGENIAL SOLUTIONS

Kenneth Schneyer

Excerpt, Skenany Textual Mesh: "We On Earth":

Generations without a home   Joined quintets dead
                    Fertility restricted
Food controlled

                                                            Pets!

    Torn from our mansions   Curiosities!
                    Nests dead
                        Nestlings slaughtered
                                            Raw materials!
Years imprisoned in ships
                            Delicacies! Distractions!
    Denied the unbroken web   Denied communion
        But always remembering   Awaiting the day
        But always planning   Awaiting the day
Passing on what we can   Awaiting the day
                    Humans cannot know
            Humans will not understand
                                    Those who eat our flesh
        They have no grief

Excerpt, Oral History of Mary White:

When I was very little—I must have been three or four—I asked my father why we had a Naichian cleaning our house instead of a robot. Our Naichian—no, I don't think I remember her name—was twice as big as me, and looked like a giant green beetle. I'm sorry, I don't mean to offend you, but that's the way it seemed to me. I said I was little.

My father said something about Naichians being better cleaners than robots. That didn't make sense to me even then, because I knew robots could do all sorts of things. I said so, and my father replied that it was important to give the Naichians work, because they no longer had their home. When I asked where their home was, he told me that their planet was now full of humans, and no Naichians lived there anymore. I asked why the Naichians left their home and came here, and my father looked sad and said that it was a long story.

There were lots of questions my parents wouldn't answer when I was that age, or answered in ways I guess they thought were "appropriate" for me to hear. Another example? Well, I once asked my mother why people only came in one color, instead of the many different colors of Naichians, Pheätioni, Xicoménese, cats, and dogs. I think I must have heard something from one of my friends, or maybe overheard one of their parents, that made me think people once had more colors.

My mother had just arisen from doing her duty to my father, and was very quiet. She started to say, "The world used to be different." Then she stopped, frowned, and said, "Not—" I think she was searching for the right words for a four-year-old. "Not as good. The world wasn't as good before as it is now."

"How?" I asked. "Are different colors bad?"

"It wasn't just colors," she said. "People believed all sorts of strange things, and they—well, there were women who didn't act like women, and—" She stopped.

I was confused as any child would be at such a vague explanation, but she didn't continue. By the time my parents might have explained the past and the present to me more cogently, everything had changed.

Yes, I agree, changed for the better. But I don't think my parents saw it that way. No, I never asked them, and they've been gone a long time. How can I know for sure?

Excerpt, The Human Affliction, *by Oma of the Lespentai:*

It is ultimately pointless to argue whether travel by star drive warped human character, on the one hand, or flawed traits in one ethnic and cultural group impelled humans to interstellar flight, on the other. Regardless of the mechanism of causation, one human sub-civilization began systematically absorbing and eliminating all competing sub-civilizations within—possibly before—the initial century of Terran interstellar exploitation. By the time the first conquerors (for thus we must call them) arrived on Xicomé, there was remarkable homogeneity among humans in belief, cultural norms, gender classification, sexual practice, and general appearance. Unfortunately for the Xicoménese, as well as for every other race that encountered humans afterward, this sub-civilization was utterly confident in its own destiny and superiority, and regarded the subjugation, humiliation, torture, and mass-murder of entire species as its natural right.

As sometimes happens among privileged communities, however, insulation from material hardship encouraged the development of abstracted inquiry into a spiritually enlightened framework. In the five or six decades prior to the Revolution, humans had begun to seek "goodness" in all its various permutations—intellectual breadth, tranquility, universal compassion—to fulfill their destiny within themselves as well as externally. There is evidence during that time that human philosophical orthodoxy was beginning to question the morality of human intervention on other worlds, of the forced transport of other sentient races to Earth for purposes of servitude, captivity as pets or curiosities, or use of their bodies as raw materials. Given another few decades or centuries, perhaps human behavior towards others would have changed. Like all such counterfactual speculations, however, this one must ultimately remain unanswered.

63

Excerpt, **Song of the Revolution**, *a Pheätioni epic*:

> For fives squared and fives cubed of orbits
> These waited
> In bondage and in servitude
> In humiliation and in torture
> These passed their languages
> These passed their heritages
> From hand to arm, from breath to whisper
> These waited
> The plan accreted in drops
> No more than a few words at a time
> Continent to continent
> Two generations for some
> Five-and-three for others
> These watched the moment approach
> In every city on their planet of exile
> At the same instant
> Arose fives cubed and cubed again of hands legs tentacles
> Ships in space they disabled and destroyed
> Communications they disrupted
> Power stations they commandeered
> Data stores and processors they disabled or controlled
> These killed who never killed
> Whose ancestors never killed
> In less than five days
> Theirs was the Earth
> This place they never wanted

Excerpt, Autobiographical Essay of Tsroac Dilfe:

On the twentieth day, the leaders of the rebellion met in a large conference room in Sao Paolo that that had formerly been reserved for board meetings of Terra's largest profit-making enterprise. We were "leaders" in the sense that we were the attendees of this meeting: some had actually held coordinating roles in the revolution; some had been elected by their fellows to attend; some had positions of high status within their own communities.

Representation was complicated by the cultural norms of each species and subgroup. The Pheätioni cannot conceive of representation that does not include all three of their biological sexes and all nine of their social genders. The Lespentai recognize sixteen separate racial and ethnic subclasses who all needed to be there. The Xicoménese split into a dizzying multiplicity of ethical, empirical, and metaphysical belief systems, but consented to have a mere twenty of these appear at the meeting. There were none who thought—or who would voice the thought—that strength, intelligence, dexterity, or prowess in combat should give some races or individuals primacy over others. For now, at least, we met as equals who had shared in a victory.

"For the time being," said Oma, the Lespentai who had been instrumental in neutralizing human law-enforcement personnel, "can we agree to attempt consensus on decisions made today, if any are? Our wishes and needs may vary much." There was no dissent from this proposition.

Lienn, an Xicoménese adherent of universal reflective consciousness and coordinator of the attack on the political centers of Europe, suggested that a given position—pe indicated a rostrum at the far end of the room from where pe sat—should be where any speaking was done, and that translations into written or sign should be available. Pe made the further suggestion that speakers should stand in line or otherwise speak in order. This last suggestion took a while to reach consensus, as some species do not engage in such regimented conversational structures. The Skenany, for example, speak simultaneously with several interlocutors and arrive at their decisions through the gestalt suggested by the directional pressure of the words. But ultimately it was agreed that some would be unable to hear, see, or feel such communications at all, and so we adopted Lienn's posposal.

Tollop, a Naichian, signed that she wanted to know about the question of repatriation. Despite the fact our home planets now contained exclusively human colonies, many wished to return.

"For those worlds that are not colonized at this timespace locus," wrote Peerri-O-Sreb, a Pheätioni dominant egg-host, "ships should be found. But humans in a colony are a danger. Humans may seek vengeance. Humans may seek to complete the task of obliteration. Humans may take hostages. This one does not believe repatriation can be attempted without prior resolution of the Human Question." We agreed to facilitate the return home of any whose worlds now held no humans, but to wait on the colonized worlds until some solution was reached.

Peerri-O-Sreb's raising of the "Human Question" made it impossible to ignore what we all knew must ultimately be discussed, although I dreaded it: what to do about the humans still on Earth. Several Skenany suggested integrating humans into a new, egalitarian Terra:

"—once they see—"
"—experiences inevitably alter outlooks—"
"—centuries of bad exposures—"
"—consequences of behaviors—"
"—working parts of a productive whole—"
"—one race among many—"
"—included in any just polity—"
"—be like the rest of us—"

When they had finished, Lienne said, "Their history does not suggest that humans are amendable to the sort of integration you recommend. It does not appear that they are able to be a part of a heterogeneous group without attempting to dominate it."

Oma responded, "That is not strictly true. My researches have shown that the many cultures in Terra's past enjoyed a multiplicity of social and political structures, and that not a few of these maintained long-term, diverse equilibria without the need for one group to control another."

Lienne replied, "But none of those societies or traditions survives. The monoculture that assimilated, overpowered or exterminated them is the only civilization represented by any humans who have lived during the last half millennium. Every human now living has been raised from birth to believe in the natural, biologically destined superiority of his own species, and will see any subordination of its authority as a perversion that must be overcome."

Tollop signed, "We could leave Terra to the Terrans and be done with them. Or we could isolate them on some other world."

Lienne gave the bass *huff* that I now understand to be the Xicoménese gesture of negation. "Leave them alone and their desire for domination will thrive, fueled by the sense of having been robbed of their birthrights by unworthy and inferior aliens. They will return in a few centuries, determined to exact revenge and set things to rights."

Rabi-I-Gald, a Pheätioni transformative inseminator, wrote, "Humans may be controlled permanently. Humans may be kept in camps and closed communities. Humans' actions and words may be heavily directed. Humans may be disallowed the power to dominate."

Tollop signed, "I like Rabi-I-Gald's suggestion. They cannot exercise their destructive and oppressive tendencies if they are under our direction."

But Oma said, "Such control is ultimately unrealistic. *We* were under the humans' very tight control, and yet we preserved our desire for liberation over the centuries and awaited the opportunity to substantiate it. If enough time goes by, the same lingering desire for domination and revenge will win out, and the result will be slaughter."

Seven or eight Skenany said:

"—centuries of retraining—"

"—enculturation of our values—"

"—transformation of human psyche—"

"—careful program of indoctrination—"

"—culture can be unlearned—"

Oma's tentacles waved thoughtfully. "To accomplish what the Skenany are suggesting would require separating human children from their parents at a very young age, and possibly forbidding them any contact with the existing adult generation for their entire lives."

Peerri-O-Sreb wrote, "Measures could be insufficient. Fragmentary information about the dominance humans achieved in the past could invoke a mythological response. Humans could imagine past glory. Humans could feel a need to recapture said glory. This one can see no safe solution that includes human existence."

There was a long pause after Peeri-O-Sreb's last comment. Then Tollop signed, "I request clarification. Do you suggest that we arrange a future that excludes human existence?"

Peerri-O-Sreb replied, "This one suggests the lack of a realistic alternative."

Spontaneous responses erupted from more than a third of the representatives, crossing over and mixing with each other to prevent any sort of comprehension, although it is possible that the Skenany followed all of it. When it had calmed down, Kysttor, a Xicoménese adherent of the soul-directed multiverse, came forward and took the rostrum.

"There is no empirical need," pe said. "That can justify genocide."

Lienne huffed again. "*Your* ethical framework would deny us the right to take any action that harms the humans for our own protection, even the steps that we have taken heretofore."

The discussion might then have devolved into an internal dispute over Xicoménese belief systems, but Kysttor leaned back and scratched perself. "Possibly true, but irrelevant. I respond not to all possible actions, but only the extremity of obliterating an entire species. My sole contention is that such action cannot be justified."

Tollop signed, "If a species of plant, animal, or bacterium is so dangerous that it will wipe out many other species, its elimination is regrettable, but necessary to protect others."

Kysttor said, "Assuming without deciding such to be true, the logic that applies to non-sentient life forms cannot be applied equally to those who have minds. A mind deserves to be treated as its own inviolable universe."

"Yet," said Oma, "humans themselves would not grant such inviolability to you, nor to any of us, as their own behavior demonstrates."

Kysttor replied, "The behavior of unethical beings is not a basis for the behavior of ethical beings. Their treatment of us does not, by itself, justify our treatment of them."

Oma rejoined, "I do not mean to suggest so. But their behavior, and particularly the likelihood of their actions in the future, define a pragmatic situation with which we must contend."

Several Skenany said:

"—too many years of servitude—"

"—nonzero risk is still a risk—"
"—justice not the only goal—"
"—how to be certain—"
"—ethical obligations reduced—"
"—collective punishment for collective crime—"
"—safety again—"
"—never again—"
"—certainty—"

The debate on this topic continued for many hours. For a time it seemed that Krysttor and those who agreed with per would refuse to allow consensus. Then Rabi-a-Gald wrote, "Krysttor does not wish extermination. This one understands. Promises Krysttor that humans will not try to retake what they think is theirs? Promises Krysttor that humans will not be strong enough? Promises Krysttor that this one's children's children's children will not be enslaved? Wishes Krysttor this one to accept that risk?"

Excerpt, Skenany Textual Mesh: "We On Earth":

To kill without killing

Attrition!

Safety without violence

Species death!

No oppressors remain

Add to their food!

Years upon years it takes

Fertility abolished!

They watch their own destruction

None is destroyed.

All are destroyed.

Excerpt, "Reports of the Revolutionary Committee on Public Safety":

Production, distribution, and introduction of the additive have proceeded according to schedule, with some exceptions in individual regions noted on the table below. There has been practically no human reaction to the additive; it appears that most humans are not aware that it is there. Some few have noticed a change in the flavor of their food, which they regard as evidence of poor quality control, and have refused to consume meals on the grounds that they are spoiled or otherwise unwholesome. But as no food without the additive is available to them, and their peers who consume it exhibit no ill effects, it is expected that these humans will eventually consume the additive as well.

Some minor disruptions of the process have occurred. Seven different Xicoménese adherents of the soul-directed multiverse have attempted, at different times and places, to sabotage production, divert distribution, or inform humans of the contraceptive nature of the additive. In each case the attempt was unsuccessful.

This particular Xicoménese sect was never fully reconciled to the plan, although their representative, Krysttor, did not block consensus when it was proposed. Their contention is that no being should be subjected to radical changes that alter its life path without its own consent, regardless of the need. When confronted with the fact that any act overthrowing human power is necessarily a radical change in their life path, and that humans are likely to renew their prior destructive and exploitative behavior, the perpetrators asserted that none of these are justifications for so global act as species-wide sterilization. Some of these Xicoménese have indicated that they will continue to resist our efforts in this area. For that reason, the perpetrators have been barred both from further contact with humans and from any facilities related to the process.

Evidence of the additive's effectiveness will not be available, for several months, and complete efficacy will not be confirmed for at least two years. It is recommended that additive production and distribution continue for at least that period, to ensure full compliance.

Excerpt, Oral History of Mary White:

No, I never expected to be the last living human. For one thing, there were children at least five years younger than I at the time of the Revolution. You'd have thought that some of them would outlive me. But I've had an unusually long life; must have had good genes.

That's funny, isn't it? "Good genes" used to mean that you'd pass the traits down to your descendants. We used to think that we all had better genes than anyone who came before us. We were the result of natural selection, survival of the fittest.

But if nobody's ever going to have descendants, then what difference do your genes make?

Bitter? I suppose. Sometimes I wonder, wouldn't it have been kinder just to kill all of us, the way you killed the humans in the space fleet and the planetary colonies? Why introduce a permanent contraceptive, so that we could slowly die out? What was the point in giving us 100 or 120 extra years to remain alive as a species, knowing what we've lost, knowing what was going to come—or what *wasn't* going to come, what will never come again?

I agree, I agree, it was kinder than what we did to you. I don't mean to defend the cruelty of my ancestors. But is behaving better than we did really the measuring stick you want to use?

No, I do understand the point. You wanted us to think about it. You wanted us to know what it meant. And the reason you're talking to me now is to see whether we got it, whether we did understand. As if I'm a representative sample.

Excerpt, **The Human Affliction,** *by Oma of the Lespentai:*

Some critics have suggested hypocrisy in the ceremony held on the surface of Terra when the last Earthbound human died peacefully in her sleep. Representatives of all the victorious species, sexes, genders, and belief systems honored human achievements in art, literature, science, and philosophy. They remembered human moments of valor and self-sacrifice. They spoke of the love of human parents for their children, of human life partners for each other. They felt the bitterness of the necessity that had brought them to this point. Those who could weep, wept.

Then every trace of human nucleic material that could be found on every planet was disrupted, even to the point of exhuming and vaporizing skeletons from ancient cemeteries.

Current scholarship debates the extent to which any of our respective cultures have recovered from the trauma of two centuries of misery. Numerous irrationalities and small cruelties have crept into the customs and traditions of each, and our current freedom from human oppression does not, apparently, free us from its influence. Further, the necessity of so complete an obliteration of an entire species could not help but leave its mark on us. No matter how fervently we may wish to recover our spiritual and ethical origins, we cannot wash the dust of our act from our limbs. We strive, however, for the self-awareness to understand that we are never free of the past, that both the evil done to us and the evil we must do lives in us always.

GREEN GIRL BLUES

_____*Martin L. Shoemaker*_____

"ARE YOU NIKO? They say you do mods."

The man she'd called *Niko* leaned back in his booth and stared at the girl, assessing the threat. He also looked around the bar to see who else might be watching. It was a small, dingy place, like he'd found near spaceports on a hundred worlds. He liked to lay low in quiet places like this while he drummed up business.

The man subtly moved his hand, shifting his sleeve so that the 'plaster hidden within would have a clear shot. He had never shot a girl that young, but it might come to that: either she was naïve, or he was getting set up by the Lund City police. She knew his current name, and not many on Pedersen did, but her approach was pretty awkward for the police. She could be just a kid, and somebody had blabbed. In that case, the man called Niko needed to decide: was it time to leave this world before trouble found him? Still, she might be a plant.

Niko snickered softly. She was *homo sapiens pedersens*, so of course she was a "plant". Pedersen's human settlers had found it ill-suited to crop growing—but well-suited to mining, energy, and trade—so they had engineered a gene mod: chloroplasts in the epidermis to synthesize nutrients from simple molecules plus light. So, like all the natives, the girl was a lovely shade of green.

Scan, he thought, and he tensed as his sensor web sent out a brief pulse. Somebody could be watching for a scan pulse, so he was ready to move. He saw the bartender, a waitress, and five patrons (three from off-world). He could fight his way out if he had surprise on his side, but it could get sticky.

No one showed any reaction. The pulse echoed back, and the results showed no weapons. Genotype read as unmodded *pedersens* female, approximate age of fifteen years—a minor on Pedersen.

The police in Lund City were no saints, but they didn't enlist juveniles. Niko kept his voice casual. "People say lots of things." He narrowed his gaze. "Some they shouldn't. And some don't know what they're talking about. Who're you?"

"I'm Sarah Sm—Sarah. That's all you need to know."

He started a search on the partial name. "Well, Sarah," he said, "you're drawing attention. You'd better sit down." She moved to sit across from him, but Niko raised his hand. "Nah. Over here by me."

"What?" Her face flushed, a murky brown shade as blood rushed to the surface.

"Sit." Niko smiled. Sarah swung to slap him, but he grabbed her wrist, pulled her closer and lowered his voice. "I won't hurt you, but I won't get hurt *for* you, either. Pretty young thing like you comes into a dump like this, and people notice. They'll assume you're either buying or selling, and I don't want anyone thinking that *I'm* selling. So smile and sit like we're arguing over price. I won't touch you, you don't try to slap me, but we have to play this game. Act like they expect, they'll forget you were ever here. You'd like that, wouldn't you?"

Sarah bit her lip, but she nodded. Niko let go of her wrist, and she sat on his side of the booth. Not too close, but that suited him. He wanted room to use his 'plaster if he had to.

A cop would've played along sooner. A thrill-seeker would've run by now. Niko began to suspect Sarah really wanted a mod. He lowered his voice further. "I don't do cosmetics, girlie. If you're looking for a boob job to catch the boys, keep looking."

"No!" Sarah shook her head. "I want a *real* mod. I want—I don't want to be green any more. I want to be a different species, and get off this world."

Niko's eyes narrowed. She *did* know something. This bar was small, out of the way, and too run-down to be connected to the local criminal element. His scouting showed that neither the Møller nor the Bruun families ran the place, though the owner probably paid protection to the Bruuns. So Niko came here searching for clients, but not often. Somebody had put the pieces together, or a client had blabbed. He had to know more.

Gently he asked, "And you came to me? Who you been talking too, girlie?"

Sarah looked down, her dark green hair falling in front of her eyes. "Svend."

"Svend?" There had to be ten-thousand Svends here.

"Svend…Bruun."

Niko shuddered as he modified his net search: *Sarah Sm* AND Svend Bruun.* The eldest son of the Bruun family was a mean one. He ran the family's street crime, including…Niko eyed Sarah again. "Aren't you a little young for one of Svend's girls?"

Sarah looked like she might try to slap him again. "It's not like that! I just…run errands for his people. I'm nobody, so nobody notices me."

Niko eyed her carefully. She was growing into a very attractive woman, and people always noticed them. Soon she would be useless as a courier, and Svend *would* put her to work on the streets. No wonder she wanted to escape.

One of his clients must have a connection with Svend, but who? For now, Niko had only one lead. "I'm no charter pilot, kid. You'll have to get off Pedersen yourself. But assuming I could get you modded…. That kind of work ain't cheap. You got money?"

"No," she said, but Niko saw a cagey look in her eyes. She had *some* money. "But I have…information."

"Information?"

Sarah whispered. "On the Bruun family. Jobs they've done, people they've hired." She swallowed. "That stuff's valuable, right? To someone with connections?"

And to Niko. Maybe it could tell him who was leaking word about him. It might put him crossways with the Bruuns, but he would take that chance. "It might be."

"So you get me modded, and get me off Pedersen."

"I said—"

"You must have connections, right?" She looked at Niko. "I'll give you a datacrypt. When I'm safely in the spaceport where he can't touch me, I'll send you the key."

Niko frowned. "And I'll open the datacrypt and find it empty. No, I need payment in advance."

"Take it or leave it," she said. "What I know could identify me to them. I have to be safe before I release it."

She looked fearless. Green-eyed ice. But something about those eyes.... Niko chanced one more pulse. Heart racing. Muscles tensed. Sarah was terrified of something.

Niko charged clients good money, but he wasn't going to rip off a scared little kid. He was a criminal (on some worlds), but he had standards.

He wrote an address on his napkin and slipped it into her hand. "Tomorrow. 10 a.m. If you're five minutes late, I'll be gone. I'll call you 'Amy'. Any other name, get away fast. It means one of us is being followed." He looked away. "*Now* I'm gonna grab you a bit, for show. And now you can slap me, and run out. Don't stop for anyone."

Ten seconds later, Niko sat alone in the booth, rubbing his cheek. She knew how to slap!

Niko tipped the bartender to summon an autocab. When the cab dropped out of the sky, Niko climbed into the seat, pulled the door closed, and tapped a random village far west of Lund. That gave him plenty of time to make calls. Airborne in an autocab was as close as he could get to a secure line on short notice.

Niko pulled a node address from his net and opened a chat channel. "Hi, Zeke," he sent, "this is Mitch." He assumed that the pilot's name was not Zeke, any more than his was Mitch—or Niko, for that matter. Throwaway identities were common on the shady side of society. *Mitch* was a name only the pilot knew.

"Mitch, my friend! How are the kids? How's Amy doing in school?"

Amy was further confirmation, another code word shared only with the pilot. With their identities mutually established, they got down to business. An eavesdropper would read local vacation plans, but actually, Niko arranged transport off Pedersen for him and Sarah—and for his considerable stock of gear. He would need his mod vat for this job, and that would take a lot of cargo space.

The departure time was the only major hiccup. The Pedersen Traffic and Customs Bureau was highly regimented. "Zeke" could only offer a couple of launch windows just before noon. Niko wasn't meeting Sarah until ten, leaving barely enough time for a quick cosmetic job to conceal her until they got off world.

Niko closed the chat and tapped the control pad to reroute the cab. But instead, the cab started dropping rapidly.

The autocab settled to the ground on a dark street in the country. The external lights came up, revealing a tall, thin Pedersen woman standing straight and ready to move. She wore the white-and-green helmet and jacket of Pedersen Traffic and Customs—and a pistol in her hand.

Niko sat in a plastic chair behind a metal table in a small room lit only by flickering illumination panels in the ceiling. Pedersen technology was mostly low, early to mid-twenty-first century by Terran standards. More reliable lighting was practically free on more advanced worlds, but too expensive for a government office here.

Niko wasn't restrained, and the customs officers hadn't roughed him up. They had taken his 'plaster, but it was disguised as an atmosphere compensator, a pump that ran air through a particle reservoir and up to his neckline. They looked it over and didn't notice anything unusual, but they took it anyway.

The inspector stood on the other side of the table and glared down through her visor. Her badge identified her as Inspector Carina Ravn. She towered over him, and he suspected her ancestral DNA had a strong Netherlands strain. So far, she had spoken only curtly to Niko and the two officers who had escorted him.

The officers left, and Niko was alone with the inspector. She pulled off her helmet and set it on the table, revealing a curly green mop of hair. "So let's go over this carefully, Mr.—" She checked his ID. "—Amédée Charlemagne. From Moreau?"

"From Frank," Niko said, with a long *a* sound. He had chosen the French-settled world because almost no one ever left there.

"And you trade in refined minerals and miniaturized devices."

Niko tried to seem friendly. "Nah, I'm a broker. I find what each world does best. Your people, you do the finest miniature work in this sector. Then I broker deals, and others do the shipping."

Ravn paced in front of the desk. "The bartender thought that your name was Niko something."

Niko cursed inwardly. He hadn't expected the bartender to give him up so easily after such a large tip. "Ah, just a nickname I picked up in the Tauran system."

The inspector raised an eyebrow. "The Tauran system?"

Niko cursed again. The inspector was brighter than most customs officers. "I deal all over Manifold Space. If it's imported, Taurans will pay extra just to lord it over their neighbors."

"But you're not Tauran?"

Niko pulled back his sleeves. "See any fur?" There hadn't been any for decades, not since his first mod. "I'm a Frank, native born." He took a deep breath. "So forgive me if I'm slow. Your air is…weak, ya know?"

"I see." Her brow furrowed. "So Mr. Charlemagne, why did you have the bartender summon and pay for your cab?"

Niko had expected that question. "I…owe a customer some money." When the inspector turned to look at him, he hastily added, "I'm gonna pay, I just need a little time. A deal fell through because the shipper got delayed, and their cargo spoiled. I lost a lot of dough on that one, and I'm still digging out. Last time we met, they threatened to break some bones! So I'm keeping a low profile until some other deals come through and I can repay them."

"And your customer would be…?"

"None of you concern, Inspector Ravn." No broker would share such information without a good reason. "The goods were made off Pedersen, the load was picked up off Pedersen, and it never passed through Pedersen space. Unless you claim jurisdiction in other systems, I got nothing to say."

"Fair enough." Again with the brow furrow. Then she spoke in a more casual tone. "Curious thing about that bar: we picked up some rumors that a modder does business there."

Niko acted surprised. "You mean a gene doc? I hadn't heard that. But then, I'm not from around here. I heard that that was illegal on Pedersen, but it's a customs concern?"

"It can be," the inspector answered. "The Genome Authority has its rules. It's my job to enforce them. We're a young settlement, only in our fourth generation. We must establish sufficient genetic diversity to ensure our long-term viability. So, at least for another generation, emigration is regulated, and modding is forbidden. As much as our youth might wish otherwise, travel off world is—" She paused. "—strictly controlled. We need to stabilize our genotype before we let anyone tinker with it again."

Niko was impressed. She understood the basics well. His only disagreement wasn't with her, it was with the Pedersen Genetic Council. His analysis told him their genome was stable already. "I see," he said slowly. "Well, if I knew anything about a modder, I'd tell you, inspector. I have nothing to hide."

"But we're not talking about just any modder," she said. "The man we want could pay for your silence. I may be stuck on this planet, but I *do* have sources off world." She leaned over the table and said in a lowered voice, "We're talking about Sandoval."

"Sandoval?" Underneath Niko's calm demeanor, every alarm in his network went off. "Wasn't that some...character in a show?"

The inspector didn't budge. "Yes, there was a video series, but it was based on a real person. Sandoval, the most wanted modder in Manifold Space. Surely you've heard stories of the Gene Wizard."

More alarms. "I prefer sports. You never know what will happen."

The inspector straightened up. "You didn't miss much. Badly written and overacted." Niko resisted the urge to agree with her. "But somewhere out there is the real Sandoval, wanted in fifteen systems."

Seventeen, Niko noted to himself. "And you think he might come to Pedersen?"

"Rumor is that he's in this sector. Maybe here already."

Niko had to get farther away from Pedersen than he had planned. "I wish I could help, but I broker goods, not services. Certainly not modding. So can I return to my hotel? I'm tired."

Ravn paused. "I have no more questions, but my superiors may in the morning. Perhaps we should hold you."

Niko would have little time to pack and ship his gear. It was time to push back. "I know my rights. If you're holding me, I wanna talk to the ambassador."

The inspector frowned. "I don't believe there's a Frank embassy on our world."

"No, but we have a reciprocal arrangement." Niko smiled. "With Terra."

Ravn turned a very pale shade of green. The home world was Pedersen's major trading partner, and the Terrans were known to throw their weight around just because they could. Niko was betting that a local customs inspector wouldn't want to draw their attention.

And it seemed he was right. She folded her arms, shook her head, and said, "That's not necessary. We can release you—but check with me before leaving the planet. Just in case I have more questions."

"Understood, inspector. We'll talk again," Niko lied smoothly. In a few hours, he would be off Pedersen, and he would never see her again. "Now please, I'm getting queasy. Can I have my compensator?"

An agent escorted Niko to the nearest tram stop on the west side of Lund. The trams were risky late at night. For every honest worker or late-night partygoer, there was a mugger or worse. Niko checked the reservoir on his 'plaster: two uses, three if he was careful. He adjusted his sleeve, and he boarded a tram for Lund's expensive tourist district where one of his hotel rooms was found.

The tram held eight other passengers, including two off-worlders. One was from Kleve, recognizable by his cumbersome water helmet. Next to him, a Tauran stood in the aisle. Her casual party dress exposed too much light-golden fur. Niko understood the urge to dress lightly and keep cool in fur, but it wasn't wise. A large young Pedersen in dirty overalls stared at her.

Then Niko realized the youth was also watching *him*. The man was dressed for rough labor, but he had a brooding look beneath his heavy green brows: suspicious, angry. Predatory.

Niko checked the tram map, and he decided to get off. It was two stops before his destination, but he liked his chances better on foot. He rose, ready to leave in a hurry—and the angry youth rose as well.

Niko responded from long habit, sending out a sensor pulse. The man had a gun holstered in his overalls, and a knife in his hand. He snaked through the passengers, past the Klevan and the Tauran.

When Niko saw the man start to lunge, he raised his left arm, aimed the chloroplaster, and thought a command: *Fire.*

Fine golden particles shot out, engulfing the man's upper body. He started to cough. The particles were in his lungs, choking him, but it was the exposed skin of his face and hands that forced him to the tram floor. The chloroplasts in his epidermis did more than just manufacture nutrients. The Pedersen gene engineers had adopted the chloroplast production codes from existing plants; and in plants, chloroplasts were a primary element of the immune system. They swarmed to the site of infection, firing off defense-signal molecules… and they actively killed off infected cells. Niko's tailored allergen particles made the man's immune system declare war on itself.

The man writhed and cried out in pain. Green blotches bubbled over his skin. It probably wouldn't be lethal, but Niko didn't care either way.

Some of the other passengers leaned over to see what was wrong with the youth, but then turned away as the residual allergen burned their skin. Three of them eyed Niko suspiciously. Another sensor pulse showed more guns.

Just then the tram reached its stop, and a dozen Pedersens started to board. Niko forced his way through them. As the last passenger stepped in, he leaped out, the doors sliding shut behind him. He rushed off the platform, sighed, and turned back to watch the tram leave. The three armed men were in the window, watching him as the tram pulled away.

Niko dashed up the escalator and out to a shaded business street, decorated in fake plastic trees. The dawn showed a few people on their morning commute. He ducked into a side street and peered back around the corner of a building, focusing his irises to zoom in on the tram station.

So much for delaying tactics. The three men appeared at the top of the escalator. Despite Niko's concealment, one saw him and started running his way. Niko resumed running as well.

When he heard the loud crack of an old-fashioned firearm, Niko thought a command: *Flush*. A small reservoir of epinephrine started dumping into his bloodstream. He would pay for that later when the exhaustion and the shakes hit, but he wanted to live that long. He sped away from his pursuers and around the next corner.

The 'plaster had only one use left, so Niko had to rely only on his legs, his wits…and a top-of-the-line internal data net. He launched the Chaos algorithm, a thousand attacks on every computer system within reach. Each attack was *designed* to fail. It triggered burglar alarms all along the block, and on nearby blocks as well. Lights flashed. Bells rang. Vehicle horns blared. People looked out doors and windows. Soon the police would appear, and the pursuers would have to deal with them.

Niko, though, would be nowhere in sight by then. He had one more trick, one he had hoped to save for breaking into the spaceport. Beneath the streets ran a cargo tram system, and Niko had paid good money for a security code for it. He saw an access plate ahead, and he sent out the code. The plate slid aside, he dropped down in, and it slid shut.

His code was only good for one use. Niko could run through the tunnels to the port, sneak in right under the nose of customs, and wave goodbye to Pedersen.

But he couldn't forget the fear in Sarah's eyes, nor the determination in her face. He suspected a lot of people had let her down in her short life. He refused to be another one.

Niko exited at a hidden spot half a block from the meeting place. There were only minutes to spare, and epinephrine anxiety made thinking difficult.

He saw no hunters, but he did see Sarah. She had dressed better this time: less flashy, more likely to blend in. There was a chill, and she paced back and forth with her hands in the pockets of a light jacket.

Niko hurried up to her. "Hi, Amy, sorry I'm late. We're going to miss the start of the show." He kept walking, and she fell in beside him. At a lower volume he added, "We gotta get to the Concordia hotel, one block south and four down. We may be followed, so if I tell you to move, don't argue. Got me?"

"Uh-huh," she said, and they kept walking. He had another room at the Concordia, chosen because the service yard there backed up against the spaceport fence. But first they had to survive to reach the hotel. Who had shot at him? The police were unlikely to knife first and ask questions later. Was it the Bruun family?

Before Niko could ponder that, he heard a voice behind them shout "Dagma!" He turned and far away saw a tall, heavy-set Pedersen man pushing through the crowd. His heart started to race again.

Then Niko felt a tug on his arm. He jolted, but then realized Sarah was pulling him into a dress shop. "What?"

"Trust me, I know what I'm doing," she answered. Then in a louder voice, "This is the *wrong* store, you idiot. Look!" She held up a sleeve. "These are kids' clothes! They're nice—" She stopped and smiled at a green-skinned female clerk. "—but they won't fit mother. I'll never find a gift for her. Take me somewhere else."

Niko's mind raced, and he realized her game: pampered princess and clueless servant. The clerk wouldn't suspect that they were hiding in the shop. "I'm sorry, miss, where shall we go next?"

Sarah was already moving through the store, right past the clerk. "There's a great place in the next block, and there's a rear entrance here. And don't touch anything. I don't want to pay for anything you get soiled."

Niko hurriedly followed Sarah out the door. "That was brilliant, kid," he said. But she was already moving. Where was she going in such a hurry?

Then he remembered. The Concordia. The danger. Damn epinephrine hangover. Lucky *she* was thinking straight. He ran to keep up with her.

Then as they neared the hotel district, Sarah started running as well, and he really started feeling the fatigue.

He was trembling and gasping when they reached the side door of the Concordia. He almost dropped his key card twice before it let them in. He pulled the metal door shut behind them, fell against the wall, and spent seconds catching his breath—seconds they couldn't spare, but the epinephrine left him no choice.

Sarah pulled at his arm. "Come on! Can't stop now."

Niko nodded, and he straightened, but he still shook all over. He led the girl to his windowless ground floor room and keyed them in.

His spare kit was near the door. He swung the door shut and locked the deadbolt. For good measure he pressed his taser against the electronic lock, shorting it out. Gasping still, he pointed at the big chair. Sarah looked at it, realized what he meant, and slid it up against the door.

Niko fell upon the bed. He *had to* treat his exhaustion, or he would collapse. Pawing through his kit, he found a quick-acting sedative. He jabbed himself with it and waited for his tremors to subside. As soon as he had control, he found ampules to treat his racing heart and his blood pressure.

Once Niko's pulse dropped into a normal range, he packed up his kit and got off the bed. Then he pointed at it. "This, too." She nodded, and they moved the bed up against the chair.

Niko turned to the heating panel in the rear wall. Normally these were sealed units, but he had unsealed his. With a quick twist, he removed the screws that held it in place. Then he gently set it down outside, avoiding any noise.

Sarah squeezed into the narrow opening. As she climbed through, Niko heard distant shouting from the corridor. Again, the booming voice: "Dagma!" It was followed by a crash of breaking glass.

Dagma? Niko started another search as he followed Sarah through to the service yard, a small paved area stacked with crates, tools, and artificial plants. He stuck the heating panel back into place, and then he and Sarah pushed a heavy crate in front of it.

"All right, over here." He brought smaller crates to the fence, and Sarah stacked them to form makeshift stairs. When the crates reached within a meter of the top, he said, "Hold it."

Just then, they heard crashing from his room, and Niko wondered how long the door would hold. "Hurry!" Sarah said softly.

Niko climbed until he could examine the top of the fence. There were power lines and spy eyes. He reached out a sensor pulse to touch them, and found stun beams concealed within. He could shut the systems down locally, but not for long before port security would detect them.

There was a louder crash from the room, followed by a thump. The blockades were falling, one by one.

Niko motioned Sarah up next to him. "OK, kid," he said, "when I say so, get your ass over that fence and don't stop to climb down. You can take the fall. Find cover and wait for me to follow." Another crash, and the heating panel shuddered. "But if I don't join you in thirty seconds, make your way to Pad 34, Berth 9. Find the pilot. Tell him you're Amy, and Mitch sent you. Got that?"

The large crate shifted a couple centimeters. Sarah nodded, and Niko thought a command through his network. When the spy eyes went down, he said, "Go!"

Sarah grabbed the fence top and vaulted over in one smooth motion. Niko liked her style, and he hoped she would get away.

He was less hopeful for himself. The big crate moved a little more. Soon the man behind it would squeeze an arm through and get more leverage. Niko made one last attempt to slow the man down more: he kicked down a few of the crates in his stairs. Then he grabbed the fence. He wasn't as spry as Sarah, but he hauled himself up to the top and looked down.

And he saw Sarah struggling to escape the grip of Inspector Ravn.

Niko paused, suspended between dangers. The crate made a scraping sound as it slid on the concrete, and one arm groped through the opening.

The kid would delay the inspector; and what could they charge her with? He could escape the yard before the big man came through. He should just run.

Niko swung his legs over the fence, dropped down into the spaceport, and landed in front of Inspector Ravn.

He was unsteady, an aftereffect of the epinephrine, but he straightened and turned to Ravn. "Let her go, inspector. It's me you want. I'm...your modder."

The inspector laughed. "Give *her* up? If you were really Sandoval, maybe the reward would be worth it, but we know better, right? You're just a petty modder. Don't you know who she is?"

Just then his search engine pinged with the answer. "Dagma Bruun."

"Uh-huh," Ravn said, and the kid deflated. "Only daughter of Povl Bruun, the boss of half this city. We've got her on breaking and entering into a spaceport. That's an *interstellar* crime. Papa will do anything to protect her from that kind of trouble. It's the first real leverage we've had over him."

Niko heard a long scrape of plastic on concrete. "And that's Svend, I suppose."

Sarah—no, Dagma—nodded. For the first time Niko saw tears on her face. "Please…. What he'll do…"

Niko looked at the kid, then at Ravn. "Stay calm, inspector. I'll give you what you want, and more. Dagma…" He looked back at the girl. "Gently take out my payment and show it to her."

Dagma looked at Ravn, and the inspector let go of her wrist. The girl reached into her pocket and held out a large silver card.

"What's that?" Ravn asked.

"A datacrypt. Let her go and it's yours."

Ravn eyed him suspiciously. "I can take it now. *And* both of you."

"Uh-uh," Niko stared straight into her eyes. "I can pulse it from here, wipe it clean, and you'll lose everything." It was a bluff. That model of datacrypt was double hardened. But he hoped the inspector didn't know that.

"Everything?" she asked. "Meaning…?"

"*Everything*. Every note she has on the Bruun family operations, it's all there. Dates and places, operators and victims. She knows it *all*." Dagma nodded.

"You're an honorable woman, inspector," Niko continued. "If you give your word, you'll keep it. Once Dagma gives you that information, you *have to* let her escape. She won't be safe here anymore. You can have the datacrypt—" His voice wavered. "—but let me get Dagma off this world."

Ravn glared at him, her lips drawn into a hard line. "I could let *her* go, but I have more questions for you."

For an instant, the inspector stared at Dagma. The woman was distracted, and Niko saw a chance to surprise her with the 'plaster. But that would engulf Dagma as well. If she had an allergic reaction, he could never get her to Zeke's ship in time. He had no choice. It was all up to the inspector.

Then Ravn nodded. "We have a deal. Give it to me." Niko nodded as well, and Dagma handed over the datacrypt.

"Now what?" Dagma asked, trembling.

"Same as before," Niko answered, "Pad 34, Berth 9, Amy, Mitch. But inspector, can she get there without getting stopped? She has no credentials."

"These are your credentials," the inspector said. She pulled off her helmet, once more revealing the curls beneath, and handed it to Dagma. "Put this on." Then she took off her jacket and handed it over as well. "Act like you're in charge, and those'll get you past most of the port staff. If anyone stops you, give them code Z921, and tell them you're on an errand for Inspector Ravn. They'll contact me, and I'll clear you."

"Z921," Dagma repeated. "Pad 34. Where is it?"

The inspector pointed. "Over on the south field."

Dagma turned away, then turned back. "Niko, I—Thank you."

Niko kept his face impassive. "Get moving, kid. Don't miss that launch." She started jogging away, and Niko shouted after her, "Tell Mitch if he doesn't take good care of you, I'll kick his ass."

Dagma looked back with a brief smile and then kept jogging. Only when her back was to him did he let himself smile in return.

Niko and the inspector watched the dwindling figure picking her way toward the berths. Then a scraping sound reminded him that they weren't out of trouble yet. "Inspector," he said softly, "you're about to have a visit from Svend Bruun."

"Oh, really?"

Niko nodded and turned back to the fence. Ravn turned as well to see elegantly coiffed green hair rise over the fence. She reached for her gun, but Niko gently said, "He'll run. Look away, pretend we didn't see him." She frowned, but she did as he said. "Did you know your security is vulnerable to a Q-modal cyber attack? Someone with the right software can shut them right down."

"No!" The inspector's eyebrows raised. "Really?"

Niko nodded when he heard heavy shoes thump against the fence. "Or turn them back on." He thought the command, and vibrant *pops* of multiple stun beams sounded behind them. They turned to see Svend fall into the spaceport, unconscious. "What was it you said? Breaking and entering into a spaceport, an interstellar crime?"

"It couldn't happen to a nicer creep."

87

Ravn opened a comm to summon a pickup team. When she was done, Niko held his arms out, wrists exposed. "Well," he said, "we had a deal. I'm an honorable man. Take me in."

Ravn laughed. "An honorable modder, imagine that. You're sure you never watched 'The Gene Wizard'?" Then she laughed again, shaking her head and ignoring his wrists. "You didn't have to save her. You could've gotten away, gotten lost in the city. But that character in the show…. 'Never double-cross a client, especially not when they're in danger.'"

Ravn leaned in closer, and she whispered. "I lied. I *loved* that show when I was a kid. I wanted to be Sandoval, or one of his clients…to change my life, to be someone else and get off this rock." She stepped back and spread her arms. "But this—" She waved her hands, gesturing at her uniform. "—this is as close as I'll ever get. In the Traffic and Customs Bureau, once in a while I get out to the orbital platform. Twice I went on extraditions to other stars…but I didn't have the guts to sneak away and just keep going." She turned and looked at the fading speck that was Dagma. Niko thought he saw moisture welling up in her eyes.

He lowered his wrists and cleared his throat. "You didn't have to save her either. You could've stuck with your original plan, used her for leverage. It would've worked."

Ravn snorted. "Or I could've just taken the card. Pulse wipe? On a *silver* datacrypt? Not a chance."

"You knew I was bluffing? But then…"

"For a moment, I was a kid again, wanting to believe that the Gene Wizard would pull off a miraculous save. And then your plan…. It was the right thing to do. She would've been a prisoner, locked away until Povl married her off to unite with another family. No."

Niko stared at Dagma, dialing his lenses to maximum zoom. "She'll still stick out like a…well, like a green thumb. Not many Pedersens in Manifold Space. If Povl wants her back, he'll find her."

"No he won't," the inspector said. "Not after you mod her."

"What?"

Ravn slapped his shoulder. "Get moving. We can't hold that launch window all day." Then she smiled. "Get to your ship, Charlemagne. Or Niko, or whatever your name is."

Niko smiled. "You're a good person, inspector."

They shook hands, awkwardly, and she said, "I'd ask if I'll ever see you again, but you're a modder. I won't recognize you if I do, will I?"

Niko squeezed her hand. "No, you won't. But I'll recognize you. And I won't forget you."

MINDJACK

_____Jody Lynn Nye_____

STIRRING. DISTURBANCE. *shooting pain in the head*. Kirsta moaned and writhed, trying to make the sensations go away. They continued, adding sounds to the assault. She fought back against the advancing monsters with long, blue fur, their shaggy arms outstretched to claw her to death. One raced ahead of the pack, its jaws engulfing her face.

"Kirsta!" it bellowed. "Open your eyes! C'mon!"

She sat up, panting. The monster was gone. She was in a brilliantly lit white room, surrounded by mounded oval shapes.

"*Bozhe moi*, that was a good one," the thin, sallow-skinned man said, kicking his legs on the bunk next to hers. He had shiny dark hair and beard cut to a few millimeters in length. "I'm going to save that for later."

"Shut up, Sergey," said the taller man. He had curly blond hair framing a long, narrow, dark-skinned face. He pushed aside the life-support mask and the massage sleeves, slipped an arm under Kirsta's shoulders and helped her to sit up.

Are you all right? he asked through the link. *Do you know who you are? Do you know where you are?*

Kirsta's mind cleared almost at once. Those were the standard questions. It took a moment to recognize her shipmates, but it all came back to her. She nodded.

I am Kirsta Melanitis, chief medical officer of Earth Podship South America, *part of the fleet en route to Goldfarb in the Leo cluster.*

Right! Senior Medtech Omar Graib hugged her and grinned over his shoulder at Sergey Ostropov, a senior computer technician the same age. It looked as if they were still together. She was glad. They were a great couple. *Still haven't killed each other*, Omar thought.

It was weird being awake without dozens of other minds and voices echoing through her consciousness. She never thought about how isolated the ships were, way out in the void, hurtling at near-lightspeed toward Leo, except at moments like this. She smiled at Omar and Sergey, glad of their company.

"How long's it been this time?" Kirsta asked.

Omar smiled, his bright white teeth stunning in his sable-brown face. "Sixty years. We've been awake four. We'll be with you one more year before we go down again."

Kirsta sighed with relief. Her third rotation since leaving Earth, but the longest yet, and she felt just fine.

"Only 830 to go. How do I look?"

"*You* look fine," Omar said, with unconscious emphasis. She caught the sensation of anxiety, and it triggered an increase in her own.

"Uh-huh. Who doesn't?"

"Noreen Koh," Sergey said. He had always been blunt. "She's dead. Some kind of neural collapse. SANDMAN didn't catch it until it was too late. I'm sorry. I liked her, too."

In her mind, Kirsta had a vision of a desiccated body in a narrow oblong shell like the one in which she sat, hardly recognizable as the quick-moving, intelligent psychologist she had come to like and respect.

"Damn." As she had been trained to do in each of her awakenings, she worked her arms and legs slowly, then moved her head from side to side. Her neck cracked. Sergey jumped.

"That hurt," he said. "Close your eyes next time, eh?"

"Sorry," she said. "How are the other ships?"

"Good," Omar said. "Shift Three is becoming operational on all six of the others. All systems green."

"That's terrific," she said, stretching her arms out and feeling the muscles and nerve endings come to life. "I can't wait to talk to everyone! Let's get the rest of Phase Three up."

Omar and Sergey glanced at each other nervously.

"Come have some breakfast first," Omar said. He helped her up, and recoiled, wrinkling his blunt nose. "Ugh! Maybe you should take a shower."

An hour later, Krista sat in the refectory, empty except for the three of them. She had put on one of her favorite coveralls, rainbow striped with strands of glittering crystals clacking together on the hems of the sleeves. Her sleek, short black hair was still wet from a rare, precious water-shower. That was a privilege only available after waking from deepsleep, partly to sluice off the accumulation of dead skin cells, partly for the experience. The sensation of dozens of gentle threads of water striking her body all over sent a frisson of pleasure quivering through her nerves. She checked her stats. During the sixty years, her hip-heavy figure had lost two kilograms. Her hair was five centimeters longer. One of her secondary molars needed attention, as the gum beneath it had receded .5 millimeters.

Krista took a fragrant, slightly bitter sip from her cup. The colorful, almost jarring décor in the refectory blasted her eyes like a second dose of caffeine, but it was intentional. She and the rest of the crew on all seven ships had to absorb all the stimuli possible while awake to ensure arriving healthy on Goldfarb.

Even after three long periods of hibernation, she found it hard to believe that she'd been asleep longer than a night. The dreams had been pretty vivid, but they were supposed to be.

Dr. Charlene Goldfarb of Stanford University—*the* Goldfarb, for whom the new planet was being named—must have received transmissions by now to assure her that her processes were proving successful. She had spent over two centuries working on ways of transporting large populations of human beings between Sol and Alpha Centauri. With the data from uncounted experiments in cryogenic preservation, hypnosis, generation ships and other systems before her, she lit on the fundamental flaws in each.

To make a really long-haul expedition work, adaptations to both environment and the humans themselves had to be initiated. The first of Goldfarb's breakthroughs, *deepsleep*, mimicked the brain activity of very small children. The system suspended subjects into deep delta-wave sleep, but slowed bodily processes down to near immobility.

In a few extreme cases, subjects' hearts beat only a few times a year. Problems arose when studies began on animals with higher cognitive function. Their brains started out with healthy theta and delta waves, but over increased intervals, those neural functions decreased dangerously. It seemed that the brain became bored with its own dreams in the deepsleep shell. After a time, the mind had worked through all the stimuli and memory it had stored during its waking period, then began to twist the brain's emgrams almost into a moebius loop, looking for something new to explore. Starved for input, the brain deteriorated. When these subjects emerged from deepsleep, there was a greatly increased incidence of psychosis, sometimes resulting in fatalities. Nearly all of the volunteers on the first human trial regressed to an almost anencephalic state of being, locked in and unable to communicate with others. Human beings could not sleep for centuries until they reached their destinations. Otherwise, the ship would arrive with a population of healthy bodies with no higher brain function.

Goldfarb's solution was to wake the subjects at designated intervals, and subject them to a period of intense stimulus, so when they went back into their pods they would dream vividly, keeping their minds as healthy as their bodies, surfacing only to refresh the temporal lobes with new stimuli. Because the travelers would need to wake up frequently for their mental health, their lifespans were increased by inducing regeneration of genetic telomeres, thereby delaying age-related cell deterioration by centuries. The splicing also created a population whose hypothalamus accepted input readily and dreamed intensely for longer periods.

Like many scientists, Goldfarb was her own primary guinea pig. When she waved the fleet farewell, she was nearly four hundred years old. Krista and her colleagues could expect to be in their early two-hundreds on arrival, with almost a century of fertility ahead of them.

"We've got the holochamber set up for you with some new experiences," Omar said, pouring her another cup of coffee. "*Africa* sent over a squirt that you just won't believe—jousting, from some medieval recreation society in Malaysia. I don't know who was hoarding that all this time, but you'll love it. You ought to get your first stimulus session in as soon as possible."

During each mandatory waking period, settlers were assigned a range of activities, such as martial arts, creative arts, sports, tournaments, shows, music, educational seminars, immersion in sensory overload in the holochamber, new foods, perfumes, textures, and encouraged to participate in personal relationships, for a period from one to five years, depending on their personalities and the contracts they had signed on Earth. Omar and Sergey's relationship had come out of one of those early sessions. It had continued, whereas Krista had been dumped by her first affair and grew away from the second by mutual consent. No experience was wasted. Plenty of input to process in deepsleep meant keeping the mind healthy.

"Looking forward to it," Krista said, glancing around at the empty tables. "So, what's the delay on getting the rest of Phase Three out of bed? There are only forty-five others. Do you need my help waking them up?"

"Well, we wanted to talk to you in private first," Omar said, drumming his long fingers on the tabletop. "Before there's anyone else up who can read our thoughts."

"A heart-to-heart," Sergey added, sitting stiffly next to his lover.

Their mental states were an emotional jumble, full of woe and strange images, so Krista assumed they wanted to talk about their relationship.

To ensure safety for the travelers, Goldfarb built SANDMAN, the central computer system that monitored all the humans in deepsleep and maintained their body functions throughout. Based upon American, British and Japanese technology of the 21st and 22nd centuries, SANDMAN could read their thoughts, both sleeping and waking. To the shock of subjects in early trials, the link to SANDMAN meant that the subjects could also read one another's thoughts. Goldfarb was surprised but pleased. Another problem the project coordinators wanted to avoid was isolation. Space travel was dangerous. The small sample of fellow beings on any crew meant that the interactions had to be more intense by comparison with the casual relationships. Telepathic and telempathic connection jumpstarted intimacy among the crew.

When reading someone else's mind was as easy as hearing them speak, it created a new problem: a lack of privacy. Everyone's thoughts, complimentary or otherwise, were open to everyone else. While the settler candidates had been analyzed and interviewed to make sure they were reasonably compatible, no one gets along all the time. So they required an out, a private room, where they could keep their thoughts to themselves. Mechanical devices, like a box to put over one's head to shut out the others, were impractical. Goldfarb used a far simpler device, that of shutting the eyes. When SANDMAN detected closed lids, it stopped all mental input and output from a person, allowing them to get their thoughts under control. That meant dreams were off limits, as was any pondering one did awake with closed eyes. As a medical officer who could not avoid interaction with the crew, Krista made frequent use of her private space, as when some of her fellow passengers just pissed her off to the point where she needed either a timeout or a blaster. Each ship had its own SANDMAN, making each a unique familial group and adding to the cohesion of internal society.

"Fine," Krista said. She glanced at the wall chronometer. It was programmed to phase through numerous different representations of the time, intended to make the crew puzzle out the reading and exercise the problem-solving neurons. This one was easy: ten dots on one side and eight on the other. It had been just over an hour since she had awakened. A respectable interval for revival. Now she had to get to work.

"Can our talk wait until I've checked in with the other ships and got a progress report on the health across the fleet? I need to hear from all the Phase Two medics before any of them doss down again."

"Uh, could you wait for a while?" Sergey asked, nervously.

"Why?" she asked, suspicious of the guilty looks on their faces. She tried to activate the link, but both of them closed their eyes. "Dammit, what did you two do now?"

"We got bored," Sergey admitted, but he still kept his eyes shut. "Promise you won't get mad?"

Kirsta moaned.

Screw human nature. It was the one thing that neither the nerds back on Earth or the sophisticated computers could foresee or control. The podship system was supposed to be nearly foolproof, but as anyone could tell you, proclaiming something to be foolproof only meant that the really determined fools would test that hypothesis to destruction.

"All right," she said, with a sigh. "Let's hear it. What did you do?"

"Well…" Omar began, cracking his knuckles. "You know, after a while you've seen all of the holos on the ship, listened to all the music, and eaten the disgusting new dishes SANDMAN thinks you ought to try?"

"Yes?"

"And, well, you've done cuddle-puddles and boxing matches and freaked out on flashing lights and hallucinogens, and you totally hate group sports, and none of the books or movies left in the library appeals to you?"

"And you can only make love so long before everything hurts," Sergey added. His eyes were still closed, so thank God she didn't have to relive one of their energetic encounters again.

"TMI!" Krista declared. "Get to the point."

"I thought it would be kind of interesting to see what other people were dreaming about," Sergey said, almost casually. "We kind of started peeking in."

Krista was horrified. "How in hell did you do that? SANDMAN is code-locked."

"Come on, girl, I'm the assistant chief Information Officer. I *installed* SANDMAN. If I have to check out a file to make sure it isn't corrupted, it's not technically snooping, is it?"

"That's splitting hairs," Krista said, impatiently. It was a terrible invasion of privacy. Well, what was done was done. "Okay, I suppose that the people whose dreams you were tapping are among the group we're supposed to wake up today, and you need me to mediate between you?"

"Not exactly," Omar said. Both of them opened their eyes.

Thanks to the link, she saw the awful truth even as Sergey said it.

"It was your dreams, Krista."

"*What?*"

"You've got a really creative imagination," Sergey said, giving her his most charming smile. "Even after sixty years, it's still clicking away. Your dreams were far more interesting than anyone else we tapped on Phase Three. Or Phase Four."

"It means you're unusually healthy," Omar added. "We enjoyed it so much that we started adding a little stimuli. All in the name of medical science, of course."

Kirsta sat hunched over as if someone had punched her in the stomach. She dragged in a breath.

"What *kind* of stimuli?"

"Strong odors. Perfumes, citrus peel, rubber foam. One time, Sergey waved a dirty sock in front of your nose. It took a long time, but you reacted."

Dirty socks. She remembered dreaming of that sharp, gagging odor.

"I remember that one," she said. "I think I was wandering over the surface of the Moon. It all smelled like green cheese. I met an alien—"

"—with a horn for a mouth," Sergey said, nodding. "Yeah."

Kirsta glared at him.

"How the hell do you know that?"

"Um. I was watching?"

"But my eyes were closed. That was *private*, between me and SANDMAN."

"I know. We're sorry. Please forgive us?"

Kirsta looked from one to the other. She hurt to the depths of her soul at the thought that her friends and men she thought of as responsible colleagues could break protocol like that. But she was going to have to live with them, and they with her, for hundreds of years yet to come.

"I will," she said, standing up. "I know I will. At the moment, though, you two are on my shit list. Come and help me start waking people up. They're going to know what you did, and you're going to have to live with that. Then, I have to call in to the other ships."

They hesitated.

"Now, what? Why shouldn't I call *Africa* or *Australia*?" The sheepish looks on their faces made her gasp with open horror. "Oh, tell me you didn't!"

Sergey shrugged. "Maybe we did...?"

"But they were *my* dreams! My personal dreams!"

"They were really evocative! My sister Zohra is the assistant chief engineer on *Asia*. We got to talking, and Zohra asked to see them. It was just a microsquirt of data. She took it into the holochamber. She thought it was cute! Much better than most of the videos that we use for intense stimulation. You're a real artist."

"How many did *she* show it to?"

"Not too many," Omar said, uneasily. "Only the ones who were awake...three years ago. The last section of Phase Two. About... twenty. And word got around to the other ships. Zohra's roommate sent it to his cousin on *Australia*, and *Australia* sent it to *Europe*. *Europe* added it to their stimulus program. Everybody's seen it. Then they asked if we had any more. And...we did."

Kirsta groaned. Three years. They had been tapping her mind for three years.

"You're probably the most popular person on all seven podships right now," Sergey said, brightly.

"You had the whole damned starship to play with. Why did you have to interfere with *me?*"

"We like you," Omar said. "We got curious about what you'd dream of. And we really didn't think you'd mind...this much."

"I'm sorry," Sergey said. Kirsta threw up a hand. Combined with her mental whiplash, it had the psychic force of a slap across the face. Both men recoiled. Omar looked angry for a split second, but the emotion passed, submerged in shame. Krista didn't care.

"No. I need a minute. I really need a minute. Don't talk to me!"

The sensation went beyond physical pain. She felt deeply violated. During her tenure on the ship, she had sat through mandatory psychological testing and intense examination to make sure she was coping. Krista had answered questions for SANDMAN that she would never have put in a diary, let alone told to another living creature. She had participated in sexual encounters that explored parts of her body that had never been touched, all in the name of mental stimulation and emotional health. Some of it she had enjoyed, some not. But her dreams were always her own. No one on the podships ever spoke of their nightly fantasies unless they felt like it. Dreams were between her and the computer. SANDMAN only observed her to make certain that her mind was staying healthy. The contents were sealed in files only accessible through multiple passwords and firewalls, all of which Sergey was capable of bypassing. It was his job to keep the computers functioning. Of *course* he had figured out how to break into them. But he should not have, not without her consent. It was rape. It was burglary. She had been *mindjacked*. Krista was furious.

"Krista?"

Krista sprang up from her chair.

"Leave me alone. I…. I don't think I can ever forgive you. Either of you."

"Krista! Come on, Krista, we're your friends." Omar tried to tease his way into her mind, sending soothing thoughts her way.

She just wanted to be alone with her pain.

She shut her eyes, closing them out. Feeling with hands and mind, she stumbled toward the refectory door.

All of Krista's senses had been enhanced since she was an embryo. There was no need to use her eyes for anything but detail work and reading. Her sense of touch extended like a bat's out to all solid objects around her. She felt the texture of the walls and floor, and stalked away from them, confident that she wouldn't slam into a wall or the edge of a door, but at that moment, she didn't really care.

SANDMAN, get me to the holochamber.

Obligingly, the computer began to nudge her forward. When Krista felt a rush of air indicating a corridor, SANDMAN made the left turning feel more appealing. She took it. A few more turns and a lift ride up a level or so brought her into the womblike chamber. Krista let herself open her eyes then. At the periphery of her mind, she sensed Omar and Sergey, rueful, beginning operations to activate the rest of Phase Three. Krista knew she ought to be in the deepsleep chamber alongside them, but she needed distance. Maybe a holo would take the edge off her anger.

The menu appeared in midair. Tiny rotating images from each of the experiences indicated what took place in those recordings. The seventh one down on the second column showed a horn-nosed, blue-faced alien. Her dream! Krista swiped at it with an angry gesture. It disappeared, to be replaced with an orchestra conductor in a severe black gown.

"SANDMAN, how many of these files list me as the creator?"

The air cleared except for eight icons, including the horn-nosed alien. The date-stamps showed that they had been added one at a time over three years, the latest only a couple of weeks old. But Sergey had said they had tapped other people.

"How many files were added in the last three years?" she asked.

Her icons snapped into a column at the left, while more columns appeared, each headed by the image of a face. She recognized all five of the members of Phase Three and two from Phase Four. None had more than one or two recordings. Sergey and Omar had a lot of apologizing to do. Krista knew she ought to go back and mediate the inevitable confrontation. She wasn't happy about it, but it was her job.

Out of curiosity, she touched an icon belonging to a Phase Four member, a biochemist from Alpha. The room filled with black and white diagonals and rows of fluffy white bunnies with pink eyes. One of the bunnies was five times the size of the others, but instead of dominating the group, it huddled away from them in fear. Dreams rarely had coherent story structure or much in the way of continuity. The room changed to an undersea scene of jellyfish battling against dangling clumps of seaweed. In addition to the audio/visual input, she sensed discomfort and frustration, along with outright fear of confinement. She began to derive insights from the recording.

As a psychologist, she detected some deep-seated insecurity about body image in this chemist. Xe was intersex, dealing with identity issues. The biochemist wouldn't be awakened until five years after Krista went back to sleep. She'd leave notes for Dr. Mundiat, the psychiatrist who oversaw mental health in Phase Four. Maybe, and she very much hated to admit it, maybe Sergey and Omar were on to something.

She closed the file. More icons bounced up and down, demanding her attention. Krista almost reached for one, until guilt overwhelmed her. Really, she should not have opened other people's files. It didn't matter that her own were on display all over the fleet. With determination, she pushed all the stolen files aside and chose an experience that dropped her onto a freezing ski slope under clear blue skies with a fir tree rushing toward her. Still, she thought as she edged leftward to avoid the collision, fresh, cold air battering her face, she would have to refer the question of useful access to Lt. Commander Sekurka, the First Officer, who even now was probably coming out of stasis. Fairness demanded that she acknowledge that there was some diagnostic benefit to having another human look over the contents of people's dreams.

Or not. Her enjoyment of the ski slopes was interrupted by overwhelming sensations of fury and guilt. She stopped the recording to listen. Lt. Commander Sekurka was awake, all right, and he immediately comprehended what Omar and Sergey had been doing.

You could destroy the entire colony with meddling like that! Our society was based on trust that we'd have privacy! Sekurka bellowed.

Mental images of the two men being stuffed into a deepsleep pod that was sealed with molten lead flooded her mind. She had to intervene. No penalties had been set for dream-violation, and Sekurka felt as if he was going to overreact grossly.

"Shut down!" Kirsta ordered. The winter images receded. Sending soothing thoughts ahead of her, Kirsta headed for the lifts.

The situation worsened while she rushed toward the Phase Three deepsleep chamber. All forty-five of the pods had been triggered and were in various stages of releasing their occupants. Six—no, eight—no, ten of the sleepers were awake. Even in their drowsy stage, they were shocked by what Omar and Sergey had done. Krista's mind was bombarded with images. The two men were being torn to pieces, frozen to death, or riddled with laser fire by the angry settlers.

"Help us!" Omar pleaded, reaching out to Krista when she appeared. The crowd around them had not yet taken any physical revenge, but Life-Support Specialist Bodine looked as if he was about to tear a pod out of its moorings and hit them with it. She rushed to get in between them and the newly awakened crew. Everyone on both sides started shouting at her.

"All right, all right!" Krista shouted, holding her hands in the air.

"What did you know about all this, doctor?" Lt. Commander Sekurka demanded, looming over her. His craggy face was still dusty with accumulated skin cells. The shock had hit him even before he had a chance to clean up.

"They violated protocol, sir," Kirsta said. She allowed the others to share her feelings of frustration. The crowd seemed to calm a little as they realized she felt the same way they did. "They were curious. I can understand that, to a certain extent."

"How?" Bodine bellowed. "How could they do it?"

"Haven't you ever wondered what people dreamed about?" she asked, dampening her emotions and projecting cool reason. Bodine's deep red complexion cooled slightly. "I have, but I'd ask instead of doing what these two have done. I know you're angry. I was angry. I *am* angry. But it's not up to us to decide on a punishment for them. It's up to the command staff. Lt. Commander, I'm at your service if you want to confer."

"Right," Sekurka said, straightening his sleep tunic. "All right, you two. We're going to the conference room right now!"

The officer marched the two miscreants out of the sleep chamber.

With SANDMAN's help, Krista kept urging calm thoughts on the rest of Phase Three. She ushered the first dozen off to the showers and brought coffee for the ones who couldn't face jets of water first thing after waking up. Her first shipboard love, Ensign Pauline Sai, helped assign shifts in the holochamber and the gymnasium.

"Did you feel anything when they were reading your dreams?" the petite woman asked, as the two of them closed the now-empty pods and set them on 'sanitize.'

"Not really," Krista said. "They made me smell things, but that's all."

"Why don't you want to punish them? I can tell you're sympathizing. Everyone else wants to kill them!"

Krista shook her head.

"Even after the indoctrination we've all undergone, I don't think I'd have been mad about it if they had asked me first. I mean, some dreams are really personal, but they were more interested in the weird stuff. Monsters, flying dreams, going outside naked, those kinds of things. Don't get me wrong, I'm still mad. I've just had an hour or two to think a little harder about it. Have we been wrong?"

"No!" Pauline said, her small face set in a grimace. "They were stealing your private thoughts! What good could it possibly do?"

Krista smiled ruefully as she discarded a used respiration mask filter and replaced it with a fresh one. "Maybe they just didn't have enough of their own."

A couple of very tense hours later, Omar and Sergey returned to the sleep chambers. They were wearing plain khaki jumpsuits. Instead of maintenance robots, they pushed a mop cart and a vacuum unit.

"You can go now," Omar said, his narrow jaw set. "We're on maintenance duty for the foreseeable future. We're first call for spills and vomit."

"You earned it," Pauline said, her thoughts and expression ice cold. She patted Krista's arm. "I'll see you later. I don't need to be in the same room with these two."

Around them, Krista could feel the ship coming to life with all the other minds. The crewmembers in the holochamber were having a hell of a party. Bodine was rediscovering scotch. Sekurka was having a lively but not very happy conversation with his counterpart on *Africa*. All of them were throwing mental daggers at Sergey and Omar. The two men winced with every fresh onslaught. Though she had her own grievances, she felt sorry for them.

"I'll stay," Krista said. "I'm almost done with the filters in here. I ought to go check on Phases Four and Five while I'm at it."

SANDMAN monitored all twelve of the phase chambers. To keep the ship's resources and recycling units from being overwhelmed, one phase was brought out of stasis at a time. Only a few people stayed awake to brief the next section of the crew. As representatives of the medical and computer departments, Omar and Sergey were the designated reporters this round from Three to Four. Normally, there would be five or six people. The fact that those two were left to their own devices almost certainly was the reason they'd abused their position. No matter. She could tell by their behavior that they would never violate privacy again.

Krista left them cleaning up in Three and went down to the next level to Four. The long, white enamel capsules had clear windows over the occupant's head and shoulders. Their eyes were covered with light pads that kept the tissues moist. A mask covered the rest of the face, keeping a light but oxygen-heavy mix available for the extended breaths drawn during deepsleep. It was so quiet in the white-walled chamber that she could hear her breathing and footsteps.

The others' actions had left her with a lot to think about. How much of her dreams belonged to her, really, and how much was the result of exterior stimulation? She would write up a proposal to investigate the phenomenon, but she'd probably have to wait until the captain came out of his current sleep period to have it approved. Oh, well, patience was something the colonists all had to cultivate on a thousand-year journey.

She became aware of the peeping of a muted alarm. She ran around the chamber, seeking out which of the capsules was malfunctioning. No lights were visible on any of them.

"SANDMAN, where is the alarm?" she asked aloud.

"Four stroke twenty-three," the calm voice said, and an image appeared in her mind of the numbers. "Life support system is functioning normally. Subject is in distress."

Phase Four? Krista ran for the lifts.

Omar, Sergey, down to Four! There's an alarm!

In the tomblike quiet of the Phase Four chamber, a single red light shone from the top of a capsule at the far left rear. She ran to open the capsule. The occupant was a middle-aged man, muscle running to fat, with a thatch of gray hair. Krista knew him. The two of them had been awake at the same time during her first rotation.

"Who is it?" Omar asked, racing into the room. He pulled the emergency kit from the wall panel.

"Chief Engineer Marquez," Krista said. She scanned the life signs on the side of the capsule. "It doesn't look like anything is wrong. Temperature normal for deepsleep. Wait, respiration, once every twenty days, heartbeat every three. He's slowing down. That shouldn't be happening."

Sergey peeled back the eye cover and pried open one of the man's dark brown eyes.

Krista slapped his hand away. "What are you doing?"

"Checking his dream state," Sergey said. "He's within four years of waking up, right?"

"So?"

"So," Sergey said, urgently, willing her with all his emotions to understand, "he might be running out of dreams."

"Ridiculous!" Krista exclaimed.

"No, it's not," Omar said. "We've had a lot of experience looking into people's minds over the last three years. He's older. His imagination might not be as flexible as young people's. Don't look at me like that! It doesn't matter now how we know it. Can't you check?"

"I...I don't know how, if SANDMAN doesn't," Krista said.

"Step back!" Sekurka barked, storming into the chamber with two lieutenants at his heels. He gestured forcefully at Omar. Even Krista could feel it. "Get away from that man. Now!"

"Sir, he's in distress," Krista said. "SANDMAN says that his life support is normal. I don't know what's wrong."

"His mind's empty," Sergey insisted. "His body won't die, but he'll shut down. His programming's become corrupted, just like a computer."

"Leave the room," the officer snapped, but Omar and Sergey didn't move. Sekurka looked at Krista. "What can we do for him? Can we bring him out of deepsleep?"

"You can, but he'll be pissed off about it," Lt. Borgqvist said. She was a tall, thin woman with long golden hair and almond-shaped eyes who wore engineering insignia on her gold-and-blue paisley sleeve. "He resents every minute awake before we get to Goldfarb. He only takes a year of intense stimulus before dossing down again. He's fifty years older than I am, and he wants to make it to Goldfarb as young as he can be."

"SANDMAN, is that true?" Sekurka asked the air.

"Affirmative."

"Sir, if we don't wake him up, he won't make it to Goldfarb," Omar said. "His mind is sputtering to a halt. Noreen Koh died, probably from the same problem."

Sekurka turned to Krista.

"You're the psychologist. I don't want to lose our chief engineer. Can we do something for him without waking him up?"

Sergey stared at her. In Krista's mind, she saw him and Omar leaning over an open capsule. In her vision, they were giggling, but she ignored that part of it.

"Sir, I request formal permission to inspect Chief Marquez's inner thoughts. I need to figure out what we're dealing with."

"No!" Sekurka burst out. But the beeping continued.

"Please, sir. I know it's unorthodox. This is an exceptional circumstance."

The officer looked trapped. Krista felt sorry for him, but she added her own sense of urgency to her plea.

"All right. Go ahead."

Krista bent over Marquez. As she had seen Sergey do, she opened his eye. Immediately, SANDMAN opened access to the man's mind. Krista felt as though she was trespassing, but persisted.

An ordinary waking mind was filled with sequential chaos of the task at hand, personal concerns, external stimuli and a persistent low-level awareness of bodily processes and physical condition. This was the first time she had been allowed to peer into the mind of some-one in deepsleep. Marquez's thoughts were far more low-key, with no conscious activity whatsoever.

This is what SANDMAN sees all the time, she thought. Omar, on the other side of the coffin-shaped capsule, nodded. Krista allowed herself to go further.

She assumed from the open thoughts of her two friends that she ought to be seeing a weird, three-dimensional movie, not unlike one of the stimulus videos in the holochamber. Instead, for as far as she could see in any direction, there was a roiling grayness, as though everything in his mind had gone to mush.

"That can't be healthy," Sekurka said, suddenly. Krista realized that everyone in the room, and probably all of the crew awake on the South America was peering over her psychic shoulder.

"No, it isn't," Krista said. "Sergey's right. We're going to have to wake him up and put him on a stimulus program right away." She reached for the controls.

"Don't, Krista," Omar said, his big hand covering hers. "Why don't you just give him some of your dreams? You're the most creative mind in the room." The others shuffled and coughed in embarrassment.

"Why can't we use the recordings you made?" Krista asked.

"Not the same," Sergey said. "We stripped out all the theta and delta wave data. If you want to save him, we'll have to put you mind-to-mind. It's not like this is the first time you've shared your dreams."

"I hate you," she said, feeling her cheeks warm with embarrass-ment. "All right. Jack me in."

"SANDMAN, bring subject Phase Four, bed twenty-three to al-pha wave level," Omar said. The pulses issuing through the capsule sped up perceptibly. On the scope, the frequency rose from six hertz to nine. Marquez's eyelashes fluttered almost imperceptibly. On the capsule's scope, she watched his brain wave indicator lift from theta to alpha, almost to the edge of waking up. Sergey took over the control panel and began to enter codes. Krista stared at him wide-eyed. So that was how he got into the system!

"Relax," Omar said. "I need you on the edge, too. Pretend you're going to sleep." He aimed soothing thoughts at her. She felt a peaceful drone come from him, coupled with the vision of a green meadow under a blue sky.

Krista concentrated on him, ignoring the other people in the room, trying to will herself to relax. It wasn't easy, but she did her best, concentrating on the vision. Then, a gigantic green-plaid shark popped up and offered to give her a ride. They leaped through waves of stars smelling of disinfectant. She startled, then found that her forehead was resting on the edge of the capsule.

"You are almost too suggestible," Omar said, steadying her. "You've been out twenty minutes."

"How's Marquez?" she asked. She looked down at the engineer, who lay still as a statue, eyes were wide open and staring at the ceiling. "Is he…?"

A long, long guttural tone erupted from the capsule, like a saw blade being drawn across a thick log coated with molasses and epoxy for half of eternity.

"Snnn—nnn—xxx—nnn—hhhhhhhh…"

"What in hell was that?" Sekurka demanded. Krista burst out in giggles.

"He's snoring," she said.

She checked the scope for Marquez's brainwaves. They had already dropped to four hertz, well within normal range. With his eyes open, she could see that the chief engineer was dreaming of riding a hippopotamus into a pale blue landscape marked out with measurements and tracings like an architectural drawing. His vital signs had straightened out. He had never come out of deepsleep.

"Well, good," Sekurka said, with a curt nod. "But I never want anyone using that process again. It's against all the principles on which our new society is based!"

"Don't dismiss the idea out of hand, sir," Krista said. "I mean, it will take some getting used to, but so has the telepathy. Look at it as another way to help us all bond as one group. I mean, no one has to contribute their dreams, or experience anyone else's, but what if they want to? No generation of humans had ever had the opportunity to form such a cohesive bond, with shared experiences like this. Not just what we experience in our waking life, but how we process it, and what revelations we get from their reactions, too. We ought to try, sir. We need each other. Why not try it?" In spite of her earlier ire, she felt the idea was not only right but inevitable. Omar and Sergey beamed and nodded enthusiastically.

Sekurka peered at her thoughtfully. He had to feel her certainty through the link. "I suppose I can propose it to the captain. Do you think the other ships will share with us, too?" Omar and Sergey suddenly exuded uneasiness. "…Too late?"

"I'd say so," Krista said, wryly.

"Fine," Sekurka said, his taciturn face easing into a smile. "Jack me in. Tonight, I'm going to sleep with someone else's dreams. If we're going to change the world, I'll need all the evidence I can get."

PICNIC ON NEARSIDE

_____John Varley_____

THIS IS THE STORY of how I went to the nearside and found old Lester and maybe grew up a little. And about time, too, as Carnival would say.

Carnival is my mother. We don't get along well most of the time, and I think it's because I'm twelve and she's ninety-six. She says it makes no difference, and she waited so long to have her child because she wanted to be sure she was ready for it. And I answer back that at her age she's too far away from childhood to remember what it's like. And she replies that her memory is perfect all the way back to her birth. And I retort…

We argue a lot.

I'm a good debater, but Carnival's a special problem. She's an Emotionalist; so anytime I try to bring facts into the argument she waves it away with a statement like, "Facts only get in the way of my preconceived notions." I tell her that's irrational, and she says I'm perfectly right, and she meant it to be. Most of the time we can't even agree on premises to base a disagreement on. You'd think that would be the death of debate, but if you did, you don't know Carnival and me.

The major topic of debate around our warren for seven or eight lunations had been the Change I wanted to get. The battle lines had been drawn, and we had been at it every day. She thought a Change would harm my mind at my age. Everybody was getting one.

We were all sitting at the breakfast table. There was me and Carnival, and Chord, the man Carnival has lived with for several years, and Adagio, Chord's daughter. Adagio is seven.

There had been a big battle the night before between me and Carnival. It had ended up (more or less) with me promising to divorce her as soon as I was of age. I don't remember what the counterthreat was. I had been pretty upset.

I was sitting there eating fitfully and licking my wounds. The argument had been inconclusive, philosophically, but from the pragmatic standpoint she had won, no question about it. The hard fact was that I couldn't get a Change until she affixed her personality index to the bottom of a sheet of input, and she said she'd put her brain in cold storage before she'd allow that. She would, too.

"I think I'm ready to have a Change," Carnival said to us.

"That's not fair!" I yelled. "You said that just to spite me. You just want to rub it in that I'm nothing and you're anything you want to be."

"We'll have no more of that," she said, sharply. "We've exhausted this subject, and I will not change my mind. You're too young for a Change."

"Blowout," I said. "I'll be an adult soon; it's only a year away. Do you really think I'll be all that different in a year?"

"I don't care to predict that. I hope you'll mature. But if, as you say, it's only a year, why are you in such a hurry?"

"And I wish you wouldn't use language like that," Chord said.

Carnival gave him a sour look. She has a hard line about outside interference when she's trying to cope with me. She doesn't want anyone butting in. But she wouldn't say anything in front of me and Adagio.

"I think you should let Fox get his Change," Adagio said, and grinned at me. Adagio is a good kid, as younger foster-siblings go. I could always count on her to back me up, and I returned the favor when I could.

"You keep out of this," Chord advised her, then to Carnival, "Maybe we should leave the table until you and Fox get this settled."

"You'd have to stay away for a year," Carnival said. "Stick around. The discussion is over. If Fox thinks different, he can go to his room."

That was my cue, and I got up and ran from the table. I felt silly doing it, but the tears were real. It's just that there's a part of me that stays cool enough to try and get the best of any situation.

Carnival came to see me a little later, but I did my best to make her feel unwelcome. I can be good at that, at least with her. She left when it became obvious she couldn't make anything any better. She was hurt, and when the door closed, I felt really miserable, mad at her and at myself, too. I was finding it hard to love her as much as I had a few years before, and feeling ashamed because I couldn't.

I worried over that for a while and decided I should apologize. I left my room and was ready to go cry in her arms, but it didn't happen that way. Maybe if it had, things would have been different and Halo and I would never have gone to Nearside.

Carnival and Chord were getting ready to go out. They said they'd be gone most of the lune. They were dressing up for it, and what bothered me and made me change my plans was that they were dressing in the family room instead of in their own private rooms where I thought they should.

She had taken off her feet and replaced them with peds, which struck me as foolish, since peds only make sense in free-fall. But Carnival wears them every chance she gets, prancing around like a high-stepping horse because they are so unsuited to walking. I think people look silly with hands on the ends of their legs. And naturally she had left her feet lying on the floor.

Carnival glanced at her watch and said something about how they would be late for the shuttle. As they left, she glanced over her shoulder.

"Fox, would you do me a favor and put those feet away, Please? Thanks." Then she was gone.

An hour later, in the depths of my depression, the door rang. It was a woman I had never seen before. She was nude.

You know how sometimes you can look at someone you know who's just had a Change and recognize them instantly, even though they might be twenty centimeters shorter or taller and mass fifty kilos more or less and look nothing at all like the person you knew? Maybe you don't, because not everyone has this talent, but I have it very strong. Carnival says it's an evolutionary change in the race, a response to the need to recognize other individuals who can change their appearance at will. That may be true; she can't do it at all.

I think it's something to do with the way a person wears a body: any body, of either sex. Little mannerisms like blinking, mouth movements, stance, fingers; maybe even the total kinesthetic gestalt the doctors talk about. This was like that. I could see behind the pretty female face and the different height and weight and recognize someone I knew. It was Halo, my best friend, who had been a male the last time I saw him, three lunes ago. She had a big foolish grin on her face.

"Hi, Fox," she said, in a voice that was an octave higher and yet was unmistakably Halo's. "Guess who?"

"Queen Victoria, right?" I tried to sound bored. "Come on in, Halo."

Her face fell. She came in, looking confused.

"What do you think?" she said, turning slowly to give me a look from all sides. All of them were good because—as if I needed anything else—her mother had let her get the full treatment: fully developed breasts, all the mature curves—the works. She had been denied only the adult height. She was even a few centimeters shorter than she had been.

"It's fine," I said.

"Listen, Fox, if you'd rather I left…"

"Oh, I'm sorry, Halo," I said, giving up on my hatred. "You look great. Fabulous. Really you do. I'm just having a hard time being happy for you. Carnival is never going to give in."

She was instantly sympathetic. She took my hand, startling me badly.

"I was so happy I guess I was tactless," she said in a low voice. "Maybe I shouldn't have come over here yet."

She looked at me with big brown eyes (they had been blue, usually), and I started realizing what this was going to mean to me. I mean, Halo? A female? Halo, the guy I used to run the corridors with? The guy who helped me build that awful eight-legged cat that Carnival wouldn't let in the house and looked like a confused caterpillar? Who made love to the same girls I did and compared notes with me later when we were alone and helped me out when the gang tried to beat me up and cried with me and vowed to get even? Could we do any of that now? I didn't know. Most of my best friends were male, maybe because the sex thing tended to make matters too complicated with females, and I couldn't handle both things with the same person yet.

But Halo was having no such doubts. In fact, she was standing very close to me and practicing a wide-eyed innocent look that she knew did funny things to me. She knew it because I had told her so, back when she was a boy. Somehow that didn't seem fair.

"Ah, listen, Halo," I said hastily, backing away. She had been going for my pants! "Ah, I think I need some time to get used to this. How can I…? You know what I'm talking about, don't you?" I don't think she did, and neither did I, really. All I knew was I was unaccountably mortified at what she was so anxious to try. And she was still coming at me.

"Say!" I said, desperately. "Say! I have an idea! Ah.…I know. Let's take Carnival's jumper and go for a ride, okay? She said I could use it today." My mouth was leading its own life, out of control. Everything I said was extemporaneous, as much news to me as it was to her."

She stopped pursuing me. "Did she really?"

"Sure," I said, very assured. This was only a half lie, by my mother's lights. What had happened was I had meant to ask her for the jumper, and I was sure she would have said yes. I was logically certain she would have. I had just forgotten to ask, that's all. So it was almost as if permission had been granted, and I went on as if it had. The reasoning behind this is tricky, I admit, but as I said, Carnival would have understood.

"Well," Halo said, not really overjoyed at the idea, "where would we go?"

"How about to Old Archimedes?" Again, that was a big surprise to me. I had had no idea I wanted to go there.

Halo was really shocked. I jolted her right out of her new mannerisms. She reacted just like the old Halo would have, with a dopey face and open mouth. Then she tried on other reactions: covering her mouth with her hands and wilting a little. First-time Changers are like that; new women tend to mince around like something out of a gothic novel, and new men swagger and grunt like Marlon Brando in A Streetcar Named Desire. They get over it.

Halo got over it right in front of my eyes. She stared at me, scratching her head.

115

"Are you crazy? Old Archimedes is on the Nearside. They don't let anybody go over there."

"Don't they?" I asked, suddenly interested. "Do you know that for a fact? And if so, why not?"

"Well, I mean everybody knows..."

"Do they? Who is 'they' that won't let us go?"

"The Central Computer, I guess."

"Well, the only way to find out is to try it. Come on, let's go." I grabbed her arm. I could see she was confused, and I wanted it to remain that way until I could get my own thoughts together.

"I'd like a flight plan to Old Archimedes on the Nearside," I said, trying to sound as grownup and unworried as possible. We had packed a lunch and reached the field in ten minutes, due largely to my frantic prodding.

"That's a little imprecise, Fox," said the CC. "Old Archimedes is a big place. Would you like to try again?"

"Ah..." I drew a blank. Damn all computers and their literal-mindedness! What did I know about Old Archimedes? About as much as I knew about Old New York or Old Bombay.

"Give me a flight plan to the main landing field."

"That's better. The data are..." It reeled off the string of numbers. I fed them into the pilot and tried to relax.

"Here goes," I said to Halo. "This is Fox-Carnival-Joule, piloting private jumper AX1453, based at King City. I hereby file a flight plan to Old Archimedes' main landing field, described as follows...." I repeated the numbers the CC had given me. "Filed on the seventeenth lune of the fourth lunation of the year 214 of the Occupation of Earth. I request an initiation time."

"Granted. Time as follows: thirty seconds from mark. Mark."

I was stunned. "That's all there is to it?"

It chuckled. Damn maternalistic machine. "What did you expect, Fox? Marshals converging on your jumper?"

"I don't know. I guess I thought you wouldn't allow us to go to the Nearside."

"A popular misconception. You are a free citizen, although a minor, and able to go where you wish on the lunar surface. You are subject only to the laws of the state and the specific wishes of your parent as programmed into me. I...do you wish me to start the burn for you?"

"Mind your own business." I watched the tick and pressed the button when it reached zero. The acceleration was mild, but went on for a long time. Hell, Old Archimedes is at the antipodes.

"I have the responsibility to see that you do not endanger yourself through youthful ignorance or forgetfulness. I must also see that you obey the wishes of your mother. Other than that, you are on your own."

"You mean Carnival gave me permission to go to the Nearside?"

"I didn't say that. I have received no instruction from Carnival not to permit you to go to Nearside. There are no unusual dangers to your safety on Nearside. So I had no choice but to approve your flight plan." It paused, significantly. "It is my experience that few parents consider it necessary to instruct me to deny such permission. I infer that it's because so few people ever ask to go there. I also note that your parent is at the present moment unreachable; she has left instructions not to be disturbed. Fox," the CC said, accusingly, "it occurs to me that this is no accident. Did you have this planned?"

I hadn't! But if I'd known...

"No."

"I suppose you want a return flight plan?"

"Why? I'll ask you when I'm ready to come back."

"I'm afraid that won't be possible," it said, smugly. "In another five minutes you'll be out of range of my last receptor. I don't extend to the Nearside, you know. Haven't in decades. You're going out of contact, Fox. You'll be on your own. Think about it."

I did. For a queasy moment I wanted to turn back. Without the CC to monitor us, kids wouldn't be allowed on the surface for years.

Was I that confident? I know how hostile the surface is if it ever gets the drop on you. I thought I had all the mistakes trained out of me by now, but did I?

"How exciting," Halo gushed. She was off in the clouds again, completely over her shock at where we were going. She was bubble-headed like that for three lunes after her Change. Well, so was I, later, when I had my first.

117

"Hush, numbskull," I said, not unkindly. Nor was she insulted. She just grinned at me and gawked out the window as we approached the terminator.

I checked the supply of consumables; they were in perfect shape for a stay of a full lunation if need be, though I had larked off without a glance at the delta-vee.

"All right, smart-ass, give me the data for the return."

"Incomplete request," the CC drawled.

"Damn you, I want a flight plan Old Archimedes-King City, and no back talk."

"Noted. Assimilated." It gave me that data. Its voice was getting fainter.

"I don't suppose," it said, diffidently, "that you'd care to give me an indication of when you plan to return?"

Ha! I had it where it hurt. Carnival wouldn't be happy with the CC's explanation, I was sure of that.

"Tell her I've decided to start my own colony and I'll never come back."

"As you wish."

Old Archimedes was bigger than I had expected. I knew that even in its heyday it had not been as populated as King City is, but they built more above the surface in those days. King City is not much more than a landing field and a few domes. Old Archimedes was chock-a-block with structures, all clustered around the central landing field. Halo pointed out some interesting buildings to the south, and so I went over there and set down next to them.

She opened the door and threw out the tent, then jumped after it. I followed, taking the ladder since I seemed elected to carry the lunch. She took a quick look around and started unpacking the tent.

"We'll go exploring later," she said, breathlessly. "Right now let's get in the tent and eat. I'm hungry."

All right, all right, I said to myself. I've got to face it sooner or later. I didn't think she was really all that hungry—not for the picnic lunch, anyway. This was still going too fast for me. I had no idea what our relationship would be when we crawled out of that tent.

While she was setting it up, I took a more leisurely look around. Before long I was wishing we had gone to Tranquillity Base instead. It wouldn't have been as private, but there are no spooks at Tranquillity. Come to think of it, Tranquillity Base used to be on the Nearside, before they moved it.

About Old Archimedes:

I couldn't put my finger on what disturbed me about the place. Not the silence. The race has had to adjust to silence since we were forced off the Earth and took to growing up on the junk planets of the system. Not the lack of people. I was accustomed to long walks on the surface where I might not see anyone for hours. I don't know. Maybe it was the Earth hanging there a little above the horizon.

It was in crescent phase, and I wished uselessly for the old days when that dark portion would have been sprayed with points of light that were the cities of mankind. Now there was only the primitive night and the dolphins in the sea and the aliens—bogies cooked up to ruin the sleep of a child, but now I was not so sure. If humans still survive down there, we have no way of knowing it.

They say that's what drove people to the Farside: the constant reminder of what they had lost, always there in the sky. It must have been hard, especially to the Earthborn. Whatever the reason, no one had lived on the Nearside for almost a century. All the original settlements had dwindled as people migrated to the comforting empty sky of Farside.

I think that's what I felt, hanging over the old buildings like some invisible moss. It was the aura of fear and despair left by all the people who had buried their hopes here and moved away to the forgetfulness of Farside. There were ghosts here, all right: the shades of unfulfilled dreams and endless longing. And over it all a bottomless sadness.

I shook myself and came back to the present. Halo had the tent ready. It bulged up on the empty field, a clear bubble just a little higher than my head. She was already inside. I crawled through the sphincter, and she sealed it behind me.

Halo's tent is a good one. The floor is about three meters in diameter, plenty of room for six people if you don't mind an occasional kick. It had a stove, a stereo set, and a compact toilet. It recycled water, scavenged CO_2, controlled temperature, and could

119

provide hydroponic oxygen for three lunations. And it all folded into a cube thirty centimeters on a side.

Halo had skinned out of her suit as soon as the door was sealed and was bustling about, setting up the kitchen. She took the lunch hamper from me and started to work.

I watched her with keen interest as she prepared the food. I wanted to get an insight into what she was feeling. It wasn't easy. Every fuse in her head seemed to have blown.

First-timers often overreact, seeking a new identity for themselves before it dawns on them there was nothing wrong with the old one. Since our society offers so little differentiation between the sex roles, they reach back to where the differences are so vivid and startling: novels, dramas, films, and tapes from the old days on Earth and the early years on the moon. They have the vague idea that since they have this new body and it lacks a penis or vagina, they should behave differently.

I recognized the character she had fallen into; I'm as interested in old culture as the next kid. She was Blondie and I was supposed to be Dagwood. The Bumsteads, you know. Typical domestic nineteenth-century couple. She had spread a red-and-white-checkered tablecloth and set two places with dishes, napkins, washbowls, and a tiny electric candelabra.

I had to smile at her, kneeling at the tiny stove, trying to put three pans on the same burner. She was trying so hard to please me with a role I was completely uninterested in. She was humming as she worked.

After the meal, I offered to clean up for her (well, Dagwood would have), but Blondie said no, that's all right, dear, I'll take care of everything. I lay flat on my back, holding my belly, and watched the Earth. Presently I felt a warm body cuddle up, half beside me and half on top of me, and press close from toenails to eyebrows. She had left Blondie over among the dirty dishes. The woman who breathed in my ear now was—Helen of Troy? Greta Garbo?—someone new, anyway. I wished fervently that Halo would come back. I was beginning to think Halo and I could screw like the very devil if this feverish creature that contained her would only give us a chance. Meantime, I had to be raped by Helen of Troy. I raised my head.

"What's it like, Halo?"

She slowed her foreplay slightly, but it never really stopped. She propped herself up on one elbow.

"I don't think I can describe it to you."

"Please try."

She dimpled. "I don't really know what it's all like," she said. "I'm still a virgin, you know."

I sat up. "You got that, too?"

"Sure, why not? But don't worry about it. I'm not afraid."

"What about making love?"

"Oh, Fox, Fox! Yes, yes. I…"

"No, no! Wait a minute." I squirmed beneath her, trying to hold her off a little longer. "What I meant was, wasn't there any problem in making the shift? I mean, do you have any aversion to having sex with boys now?" It was sure a stupid question, but she took it seriously.

"I haven't noticed any problem so far," she said, thoughtfully, as her hand reached down and fumbled, inexpertly trying to guide me in. I helped her get it right, and she poised, squatting on her toes. "I thought about that before the Change, but it sort of melted away. Now I don't feel any qualms at all. Ahhhhh!" She had thrust herself down, brutally hard, and we were off and running.

It was the most unsatisfactory sex act I ever had. It was not entirely the fault of either of us; external events were about to mess us up totally. But it wasn't very good even without that.

A first-time female Changer is liable to be in delirious oblivion through the entire first sex act, which may last all of sixty seconds. The fact that she is playing the game from the other court with a different set of rules and a new set of equipment does not handicap her. Rather, it provides a tremendous erotic stimulus.

That's what happened to Halo. I began to wonder if she'd wait for me. I never found out. I looked away from her face and got the shock of my life. There was someone standing outside the tent, watching us.

Halo felt the change in me and looked at my face, which must have been a sight, then looked over her shoulder. She fainted; out like a light.

Hell, I almost fainted myself. Would have, but when she did, it scared me even more, and I decided I couldn't indulge it. So I stayed awake to see what was going on.

It looked way too much like one of the ghosts my imagination had been walking through the abandoned city ever since we got there. The figure was short and dressed in a suit that might have been stolen from the museum at Kepler, except that it was more patches than suit. I could tell little about who might be in it, not even the sex. It was bulky, and the helmet was reflective.

I don't know how long I stared at it; long enough for the spook to walk around the tent three or four times. I reached for the bottle of white wine we had been drinking and took a long pull. I found out that's an old movie cliché; it didn't make anything any better. But it sure did things for Halo when I poured it in her face.

"Get in your suit," I said, as she sat up, sputtering. "I think that character wants to talk to us." He was waving at us and pointing to what might have been a radio on his suit.

We suited up and crawled through the sphincter. I kept saying hello as I ran through the channels on my suit. Nothing worked. Then he came over and touched helmets. He sounded far away.

"What're you doin' here?"

I had thought that would have been obvious.

"Sir, we just came over here for a picnic. Are we on your land or something? If so, I'm sorry, and…"

"No, no," he waved it off. "You can do as you please. I ain't your ma. As to owning, I guess I own this whole city, but you're welcome to do as you please with most of it. Do as you please, that's my philosophy. That's why I'm still here. They couldn't get old Lester to move out. I'm old Lester."

"I'm Fox, sir," I said.

"And I'm Halo." She heard us over my radio.

He turned and looked at her.

"Halo," he said, quietly. "A Halo for an angel. Nice name, miss." I was wishing I could see his face. He sounded like an adult, but he was sure a small one. Both of us were taller than he was, and we're not much above average for our age.

He coughed. "I, ah, I'm sorry I disturbed you folks…ah," he seemed embarrassed. "I just couldn't help myself. I haven't seen any people for a long time—oh, ten years, I guess—and I just had to get a closer look. And I, uh, I needed to ask you something."

"And what's that, sir?"

"You can knock off the 'sir.' I ain't your pa. I wanted to know if you folks had any medicine?"

"There's a first-aid kit in the jumper," I said. "Is there someone in need of help? I'd be glad to take them to a hospital in King City."

He was waving his arms frantically.

"No, no, no. I don't want doctors poking around. I just need a little medicine. Uh, say, could you take that first-aid kit out of the jumper and come to my warren for a bit? Maybe you got something in there I could use."

We agreed, and followed him across the field.

He led us into an unpressurized building at the edge of the field. We threaded our way through dark corridors.

We came to a big cargo lock, stepped inside, and he cycled it. Then we went through the inner door and into his warren.

It was quite a place, more like a jungle than a home. It was as big as the Civic Auditorium at King City and overgrown with trees, vines, flowers, and bushes. It looked like it had been tended at one time, but allowed to go wild. There were a bed and a few chairs in one corner, and several tall stacks of books. And heaps of junk; barrels of leak sealant, empty O2 cylinders, salvaged instruments, buggy tires.

Halo and I had our helmets off and were half out of our suits when we got our first look at him. He was incredible! I'm afraid I gasped, purely from reflex; Halo just stared. Then we politely tried to pretend there was nothing unusual.

He looked like he made a habit of going out without his suit. His face was grooved and pitted like a plowed field after an artillery barrage. His skin looked as tough as leather. His eyes were sunk into deep pits.

"Well, let me see it," he said, sticking out a thin hand. His knuckles were swollen and knobby.

I handed him the first-aid kit, and he fumbled with the catches, then got it open. He sat in a chair and carefully read the label on each item. He mumbled while he read.

Halo wandered among the plants, but I was more curious about old Lester than about his home. I watched him handle the contents of the kit with stiff, clumsy fingers. All his movements seemed stiff. I couldn't imagine what might be wrong with him and wondered why he hadn't sought medical help long ago, before whatever was afflicting him could go this far.

At last he put everything back in the kit but two tubes of cream. He sighed and looked at us.

"How old are you?" he asked, suspiciously.

"I'm twenty," I said. I don't know why. I'm not a liar, usually, unless I have a good reason. I was just beginning to get a funny feeling about old Lester, and I followed my instincts.

"Me, too," Halo volunteered.

He seemed satisfied, which surprised me. I was realizing he had been out of touch for a long time. Just how long I didn't know yet.

"There ain't much here that'll be of use to me, but I'd like to buy these here items, if you're willin' to sell. Says here they're for 'topical anesthesia,' and I could use some of that in the mornings. How much?"

I told him he could have them for nothing, but he insisted; so I told him to set his own price and reached for my credit meter in my suit pouch. He was holding out some rectangular slips of paper. They were units of paper currency, issued by the old Lunar Free State in the year 76 O.E. They had not been used in over a century. They were worth a fortune to a collector.

"Lester," I said, slowly, "these are worth more than you probably realize. I could sell them in King City for..."

He cackled. "Good man. I know what them bills is worth. I'm decrepit, but I ain't senile. They're worth thousands to one what wants 'em, but they're worthless to me. Except for one thing. They're a damn good test for findin' an honest man. They let me know if somebody'd take advantage of a sick, senile ol' hermit like me. Pardon me, son, but I had you pegged for a liar when you come in here. I was wrong. So you keep the bills. Otherwise, I'd a took 'em back."

He threw something on the floor in front of us, something he'd had in his hand and I hadn't even seen. It was a gun. I had never seen one.

Halo picked it up, gingerly, but I didn't want to touch it. This old Lester character seemed a lot less funny to me now. We were quiet.

"Now I've gone and scared you," he said. "I guess I've forgot all my manners. And I've forgot how you folks live on the other side." He picked up the gun and opened it. The charge chamber was empty. "But you wouldn't of knowed it, would you? Anyways, I'm not a killer. I just pick my friends real careful. Can I make up the fright I've caused you by inviting you to dinner? I haven't had any guests for ten years."

We told him we'd just eaten, and he asked if we could stay and just talk for a while. He seemed awfully eager. We said okay.

"You want some clothes? I don't expect you figured on visiting when you come here."

"Whatever your custom is," Halo said, diplomatically.

"I got no customs," he said, with a toothless grin. "If you don't feel funny naked, it ain't no business of mine. Do as you please, I say." It was a stock phrase with him.

So we lay on the grass, and he got some very strong, clear liquor and poured us all drinks.

"Moonshine," he laughed. "The genuine article. I make it myself. Best liquor on the Nearside."

We talked, and we drank.

Before I got too drunk to remember anything, a few interesting facts emerged about old Lester. For one thing, he really was old. He said he was two hundred and fifty-seven, and he was Earthborn. He had come to the moon when he was twenty-eight, several years before the Invasion.

I know several people in that age range, though none quite that old. Carnival's great-grandmother is two twenty-one, but she's moon-born, and doesn't remember the Invasion. There's virtually nothing left of the flesh she was born with. She's transferred her memories to a new brain twice.

I was prepared to believe that old Lester had gone a long time without medical care, but I couldn't accept what he told us at first. He said that, barring one new heart eighty years ago, he was unreconstructed since his birth! I'm young and naive—I freely admit it now—but I couldn't swallow that. But I believed it eventually, and I believe it now.

He had a million stories to tell, all of them at least eighty years old because that's how long he had been a hermit. He had stories of

Earth, and of the early years on the moon. He told us about the hard years after the Invasion. Everyone who lived through that has a story to tell. I drew a blank before the evening was over, and the only thing I remember clearly is the three of us standing in a circle, arms around each other, singing a song old Lester had taught us. We swayed against each other and bumped foreheads and broke up laughing. I remember his hand resting on my shoulder. It was hard as rock.

The next day Halo became Florence Nightingale and nursed old Lester back to life. She was as firm as any nurse, getting him out of his clothes over his feeble protests, then giving him a massage. In the soberness of the morning I wondered how she could bring herself to touch his wrinkled old body, but as I watched, I slowly understood. He was beautiful.

The best thing to compare old Lester to is the surface. There is nothing older, or more abused, than the surface of the moon. But I have always loved it. It's the most beautiful place in the system, including Saturn's Rings. Old Lester was like that. I imagined he was the moon. He had become part of it.

Though I came to accept his age, I could still see that he was in terrible shape. The drinking had taken a lot out of him, but he wouldn't be kept down. The first thing he wanted in the morning was another drink. I brought him one, then I cooked a big breakfast: eggs and sausage and bread and orange juice, all from his garden. Then we were off and drinking again.

I didn't even have time to worry about what Carnival and Halo's mother might be thinking by now. Old Lester had plainly adopted us. He said he'd be our father, which struck me as a funny thing to say since who the hell ever knows who their father is? But he began behaving in the manner I would call maternal, and he evidently thought of it as paternal.

We did a lot of things that day. He taught us about gardening. He showed me how to cross-fertilize the egg plants and how to tell when they were ripe without breaking the shells to see. He told us the secrets of how to grow breadfruit trees so they'd yield loaves of dark-brown, hard, whole wheat or the strangely different rye variety by grafting branches. I had never had rye before. And we learned to dig for potatoes and steakroots. We learned how to harvest honey and cheese and tomatoes. We stripped bacon from the surface of the porktree trunks.

And we'd drink his moonshine while we worked, and laugh a lot, and he'd throw in more of his stories between the garden lore.

Old Lester was not the fool he seemed at first. His speech pattern was largely affected, something he did to amuse himself over the years. He could speak as correctly as anyone when he wanted to. He had read much and remembered it all. He was a first-rate engineer and botanist, but his education and skills had to be qualified by this fact: everything he knew was eighty years out of date. It didn't matter much: the old methods worked well enough.

In social matters it was a different story.

He didn't know much about Changing, except that he didn't like it. It was Changing that finally decided him to separate himself from society. He said he had been having his doubts about joining the migration to Farside, and the sex-change issue had been the final factor. He shocked us more than he knew when he revealed that he had never been a woman. I thought his lack of curiosity must be monumental, but I was wrong. It turned out that he had some queer notions about the morality of the whole process, ideas he had gotten from some weirdly aberrant religion in his childhood. I had heard of the cult, as you can hardly avoid it if you know any history. It had said little about ethics, being more interested in arbitrary regulations.

Old Lester still believed in it, though. His home was littered with primitive icons. There was a central symbol he cherished above the others: a simple wooden fetish in the shape of a plus sign with a long stem. He wore one around his neck, and others sprouted like weeds.

I came to realize that this religion was at the bottom of the puzzling inconsistencies I began to notice about him. His "do as you please" may have been sincere, but he did not entirely live by it. It became clear that, though he thought people should have freedom of choice, he condemned them if the choice they made was not his own.

My spur-of-the-moment decision to lie about my age had been borne out, though I'm not sure the truth wouldn't have been better. It might have kept us out of the further lies we told or implied, and I always prefer honesty to deception. But I still don't know if old Lester could have been our friend without the lies.

He knew something of life on Farside and made it clear he disapproved of most of it. And he had deluded himself (with our help) that we weren't like that. In particular, he thought people should not have sex until they reached a "decent age." He never defined that, but Halo and I, at "twenty," were safely past it.

It was a puzzling notion. Even Carnival, who is a bit old-fashioned, would have been shocked. Granted, we speed up puberty now—I have been sexually potent since I was seven—but he felt that even after puberty people should abstain. I couldn't make any sense out of it. I mean, what would you do?

Then there was a word he used, "incest," that I had to look up when I got home to be sure I'd understood him. I had. He was against it. I guess it had a basis back in the dawn of time, when procreation and genetics were so tied up with sex, but how could it matter now? The only place Carnival and I get along at all is in bed; without that, we would have very little in common.

It went on and on, the list of regulations. Luckily, it didn't sour me on old Lester. All I disliked was the lies we had trapped ourselves into. I'm willing to let people have all sorts of screwball notions as long as they don't force them on me, like Carnival was doing about the Change. That I found myself expressing agreement with old Lester's ideas was my own fault, not his. I think.

The days went by, marred by only one thing. I had not broken any laws, but I knew I was being searched for. And I knew I was treating Carnival badly. I tried to figure out just how badly, and what I should do about it, but kept getting fogged up by the moonshine and good times.

Carnival had come to the Nearside. Halo and I had watched them from the shadows when old Lester's radar had picked them up coming in. There had been six or seven figures in the distance. They had entered the jumper and made a search. They had cast around at the edge of the field for our tracks, found them, and followed them to where they disappeared on concrete. I would have liked to have listened in, but didn't dare because they were sure to have detection apparatus for that.

And they left. They left the jumper, which was nice of them, since they could have taken it and rendered us helpless to wait for their return.

I thought about it, and talked it over with Halo. Several times we were ready to give up and go back. After all, we hadn't really set out to run away from home. We had only been defying authority, and it had never entered my head that we would stay as long as we had. But now that we were here we found it hard to go back. The trip to Nearside had acquired an inertia of its own, and we didn't have the strength to stop it.

In the end we went to the other extreme. We decided to stay on Nearside forever. I think we were giddy with the sense of power a decision like that made us feel. So we covered up our doubts with backslapping encouragement, a lot of giggling, and inflated notions of what we and old Lester would do at Archimedes.

We wrote a note—which proved we still felt responsible to someone—and taped it to the ladder of the jumper; then Halo went in and turned on the outside lights and pointed them straight up. We retired to a hiding place and waited.

Sure enough, another ship returned in two hours. They had been watching from close orbit and landed on the next pass when they noticed the change. One person got out of the ship and read the note. It was a crazy note, saying not to worry, we were all right. It went on to say we intended to stay, and some more things I'd rather not remember. It also said she should take the jumper. I was regretting that even as she read it. We must have been crazy.

I could see her slump even from so far away. She looked all around her, then began signaling in semaphore language.

"Do what you have to," she signaled. "I don't understand you, but I love you. I'm leaving the jumper in case you change your mind."

Well. I gulped, and was halfway up on my way out to her when, to my great surprise, Halo pulled me down. I had thought she was only going along with me to avoid having to point out how wrong I was. This hadn't been her idea; she had not been in her right mind when I hustled her over here. But she had settled down from all that lunes ago and was now as level-headed as ever. And was more taken with our adventure than I was.

"Dope!" she hissed, touching helmets. "I thought you'd do something like that. Think it through. Do you want to give up so easy? We haven't even tried this yet."

Her face wasn't as certain as her words, but I was in no shape to argue her out of it. Then Carnival was gone, and I felt better. It was true that we had an out if it turned sour. Pretty soon we were intrepid pioneers, and I didn't think of Carnival or the Farside until things did start to go sour.

For a long time, almost a lunation, we were happy. We worked hard every day with old Lester. I learned that in his kind of life the work was never done; there was always an air duct to repair, flowers to pollinate, machinery to regulate. It was primitive, and I could usually see ways to improve the methods but never thought of suggesting them. It wouldn't have fit with our crazy pioneer ideas. Things had to be hard to feel right.

We built a grass lean-to like one we had seen in a movie and moved in. It was across the chamber from old Lester, which was silly, but it meant we could visit each other. And I learned an interesting thing about sin.

Old Lester would watch us make love in our raggedy shack, a grin across his leathery face. Then one day he implied that lovemaking should be a private act. It was a sin to do it in front of others, and a sin to watch. But he still watched.

So I asked Halo about it.

"He needs a little sin, Fox."

"Huh?"

"I know it isn't logical, but you must have seen by now that his religion is mixed up."

"That's for sure. But I still don't get it."

"Well, I don't either, but I try to respect. He thinks drinking is sinful, and until we came along it was the only sin he could practice. Now he can do the sin of lust, too. I think he needs to be forgiven for things, and he can't be forgiven until he does them."

"That's the craziest thing I ever heard. But even crazier, if lust is a sin to him, why doesn't he go all the way and make love with you? I've been dead sure he wants to, but as far as I know, he's never done it. Has he?"

She looked at me pityingly. "You don't know, do you?"

"You mean he has?"

"No. I don't mean that. We haven't. And not because I haven't tried. And not because he doesn't want to. He looks, looks, looks; he never takes his eyes off me. And it isn't because he thinks it's a sin. He knows it's a sin, but he'd do it if he could."

"I still don't understand, then."

"What do you mean? I just told you. He can't. He's too old. His equipment won't function anymore."

"That's terrible!" I was almost sick. I knew there was a word for his condition, but I had to look it up a long time afterward. The word is crippled. It means some part of your body doesn't work right. Old Lester had been sexually crippled for over a century.

I seriously considered going home then. I was not at all sure he was the kind of person I wanted to be around. The lies were getting more galling every day, and now this.

But things got much worse, and still I stayed.

He was ill. I don't mean the way we think of ill; some petty malfunction to be cleared up by a ten-minute visit to the bioengineers. He was wearing out.

It was partly our fault. Even that first morning he was not very quick out of bed. Each lune—after a long night of drinking and general hell-raising—he was a little slower to get up. It got to where Halo was spending an hour each morning just massaging him into shape to stand erect. I thought at first he was just cannily malingering because he liked the massage and Halo's intimacy when she worked him over. That was not the case. When he did get up, he hobbled, bent over from pains in his belly. He would forget things. He would stumble, fall, and get up very slowly.

"I'm dying," he said one night. I gasped; Halo blinked rapidly. I tried to cover my embarrassment by pretending he hadn't said it.

"I know it's a bad word now, and I'm sorry if I offended you. But I ain't lived this long without being able to look it in the eye. I'm dying, all right, and I'll be dead pretty soon. I didn't think it'd come so sudden. Everything seems to be quittin' on me."

We tried to convince him that he was wrong and, when that didn't work, to convince him that he should take a short hop to Farside and get straightened out. But we couldn't get through his superstition. He was awfully afraid of the engineers on Farside. We would try to show him that periodic repairs still left the mind—he called it the "soul"—unchanged, but he'd get philsophical.

The next day he didn't get up at all. Halo rubbed his old limbs until she was stiff. It was no good. His breathing became irregular, and his pulse was hard to find.

So we were faced with the toughest decision ever. Should we allow him to die, or carry him to the jumper and rush him to a repair shop? We sweated over it all lune. Neither course felt right, but I found myself arguing to take him back, and Halo said we shouldn't. He could not hear us except for brief periods when he'd rouse himself and try to sit up. Then he'd ask us questions or say things that seemed totally random. His brain must have been pretty well scrambled by then.

"You kids aren't really twenty, are you?" he said once.

"How did you know?"

He cackled, weakly.

"Old Lester ain't no dummy. You said that to cover up what I caught you doin' so's I wouldn't tell your folks. But I won't tell. That's your business. Just wanted you to know you didn't fool me, not for a minute." He lapsed into labored breathing.

We never did settle the argument, unless by default. What I wanted to do took some action, and in the end I didn't have it in me to get up and do it. I wasn't sure enough of myself. So we sat there on his bed, waiting for him to die and talking to him when he needed it. Halo held his hand.

I went through hell. I cursed him for a vacuum-skulled, mentally defective, prehistoric poop, and almost decided to help him out in his pea-brained search for death. Then I went the other way; loving him almost like he loved his crazy God. I imagined he was the mother that Carnival had never really been to me and that my world would have no purpose when he was dead. Both those reactions were crazy, of course; old Lester was just a person. He was a little crazy and a little saintly, and hardly a person you should either love or hate. It was Death that had me going in circles: the creepy black-robed skeletal figure old Lester had told us about, straight out of his superstition.

He opened one bleary eye after hours of no movement.

"Don't ever," he said. "You shouldn't ever. You, I mean. Halo. Don't ever get a Change. You always been a girl, you always should be. The Lord intended it that way."

Halo shot a quick glance at me. She was crying, and her eyes told me: don't breathe a word. Let him believe it. She needn't have worried.

Then he started coughing. Blood came from his lips, and as soon as I saw it, I passed out. I thought he would literally fall apart and rot into some awful green slime, slime that I could never wash off.

Halo wouldn't let me stay out. She slapped me until my ears were ringing, and when I was awake, we gave up. We couldn't make a meaningful decision in the face of this. We had to give it to someone else.

So twenty-five minutes later I was over the pole, just coming into range of the CC's outer transmitters.

"Well, the black sheep return," the CC began in a superior tone. "I must say you outlasted the usual Nearside stay, in fact…"

"Shut up!" I bawled. "You shut up and listen to me. I want to contact Carnival, and I want her now, crash priority, emergency status. Get on it!"

The CC was all business, dropping the in loco parentis program and operating with the astonishing speed it's capable of in an emergency. Carnival was on the line in three seconds.

"Fox," she said, "I don't want to start this off on a bad footing; so, first of all, I thank you for giving me a chance to settle this with you face-to-face. I've retained a family arbiter, and I'd like for us to present our separate cases to him on this Change you want, and I'll agree to abide by his decision. Is that fair for a beginning?" She sounded anxious. I knew there was anger beneath it—there always is—but she was sincere.

"We can talk about that later, Mom," I sobbed. "Right now you've got to get to the field, as quick as you can."

"Fox, is Halo with you? Is she all right?"

"She's all right."

"I'll be there in five minutes."

It was too late, of course. Old Lester had died shortly after I lifted off, and Halo had been there with a dead body for almost two hours.

133

She was calm about it. She held Carnival and me together while she explained what had to be done, and even got us to help her. We buried him, as he had wanted, on the surface, in a spot that would always be in the light of Old Earth.

Carnival never would tell me what she would have done if he had been alive when we got there. It was an ethical question, and both of us are usually very opinionated on ethical matters. But I suspect we agreed for once. The will of the individual must be respected, and if I face it again, I'll know what to do. I think.

I got my Change without family arbitration. Credit me with a little sense; if our case had ever come up before a family arbiter, I'm sure he would have recommended divorce. And that would have been tough, because difficult as Carnival is, I love her, and I need her for at least a few more years. I'm not as grownup as I thought I was.

It didn't really surprise me that Carnival was right about the Change, either. In another lunation I was male again, then female, male; back and forth for a year. There's no sense in that. I'm female now, and I think I'll stick with it for a few years and see what it's about. I was born female, you know, but only lasted two hours in that sex because Carnival wanted a boy.

And Halo's a male, which makes it perfect. We've found that we do better as opposites than we did as boyfriends. I'm thinking about having my child in a few years, with Halo as the father. Carnival says wait, but I think I'm right this time. I still believe most of our troubles come from her inability to remember the swiftly moving present a child lives in. Then Halo can have her child—I'd be flattered if she chose me to father it—and...

We're moving to Nearside. Halo and me, that is, and Carnival and Chord are thinking about it, and they'll go, I think. If only to shut up Adagio.

Why are we going? I've thought about it a long time. Not because of old Lester. I hate to speak unkindly of him, but he was inarguably a fool. A fool with dignity, and the strength of his convictions; a likable old fool, but a fool all the same. It would be silly to talk of "carrying on his dream" or some of the things I think Halo has in mind.

But, coincidentally, his dream and mine are pretty close, though for different reasons. He couldn't bear to see the Nearside abandoned out of fear, and he feared the new human society. So he became a hermit. I want to go there simply because the fear is gone for my generation, and it's a lot of beautiful real estate. And we won't be alone. We'll be the vanguard, but the days of clustering in the Farside warrens and ignoring Old Earth are over. The human race came from Earth, and it was ours until it was taken from us. To tell the truth, I've been wondering if the aliens are really as invincible as the old stories say.

It sure is a pretty planet. I wonder if we could go back?

AN ENDLESS SERIES OF DOORS

David Walton

GARRETT WAITED FOR THE PORTAL with a scowl on his face. Safety lectures always put him in a bad mood. Yeah, okay, he got it: Kirakira was a new planet. The atmosphere wasn't all the way oxygenated yet, most of the territory wasn't mapped, and doing stupid things could get you killed. He wasn't an idiot. And it wasn't like he was planning to go hiking into the wilderness. He just wanted to party.

"Can you believe that guy?" he said. "I think he was older than God. And five tips for surviving in a low-gravity desert? I mean, come on. That's an hour of my life I'll never get back."

He was trying for a laugh, but Brooke Carrington's pretty face remained serious. "I thought he was sweet," she said. "And it wasn't an hour. It only took ten minutes."

"It felt like an hour," Garrett said. "He couldn't have been any more boring if it had been his own funeral."

The two girls in line ahead of them stepped into the portal. The doors closed behind them. A few moments later, the doors opened again, and the girls were gone.

Brooke took his arm. "Come on," she said. "It's our turn."

It was cute how excited she was about taking the portal. Garrett had portaled about half a billion times, ever since he was little. There wasn't much to it. Brooke's family, however, had funny ideas about portals being dangerous, and Brooke had never been through one, even though her parents had plenty of money. When he'd offered to take her to the Hundredth Planet celebration on Kirakira, she'd jumped at the chance.

And he planned to jump *her* as soon as he got the chance. He let his eyes roam over her figure, enjoying what he saw. Brooke was hopelessly naive—her crazy family's fault again—and she dressed a little too conservatively for his tastes, but even so, she was hot. Maybe even more so for what she left to the imagination.

Inside the portal, she gripped his arm and pressed pleasantly against him. "Nervous?" he asked.

She nodded. "A bit."

They faced the doors, which slid shut, blocking the view of the line of people waiting their turn. The light above the door flicked red, then green, and the doors opened again, this time into a wide open space under a shimmering dome.

Brooke laughed. "That's it?"

"That's it. Welcome to Kirakira."

"We just traveled like, what, 470 light years in two seconds?"

"Something like that," he said. He had no idea how far it was. It didn't seem to matter.

They threaded their way through the crowd to the bar and ordered a pair of drinks. The stars dazzled overhead, their light slightly distorted by the nearly invisible dome. The dome was an energy field of some kind, generated temporarily to make the partygoers more comfortable. Everyone at the party had paid a considerable sum to attend, and panting around the dance floor with insufficient oxygen was no way to have a good time.

"I wonder how much all this cost," Brooke said, her gaze skyward.

Garrett shrugged. Money had never been an obstacle to anything he wanted, and so he didn't think very much about it. "What does it matter?"

"Well, it's a charity, right?" she said. "It's not easy to colonize a new planet. The people who emigrate do it because their lives on Shengshi or Herschel or Satyagraha or wherever were even worse than they are here. A celebration like this gives their economy a boost. They're lucky to be the hundredth. I bet the ninety-ninth planet didn't get nearly this attention."

Her lips were so gorgeous when she talked. He could watch her all day. The tip of her tongue slipped out and brushed gently against her upper lip. "Why not?" he asked, just to keep her talking.

"People like even numbers, I guess. It's a shame they have to spend so much of what they get on the party, though. I'm sure they need every dollar."

Garrett laughed. "If there wasn't a party, why would anybody pay?"

They finished their drinks, and he pulled her out onto the dance floor. The music pounded through them, and she danced with abandon, bringing a pretty flush to her cheeks. When the song ended, she fell against him, laughing. This was going well.

"Another drink?" he asked.

Before she could answer, the lights went out, plunging them into darkness.

For a moment, Garrett thought it was part of the show, a transition to some kind of light spectacle or slow dance. Nothing happened, however, and when he looked up, he could see the stars clearly, with no distortion. What had happened to the dome? He realized that not only had the music gone quiet, but also the background hum of fans and refrigerators and other machinery. He felt with sudden clarity how small they were, two hundred people standing in the dark on an alien landscape, an impossible distance from home.

After a moment of silence, everyone talked or shouted or screamed at once. Brooke clasped his hand. "What's happening?"

"I don't know. Some kind of power failure, I guess." If this ruined his evening, he was going to be pissed. He didn't see how they expected to succeed at populating a new planet if they couldn't even keep the power on.

A light blazed out from the direction of the bar, harsh and blinding. "Ladies and gentlemen," a voice said, somewhat garbled, but amplified enough to be heard. As his eyes adjusted, Garrett could see Yumi Akiyama, the governor of the new colony, standing on a chair, her eyes reflecting the light like a frightened animal. "I want to apologize," she said, her voice shaking a little, "but it seems that the portal has gone down."

"What does she mean, down?" Garrett asked. He'd never heard of a portal going down before. He hadn't realized it was possible.

"Most of the power for our celebration came from off-planet, through the portal," the governor continued. "We can't generate enough locally to maintain the dome, but our technicians are working to get the lights back on, and as many of the other systems as possible. I'm certain this will be only a short-lived inconvenience. Please, continue to mingle, sample the bar, and enjoy yourselves."

A string of lights around the edge of the gathering sprang to life, providing enough illumination to see their surroundings again. Brooke didn't look at him. Her shoulders sagged, and her smile had disappeared. Garrett ground his teeth. Mismanagement and incompetence, that's what this was. It was unacceptable. He didn't remember how much he had paid to be here, but whatever it was, he was going to demand a refund.

"Come on," he said. "Let's get another drink."

The band tried to strike up an acoustic number, but nobody felt like dancing anymore. Garrett and Brooke sat at a small table with a brochure about the wonders of Kirakira and how much the colony there relied on the generous contributions of their benefactors. Garrett tossed it on the floor.

Ridiculous. He should have just taken her to a club on Prosperity. She would have had her portal experience, and then, after a few hours and enough drinks, he could have taken her up to a penthouse suite and finally gotten a look underneath that dress.

An hour passed. Garrett ran out of things to say, and just sat, stewing, imagining all the people he was going to sue for this disaster of an evening. He tried to check the news to see if the portals were down anywhere else, but of course, he had no connection. The portal was *down*. They were a zillion light years from everywhere.

He was bored. He hated being bored. Finally, he realized that Brooke was crying. Great. Just what he needed.

"I'm sure they'll get it back up soon," he tried. "They have technicians working on it. That's what technicians are for."

She shook her head, the tears streaming more freely now. "My parents told me this would happen. They warned me. I thought they were stupid."

"They were stupid," he said. "This is just a glitch. Come on, don't cry. Let me get you another drink."

"They always said 'What comes for free, goes away for free.' Nobody really knows the source of the phenomenon that makes the portals work, and so nobody really knows if it will last. Uncle Calvin always warned that it might just disappear one day. But I thought…it had been so many years, and they'd always…"

"Wait," Garrett said. "Uncle Calvin? You mean your uncle was Calvin Carrington?"

"Great-uncle, but yeah. He invented the portals. Or discovered them, really."

"And you think…"

"I don't think anything. I'm just afraid. I'm afraid the portals might never come back. That we might be stuck here forever."

Garrett felt like he was suffocating. He knew the oxygen in Kirakira's atmosphere was enough for life, but it didn't feel that way. He looked up, as if he could see the air from their vanished dome rushing out into space. Instead, he saw the black expanse and the stars, impossibly distant and unreachable. He couldn't be stuck here. He just couldn't.

Kirakira didn't have the hotel space to accommodate them. In fact, they didn't seem to have a hotel at all. Most residents lived in rows of prefabbed housing units with tiny, noisy generators and barely enough room for themselves. The partygoers eventually lay down against walls or under tables and slept where they were.

Some of the governor's people returned with a pile of blankets a few hours later. Garrett snatched one, though there weren't enough to go around. He and Brooke huddled under it against the increasing cold.

All the charged energy of the evening had vanished, leaving Garrett with a sick feeling deep in his gut. He didn't even want to have sex, and that was saying something. All he wanted was to see that light above the portal door turn green again, telling him he could go home. He lay uncomfortably on the hard floor, freezing despite the blanket, and waited for morning.

The next day, the portals were still down. Brooke rose and walked around, talking to other people, but he stayed where he was. His head hurt, and he felt nauseated. And besides, what was the point? After a while, a Kirakira woman told him there would be a meeting in an outdoor pavilion about a mile's walk from there, but Garrett told her he was too sick to come. Someone would tell him if the portal came back online. He wasn't interested in any other news.

Eventually, Brooke returned and told him they were planning to split the guests up, assigning them to residents' houses where they could stay until new housing could be built to accommodate them.

"New housing?" Garrett said. "We don't need new housing. We need them to fix the portal."

She gave him a pitying look. Garrett hated her for it. "Construction crews will form this afternoon," she said. "And we'll need to increase food production somehow. This colony just gained two hundred new mouths, and lost their only source of imports. They planned it all with self-sufficiency in mind—thank goodness the designers had some foresight—but there are still some products, medications and crop boosters primarily, that can't be replaced."

Garrett stared at her. She seemed more animated by the prospect of this horror than she had dancing with him at the party. "I can't work," he said. "I'm sick. I can barely breathe." He took a few labored breaths to demonstrate.

That look again. "Those too sick or young are excused," she said. "But we'll all need to pitch in if we're going to get through this."

Garrett didn't know how he had ever been attracted to her. This talk of building houses and growing food was just ridiculous. He didn't know anything about farming. The way to get through this was for the portals to come back online so they could go home.

Two days passed. Three. Five. The portal was as dark and dead as the desert landscape of this godforsaken planet.

"Nobody's even working on it!" Garrett said. "Why don't they try to fix it?"

Brooke sighed, irritation in her voice. "They don't know how. The scientists who study the phenomenon and the engineers who built the doors all live on other planets. Maybe someone on the other side is working the problem. Probably they are. But since nobody really understood how they worked in the first place, I'm not sure what they're going to accomplish. At any rate, nobody on Kirakira knows how to fix it any better than you do."

Garrett had finally dragged himself off the floor and joined a work crew, though mostly he just sat around and watched Brooke and the others build. They used a combination of prefabbed components and rock that another crew had drilled from a nearby quarry. The resulting structures were cramped and ugly. Garrett figured they'd fall down at the first strong wind.

He was dying of hunger and thirst by lunchtime, but all they gave him was a stick of dry nutrient bread and a bottle of water. It wasn't fair. He knew for a fact that some of the meats and pastries from the celebration were still locked away in a freezer. That food had been meant for the party. It wasn't fair for the colonists to take it.

By the end of the afternoon, he was sure he wasn't getting enough oxygen. He just couldn't *breathe*. A doctor measured his O_2 levels and tried to tell him he was fine, but what did she know? She wasn't the one who couldn't get enough air.

When the sun finally dipped below the horizon, their crew trudged back to the party space for dinner. The tables were still as they'd left them, the band's instruments abandoned by their microphones and speakers, the balloons and flowers long since discarded. The cold started to set in again. Garrett felt it in his bones. He hated this planet.

He glanced longingly over at the portal, and for a moment his eyes failed to register what he was seeing. The light above the doors glowed green.

"Green!" Garrett laughed and pointed. "Green!" he said. "It's green! It's online again! We can go home!"

Cheers and applause erupted around the room. Garrett hugged strangers and whooped his delight, his breathing problems forgotten. He realized his face was wet and wiped the moisture away.

A shout from near the portal caught his attention, and he turned in time to see a woman pushed to the ground. The festive mood turned suddenly ugly as partygoers crowded for the doors. At that moment, the same thought occurred to Garrett as was occurring to everyone else: The portal was online *now*. But who knew how long it would last?

He pushed forward himself as the first several people crowded through the open doors into the tiny space beyond. For the first time, he wondered why the portal wasn't bigger. Why didn't they make it the size of a freight elevator? Or an airliner? The answer was probably some technical babble about energy or particles or cost efficiency. He didn't really care as long as he got through before it turned off again.

The governor showed up with some of her staff and enforced order, stuffing as many people as possible into the portal with every cycle, but preventing a stampede. Garrett found himself waiting impatiently in a rough line, just barely resisting the urge to run ahead and force his way on. He offered a huge sum of money to the people ahead of him in line to switch places, but they refused. He checked his messages, a flood of queries and well-wishes and missed invitations.

Brooke appeared beside him. He had forgotten about her. "She's with me," he told the people behind him.

Before they could object, Brooke shook her head and took a step back. "I just came to say goodbye," she said. "I'm going to stay here."

He stared at her pretty face, the words cycling in his brain but not making any sense. "You're…"

"I'm not leaving. I'm going to stay on Kirakira. There's so much happening here. Expanding the variety of crops they can grow, understanding erosion patterns, establishing schools and libraries and community programs." Her eyes danced, and a pretty flush made her cheeks shine. "Before we came here, there didn't seem to be anything interesting to do. Nothing important, anyway. Everything I could think of had already been done by someone else, a million times over. But here it's all new, and it's all necessary. You don't need to be an expert; you just need to be willing to work. Here, they need me."

An odd feeling came over Garrett. A sense of—what—of regret? For leaving this hellhole and going back to civilization? Nonsense. It was just that she looked so animated, so alive. It pricked something deep in Garrett's brain that he didn't want to evaluate. Why would someone choose work over ease, poverty over riches? For a sense of purpose, he supposed. A sense of belonging.

Those were abstract concepts, though, not nearly as interesting as a glass of bourbon or a girl in a minidress. There was too much pain in the world to stay in one place for very long. He wanted to keep moving, to find the good things in life and enjoy them. She could be high and mighty if she liked. He wasn't going to think about it, not now that the portal was working again. If she wanted to stay, let her. It was nothing to him.

"I just wanted to say goodbye, and thank you. For bringing me here," she said. She leaned in and gave him a peck on the cheek.

The line moved forward, and Garrett scrambled to move with it, lest he lose his place. Brooke took another step back.

"Well, see you," he said airily.

She made a wry face. "Bye."

His turn. Over his shoulder, he saw her walking away, her stride purposeful and bright with energy. He shook his head to clear it. Time to put Brooke Carrington out of his mind. She was staying, and he would never come back to Kirakira, not if he lived to be a hundred. He had a lot of partying to catch up on. The portal opened, like an endless series of doors, enough to keep him moving for the rest of his life.

ANGRY ROSE'S LAMENT

_____Cat Rambo_____

What has happened, I cannot change…what will happen, I cannot decide. I am only responsible for the here and now. I will be honest in my dealings; I will acknowledge the pain I have caused. I can offer amends; I cannot demand that they be accepted. I can ask for forgiveness; I cannot demand that I be forgiven.

—LITANY FOR THE RECOVERING

ALL HIS LIFE. Paul Rutter had hated dirt. He'd been raised in a decrepit Project by a foster mother, along with six other children, and those early years had left him memories of stained sheets, maggots in the sink, and grime that you couldn't scrub away. It was one of the reasons he'd worked to become a Spacer, and when he reached his first station, smelled the tang of recycled air and water, and saw a metal hallway corroded with the effluvium that humans inevitably deposit everywhere they touch, it was a vast disappointment. But better, even so, than the roots from which he'd come. And now his career, such as it was, had brought him back to a place as dirty as he'd ever seen.

The main feature of Linko Port was grease. Greasy dirt, black as tar, lay underfoot, grinding under the boot heels of the Fleet soldiers keeping order. The smell of machinists' grease from the yard that maintained the ferries coming down from its counterpart satellite far above, circling in unison with the slime green moons, was heavy in the air. Grease and black grime coated the walls of the buildings, assembled from Alliance plastics and weatherworn native woods. Of the dozens of races using this common rendezvous point, all seemed shabby and grubby, particularly the humans.

"Welcome to Linko. First assignment planet side in a while?" his attendant asked as he checked through Paul's records.

"How can you tell?"

"It's in the walk. Spacers move their feet a little different, come down flatfooted like they're not used to the pull."

Rutter grunted acknowledgement. "What do I need to carry here?" he asked.

"Some form of ID; best not to leave your docco at home. No guns. Credit chits for tipping, if you plan on being out doing much. Your guild marque if you're dealing as a rep."

"I'm rep to the Solins."

The man's smile faded. "Yeah?" he said noncommittally. "For what company?"

"Little outfit, doubt you've heard of it." Rutter preferred to keep his cards close to his chest. Besides, RecoveryCo's humble beginnings, compared to the larger corporations, were a little embarrassing. *No matter*, he thought. They'd done well taking a small company and turning it into an active corp, capable of interstellar negotiations. The resources provided by Solin might be the company's big strike, help them struggle their way to a respectable third tier status as an all-out, multi-market corporation.

"Not one of the Big Three? Thought CocaCorp would want a piece of that."

Rutter had wondered that himself. By all accounts, Solin was a plum piece of real estate, the kind one of the big companies like General M or Bushink would snatch up as an asset. Across the galaxies, they'd grabbed small systems every chance they got. Solin did have a native intelligent race to be wooed, but there was a surplus of impoverished races deep in debt to the Companies. Very few, the ones who knew to hire themselves savvy (and expensive) legal counsel, managed to keep themselves free.

There was, Rutter figured, something out of the ordinary about Solin. Not out of the ordinary in a valuable way, but something tricky, something slippery or scandalous, some taint the Big Three wanted to avoid. He'd find out soon enough, he guessed.

"What about hotels here?" he asked.

"There's a few. Carnival's a bit swanker than most—it's where most of the visiting dignitaries stay. The regulars go for the Jewel or the Home House, which is the cleanest. Not so pricey. Only real difference is that the Jewel's closer to the bars. They're all on the main drag."

The Home House quarters were simple but as clean as promised. A holo on the wall offered him his choice of spacescape or uploading his own images. Unlike most, he didn't carry such amenities. He flipped through the settings on the bed and chose the firmest, then settled himself to look through the docco again.

The Solins resembled nothing so much as giant wasps. Colored in dull reds and browns, they had the habits of hive insects, although the details were sketchy. Morgan had promised him more information soon, but when he checked his mail, it wasn't there yet. He fired off a reminder; Morgan was increasingly forgetful lately. "Slipped back?" he wondered, and sighed, rubbing his long fingers down the bridge of his nose.

Going into the fresher to splash his tired eyes with cold water, he looked into the mirrored wall. He saw an unremarkable face, although older looking than his fifty years. Ten years of addiction to Stardrift had left him there, crevices worn irreparably into his brow and the skin surrounding his mouth, broken veins lacing the sagging skin of his cheeks. But unlike most addicts, he'd broken free, formed a company with five of the men he'd met in Rehab. Now he wondered if that had been the smartest idea; 90% slipped back into the Drift, although they'd all sworn they were part of the lucky 10%.

He slipped into the Litany, murmuring it under his breath. "What has happened, I cannot change…what will happen, I cannot decide. I am only responsible for the here and now." Muttering the familiar words, he went back to study the information he had again.

The Representative building lay on the outskirts of town, a blocky tower misshapen by the demands of accommodating hundreds of different species. Blue bubbles held the distinctive toxic atmosphere of the Anjelis, and a tank near the ground floor showed swirls of blue and green liquid. Windows were tinted in shades ranging from

149

bloody rust to bilious chartreuse, filtering Linko's dull and watery sunlight into more palatable shades. *Lucky me*, Rutter thought. Solins and humans were capable of breathing the same atmosphere, although the compromise was unpleasant to both.

The meeting room lay on the fifth floor. As he paused outside the airlock, a voice hailed him.

"You rep Rutter?"

He turned. A slight figure in Pilot's Guild green coveralls stood there. "Yes. Do you have some question?"

"Just scoping you out," the woman said. She was small, dark-haired and olive-skinned. "I flew the initial mission exploring the Solin system. Look me up afterwards and I'll buy you a drink—I'm curious about your impressions." She flipped him an ID chip and turned.

He turned the chip over in his fingers once, gazing after her, then turned and pressed his code into the airlock.

Inside the room the air was unpleasantly acrid, stinging his nose with its vinegar reek. At one end of the room the Solin clung to the wall, watching him with its faceted eyes. A small table and chair had been placed in the middle of the room for his convenience.

Up close, the impression of a wasp was diminished but it still sported two sets of paired, pale rose wings. It was unexpectedly beautiful, a creature spun of crystal or sugar, edges sharp and defined as jewels, undulled by time or dirt. A stinger ending its abdomen dripped with a clear ichor that splattered on the floor. A small pool had collected beneath it; he wondered how long it had been waiting for him.

Its eyes were equally beautiful; malachite and lapis lazuli warred for the surface of the bulbous orbs, swirling and coalescing like gaseous clouds. Two business-like mandibles sat on either side of its tiny mouth; segmented, they flexed at intervals as though impatient to be used.

The voice emanating from the waxy collar around its thorax, though, was disconcertingly human, down to a slight, indefinable accent. "You are the Representative?"

"Yes," he said, setting his documents tablet on the table between them.

"I am called Kizel. You may begin recording," the Solin said.

He raised an eyebrow. "You have no questions? You are aware of what this contract will mean?"

"Your company will offer certain amenities, payments, and legal agreements in return for rights to planetary resources within our solar system. This negotiation will be recorded, and when it is complete, which may be a lengthy process, the record will be published publicly. Our race will achieve legal status as a result of participating, and we will no longer be vulnerable to those who wish to exploit our planet."

He nodded. "I'm impressed by your command of Galactic Custom. Not all races come to the bargaining table knowing how it is structured."

Kizel buzzed, in irritation or amusement, he couldn't tell which.

"We have accumulated necessary information," it said. "Assume that we have sufficient knowledge of humans that you do not need to explain each amenity."

A worm of confusion crawled its way through his head. Most native races weren't even close to this savvy. He took out his list and began. "Item 1: In exchange for the right to extract 500 kilograms of aurium each solar year, one energy replicator unit, no older than one year from the signing of this contract..."

As the session wore on, he was increasingly puzzled by the intimate knowledge of galactic customs that the Solin displayed. At one point he made a slight witticism that he thought only a human would have caught, and the Solin buzzed.

"What is the significance of that sound?" he asked.

"Your joke pleased me," it said.

After a few hours, his throat dry and rasping from reciting the lists of what RecoveryCo was prepared to offer for the long, exhaustive list of the Solin system's resources, he signaled the end.

"We can resume tomorrow," the Solin said. Traditionally, a trade agreement took three sessions. Even when both parties knew exactly what they wanted—usually not the case—the Negotiation must be acted out.

The pilot was waiting outside the door.

"I didn't want to wait to talk to you. Hungry?" she said.

"Starving."

"There's a place near Jewel that makes a mean bowl of noodles."

He followed her to the restaurant. She walked with the swagger that he'd learned to expect from pilots, an insouciance sprung from their inviolability; harming a pilot could lead to a planet or system being put into Exile, trade withering away.

As they slid into the plastic booth, she signaled the server—a grey-skinned, four-armed Doolah—who brought them menu cards. Rutter fingered the sticky edges with distaste, but the pilot cast a practiced eye down the card and said "Number 3 if you like spicy, number 5 if you like sweet, number 12 if you like bland. The beer's crap but does the trick. My name's Angry Rose."

"Sounds like a Harmonistic name."

She shook her head. "Self-picked, I liked the sound of it. Harmonistics start with the noun, anyhow."

He studied her. Threads of scarlet worked their way through her dark hair, and her right arm wore a sleeve of faded floral tattoos. Her outfit had the slapdash look of someone who preferred no clothes when on ship.

She studied him back, her look curious but non-sexual. "What did you think of the Solin?"

He used his napkin to wipe at the table in front of him, polishing away a smear of grease as he thought about it.

"I haven't dealt with that many alien races," he admitted. "Just in training, mainly. I didn't expect them to seem so human in their thinking."

Her lips twitched. "Wanna know why that is?"

"Huh?"

She leaned across the table towards him, lowering her voice. "They're brain eaters."

He snorted but she pressed on, her voice edged with urgency. "No, it's true. That Solin you're dealing with has at least one human mind in its own. I should know, he was a friend of mine. Luke Parse."

The Doolah slid a plate of Number 12 noodles in front of him, along with his water. Angry Rose took up her chopsticks, starting on her own plate as she watched him.

"Can you explain a little more?" he said cautiously.

She claimed that her friend had been one of the first explorers to make contact with the Solins. "Then they got to him, I dunno how. They left his body there, sitting, drooling…smiling. Smiling like he was at his momma's tit. I was on the ship that recovered him. The

Solin talked to me, said he had Luke inside him now, and that Luke didn't want me to worry about him. We took the body off planet to a medfactory, but he died a month or so afterwards. Still smiling."

"How did the Solin absorb him? Did you test to see if it was really him?"

She shook her head. "I dunno much. Went a little crazy when I heard his voice coming out of it." She gave him a lopsided, half-hearted grin. "They just put me off the world, said don't come back. Not supposed to go near any of the Solins now."

He chased a noodle around his plate before his chopsticks seized it. "Why are you telling me all this?"

Her face took on an edge of hostility. "Seemed like the decent thing to do, warn folks before they met the same fate."

"I appreciate it," he said, his voice sincere, and she untensed.

"Look," she said. "If you decide to…do anything, lemme know."

"Do anything?"

"There's at least one human mind in there," she said. "Trapped in a body they never wanted to be in."

She slid enough chits onto the table to pay for both meals. "You got my contact info. Call me."

After she left, he chewed each noodle and washed it down with sips of water. He'd learned over the years that his body would falter if he didn't fuel it, although the Drift had affected his taste buds to the point where any number on the menu would have been the same to him. Angry Rose had some agenda, but he wouldn't let it compromise RecoveryCo's dealings. Too many of his fellows were depending on the company's success; let this deal fail and half of them—if not all—would let it be an excuse to go back to their old ways. Even he'd be tempted.

The thought ached at him, reaching every corner of his being. The main thing Stardrift did was make you feel connected. A warm, golden glow in which all the minds around you were tied together. No loneliness, no isolation. Knowing that you were just where you needed to be, as though the universe held you in her arms, held you close and warm and loved.

He pulled his jacket around himself, added a few chits for the tip, and left.

Back at the Home, he succeeded in reaching Morgan. Pages of information spilled from the wall printer.

"Thanks," he said gratefully to the screen where his partner's face hovered, looking much the same as always. "Hey, do me a favor...look up a name and tell me if it's got any connection with the Solins?"

"What's the name?" Morgan said.

"Luke Parse."

Morgan grinned. "Ask and ye shall receive. That's already in the docco I just gave you. Three explorers made first contact: Conchetta Alo, Tresy Cooke, and Luke Parse. Parse had some sort of accident, and died a month or two later."

"Are his med records in there?"

"You're crazy, man. You know how much it costs, getting something like that? No, they're not."

"All right," he said. "Thanks, Morgan."

They finished as they always did, saying the Litany together. "I am only responsible for the here and now."

Parse's fate nagged at him all through the negotiations. Kizel clung to its wall, head downwards, supplying details to match his own. As the dialogue grew towards that day's end, he found himself asking, against every stricture of his training, "Are you Luke Parse?"

Kizel's wings stilled before it answered. "Luke Parse is part of us, yes."

"How big a part?"

"We currently hold four minds. An elder, by Solin standards."

He frowned, trying to pick meaning out of the words. "Hold the minds?"

The greens and blues of its eyes swirled. "Like all Solins, I am made up of the minds I have absorbed. Three Solin and one human. Luke Parse."

"Can you start from the beginning?"

This time he did detect amusement in the synthetic voice.

"The beginning of time, or of my life?"

He didn't find the joke as funny as it apparently did. "Your life," he said flatly.

"When we are born, we are mindless grubs. Or consciousness-less, to be more exact. The grubs are tended with care until they

154

metamorphose into something closer than my current form, and the best physical specimens chosen. When an elder is ready to die, they go to the nursery. The infant Solin gives them the Kiss for the Dying." Its stinger twitched. "Their consciousness fades and is absorbed by the new host, who then holds their memories. Throughout an individual's life, they may be given the opportunity to absorb more minds."

"Of the dying?"

"Not usually. Older Solins like to choose their mind partner. Someone they feel compatible with."

"If they hold more than one mind in turn, don't you end up with hundreds of minds in one individual?"

"The minds are consolidated into a single personality in the process of transfer."

"I don't understand why you hold Luke Parse," he said.

"We needed to understand how to deal with the creatures that had appeared on our world."

Panic gripped his throat. "So you just killed him?"

Kizel uttered a shrill buzz of negation. "No. He requested the Kiss."

"Why?"

"It was immortality," Kizel said. "I had been diagnosed with Pax two weeks earlier. I hadn't told my co-workers—was still figuring out how to deal with it. So when the process was explained to me, I asked for it."

"To become an enormous wasp?" He caught himself. "My apologies...I didn't mean to imply..."

"Understandable," Kizel said. "But life is life. And I knew I'd be here forever, with a mind that I found...compatible. I don't know if I'm explaining it well, but you don't understand the lure."

Oh, I understand lures, he thought. "What about Angry Rose?"

The noise Kizel made was close to a human sigh. "Rose...I tried to explain after the transformation, but she wouldn't listen. She thought I didn't exist anymore."

Silence hung in the room between them like a web, torn only by the shrill whine of Kizel's wings.

At length, it said, "Perhaps we should end this negotiation here for the day."

He felt absurdly grateful.

Back at the hotel, he studied his lists. No outrageous demands had been made yet, but usually the third day was the day for tacking on the true bargaining chips. He had hoped that by being straight-forward with the Solins, he might persuade them not to engage in this last minute dance, which sometimes became absurd and killed the whole deal.

He called Morgan.

"Sah went back," Morgan said without preamble.

"Shit." He rubbed at his face, feeling accumulated grime and stubble on his face. Sah was not the man he had expected. Morgan looked drawn and weary. "Well. Not like we can control anyone but ourselves."

"I'm starting to have some doubts," Morgan admitted. "I keep thinking how easy it would be to go around the corner and just keep walking till I find someone with Drift."

Rutter laid his palm flat against the screen. "Don't do it, man."

Morgan's hand mirrored his. "Thanks." But the words were un-even and strained.

"Hey, once we get a good deal with the Solins, we'll be sitting pretty," he said.

Morgan ignored him. "It's just that I feel so alone," he said. "Re-member being in the Drift? I never felt that way there."

"I know," he said. Like his fellow ex-addicts, the absence of the artificial connections provided by the drug ate at him with a constant ache. "But we're doing well, Morgan. RecoveryCo will succeed."

"Yeah," Morgan said dully.

After he got off the screen, he slammed his fist into the wall in frustration. Every time one of them went back, they knew it dragged the rest of them a little closer. In the fresher, he stood under the cycling water for an hour, soaping and rinsing every inch of skin until he no longer felt Linko Port clinging to him like a garment.

He'd never felt that way with Drift, either. It was as though the drug removed all his anxieties, and what he would have considered filth in any other state seemed like just part of the chain of life. He thought it was the connectedness that did it—it was hard to object to something when you felt yourself so thoroughly a part of it. As though you belonged.

At the same noodle shop he had gone to the night before, he ordered the same tasteless meal. Angry Rose slid into the seat across from him, her eyes expectant. "Didn't hear from you today," she said.

He sucked in a long strand, greasy with fat. "It said he's still your friend," he said without preamble.

"Shit. That's a thing. It knows what to say because it ate his mind."

"Why are you so sure of that?"

"Luke would have never agreed to something like that."

"He had Pax," he said. "Two weeks diagnosed. That would have meant he had, at most, half a year to live."

She shook her head, dark hair falling to obscure her face. "He didn't."

"How do you know?"

"Because it's not possible. He kept clean. Look, it's just not."

"I know it's sad to lose a friend, but it's sadder still to do it when you don't have to."

"Fuck you," she said, loud enough to rouse several other people in the shop. The Doolah glanced over, but did not stir as he took another chopstickful of the noodles.

"Fuck you," she said again. "That thing isn't Luke." Sliding from the seat, she moved out of the shop with furious grace.

He felt tired to his bones. He didn't need this crap disrupting his first big Negotiation. He didn't need this crap driving him back towards the Drift. So much depended on this deal. If it failed, all the money the company had spent on training him would be wasted and the company would go down the tubes. Taking all of them with it.

Day three of the Negotiation. List after list of trades, the result of long research on his part, and consultation with his partners regarding what RecoveryCo could and couldn't afford. The Solin hung motionless on the wall, speaking its assent when necessary. He'd been warned that his voice would go; the previous night he'd spent sucking on restorative lozenges and started the day wintergreen strong, but wavered as the hours progressed. Finally he was ready to hear the additional items that Kizel would demand.

"Your turn," he said.

"Ah," the Solin said. Again, Rutter wondered at the humanity implicit in that slight hesitation. How could Angry Rose doubt this was her friend?

"We require one thing only," Kizel said.

He shuddered inwardly. Single items were usually big ticket items. A spaceship? A station? Bleeding edge technology?

Again, the hesitation before the Solin spoke.

"We require a human mind to join with us. One trained in intergalactic trade negotiations."

Cold coiled heavy in his bowels as his mouth went dry.

"Mine, in other words," he said.

"If no substitute can be found. We are willing to give up other items in return for the fulfillment of this request."

"What other items?"

"Any ten from your list."

It was a magnificent concession. The sort corporations spent their existences pursuing, hoping for the odd superstitious race that would give up more than they should due to vagaries of numbers, moon cycles, or the whimsy of their gods.

"We realize you may see this as a sacrifice," Kizel said. "But be aware of what you are being offered. Immortality within a group consciousness that will always be with you. Knowing yourself safe and secure. All your anxieties gone."

They've read my files, he thought. They know how to appeal to me.

The Solin's voice took on the intonation he associated with Luke. "It's unbelievable," he said. "You feel connected to things. Like you're suspended in light, and can reach the stars. You have access to the memories of literally thousands of entities."

"Ever do Drift, Luke?" he said, his voice harsh. "Or are you taking that out of some junkie's description of what it's like?"

"I hoped to put it in terms that you would understand—so you can know what a marvelous chance this is."

The first word that came to his lips was an unconditional no, but thoughts of the others in the company caught him in the gut long enough to catch the word back.

"I'll have to think about this," he said.

The Solin seemed pleased. "We are prepared to meet again to-morrow, if you wish?"

"Very well," he said. Honesty forced him to say more. "I'm going to say no, you know."

"We are prepared for that," the Solin said. "Be aware that you would not just be benefiting your company but our race. We are un-prepared for complex trade deals."

It was true that they had not challenged many of the items. He wondered again that none of the Big Three had approached them before suspicion seized him.

"You've proposed this deal to others?"

It buzzed briefly. "We have engaged in these negotiations forty-three previous times."

No wonder it had come down to RecoveryCo.

At first he sat in his room pretending that none of it had been said, but finally he acknowledged reality and called his partners.

"Shit on that deal," Morgan said immediately when consulted. The hopelessness in his voice gave way to anger. "Just stringing us along."

"They'd make good on it," Rutter said. "Just that...well, it's a high price."

"It's out of the question," Morgan said.

Outside the window, the greasy smoke of the port roiled like a spreading contagion.

"Look," he said. "I'm going to try to talk them into the regular deal tomorrow. Maybe they'll take it."

"I'm sure the other forty-three guys felt the same." Morgan's shoulders slumped. "Dammit, Paul, I thought...I really thought we had a chance at things. And here we are, all the work gone straight down the tube. Out more than we started with. My mother mort-gaged her holdings to fund my share. She was that excited about me going off the Drift for good."

Others had made similar sacrifices. Rutter had been lucky; he'd stopped before the Drift sucked away everything he'd owned. *All I lost were family and friends*, he thought wryly. He'd also been the one best suited to the training. The training that the Solins valued so highly.

"I'm going to grab a bite to eat," he said. "I'll call you tomorrow after the Negotiation and tell you how it went."

He paused, waiting for Morgan to begin the Litany, but the other man simply nodded and signed off.

Hunger had been gnawing at his gut like a parasite, but once outside he found his appetite had vanished. Instead he walked along the street, keeping to the more solid walkways and avoiding the dirty puddles that lay splattered across the roadway.

I should have expected this, he thought as he turned a corner and saw Angry Rose coming at him. *Perfect end to a crap day.*

"Well?" she said. She fell into pace alongside him. Her uniform was crumpled and worn, ringed with dirt around the neck.

"Well, what?"

"Found out what they want yet?"

"Is it common knowledge?"

"They've asked a whole lot of other reps the same thing."

"You could have warned me," he said.

"I tried to," she said. "Then you told me that I was wrong and Luke was still alive."

"I think he is. I think he's the luckiest man alive."

Her forehead furrowed in confusion. "What?"

He shrugged.

"So you're going to do it?"

"I don't know," he said. "It'd be giving in."

"You are one fucked-up individual," she said. "Look, you're kidding me, right?"

"Sure," he said. "Just kidding."

She thumbed a pocket open and took out a small cylinder. "This is a bio-bomb. Cost me a lot to get one that would kill a Solin and not affect any other species in the room. I want my friend avenged. But now I can't get close enough to use it. You can. You can free Luke."

"All right."

Suspicious, she glared at him. "You're going to use it, right?"

"I don't know."

"Shit," she said, but she pressed it into his palm anyway. "Tap the red button to set it going. Should take about three seconds, five tops, to work. Good tech."

He tucked it away without looking at her.

"Buy you some noodles?"

"No," he said. "I need to get some sleep for tomorrow."

"Surely there must be some room to negotiate here," he said to Kizel the next day.

"Not for this." It was regretful but firm.

He took the bio-bomb on his pocket. "See this?" he said. "Angry Rose gave it to me. She wanted me to kill you, and instead I'm giving it to you. Isn't that worth something?"

"It is appreciated," the Solin said. "We will change the number of items you may remove to twelve."

"I could just set it off right now."

"It is within the realm of possibility. I do not know what we would do then. It is most probable that we would try to start again before our system is stripped clean."

"God," he said. He leaned his forehead onto the surface of the table. *Maybe if I just don't move, nothing will happen. Maybe I'll wake up and find myself back in my old life.*

The Solin let him sit in silence until his cramping limbs forced him upright.

"We cannot survive without this," the Solin said.

"That's not my responsibility."

"No. It's not."

"I want to talk to Luke again."

"We contain Luke. You are speaking with him."

"What's it like?" he said. "What's it really like?"

"Like love," Luke said. "It's like love."

"How do I know you're not lying? Or that you're really there? Or that you haven't been altered by the minds with you?"

"You don't."

Tears ran down his face, washing away the traces of dirt left on the skin by his morning walk to the Representative Building. He thought about the others, of their hopes, of their dreams, of the losses they had already suffered to the drug. He thought about Angry Rose, and her refusal to forgive her friend for changing. And of stardrift itself, of surrendering himself to the drug, feeling that glow, feeling that connection, feeling loneliness slip away. He thought about all these things, the Litany a counterpoint behind them, before the word "Yes" echoed in the room, and the Solin moved forward, sting quivering and poised.

THE RIGHT PLACE TO START A FAMILY

_____*Caroline M. Yoachim*_____

YUNA SEARCHED THE COLONIZATION VIDS for a world Oliver would find appealing. Of the half dozen people she was dating, he was her favorite, and the only one she'd really want to bring with her for the centuries-long trip to the colonies. There were seven destination planets to choose from. "What do you think of this one?"

Oliver shrugged. "They're all too expensive. Honestly, I think we're better off staying here. Once the ships launch the overcrowding won't be so bad, and we could move into one of the arcologies. Rumor is they're even going to lift the ban, so we can have those kids you always wanted."

"Earth isn't a good place to raise kids. Not any more." Yuna was older than Oliver, and she remembered what Japan had been like before the collapse. As a child she'd gone hiking with her parents through the forest of ancient cedar trees in Yakushima, and snorkeling off the coast of Ishigaki. In the summertime, they'd let her eat ice cream made from actual milk. The colonies wouldn't have those things, obviously, but they were pristine new worlds, a fresh start. "We aren't meant to spend our lives cooped up in bunkers and arcologies."

"We aren't *meant* to do anything," Oliver argued. "When the environment changes, we adapt, and the environment is always changing.

It doesn't matter whether you stay or go, you can't recreate the world you grew up in."

"Of course we adapt. Where we live changes who we are, especially when we're young—that's why it's so important to find the right place." Yuna dreamed of a planet where her children could run across grassy fields, and climb trees, and swim in open water. A place that was wild and a little unpredictable, where her children would be challenged to reach their full potential instead of stagnating in a carefully controlled artificial environment.

One of the vids showed a simulation of Gliese 667 Cc, a super-Earth planet with dramatic cliffs and flowing rivers. There were three suns in the sky. Yuna couldn't remember the last time she'd seen the sun as more than a faint brightness in the smog. The ship traveling to Gliese 667 Cc was a generation ship the size of Hokkaido, crewed by unaltered humans who would spend their entire lives on board. Yuna didn't want to die before reaching the colony planet, but there were stasis pods available as well. She liked the idea of being suspended in a bubble outside of time, tended by humans rather than an AI.

"I really like this one," she said. "We could fall asleep orbiting Earth, and wake up to explore a brand new world. Look at the rivers, aren't they beautiful?"

"It's a simulation. Nobody knows what the planet will really look like." Oliver turned off the vid. "I was sure I'd be able to talk you out of this. There are so many unknowns. Sure, Earth has problems, but we evolved here, this is where we fit. Besides, the place isn't the important thing. Home is where you make it."

"This planet is a mess and as much as I'd like to fix it, our biggest problem is overcrowding. Some of us need to leave, and I want the adventure, the opportunity." She took Oliver's hand. "I'd love for us to go together, but if you won't come, I'll go alone."

"Our families are here," he said.

Yuna squeezed his hand and let it go. "I'll miss my brothers—and you, of course—but my future family isn't here. It's out there somewhere."

An oversized four-legged flesh-colored spider hovered over Yuna and she screamed. She tried to bat it away, but her arms refused to function. The spider backed away and rose up onto its hind legs. Away from the warm orange lights, it looked less brown and took on a bluish tinge. The color reminded Yuna of the ocean on a stormy day, a mix of blue water and churning brown sand.

"Sorry to startle you," it said. "The ship is at Gliese, and my job does wake the sleepers."

Sensation and motor control returned to Yuna's body, her limbs tingling and burning, her eyes sore and dry. As her brain cleared, she could see that the spindly-legged creature in the room with her was not a giant insect, but an oddly altered human child. "Are your parents part of the crew?"

"My generation run the ship." The spidery human grinned at her. "We don't grow to sleeper-size. You call me N-17, okay yeah?"

It took a little less than three thousand years to get to Gliese, and Yuna had known that the crew would change somewhat in the hundred or so generations that lived and died en route. She just hadn't pictured how drastic the differences would be. "You seem very changed, more than I expected."

N-17 leaned in closer. "This isn't random. We pick our evolution paths. Small is the best fit for ship cabins. We do other changes too. Come with me, see the mermaids, yeah?"

Mermaids sounded exciting, albeit a strange choice for humans traveling between the stars. Yuna was dying to see them, but she couldn't move around well enough to leave her recovery cabin. N-17 came back the next day, and the next, helping her regain her strength. By the third day, Yuna was able to maneuver well enough in the low gravity to explore the ship.

"Can we go to a replicator bar?" she asked. N-17 had left her a stack of nutrient bricks to eat in her recovery cabin, but the colony recruitment vids had advertised much better food.

N-17 frowned. "Better not. We smell like food if we hang around in there. Disgusting, yeah?"

"Don't you get tired of those nasty bricks?"

"Oh, we don't eat." N-17 spun upside down in the low gravity to show off a port sticking out of one leg, just above the knee. "Nutrients go straight in. We get you one of these, yeah?"

"Maybe." Yuna could wait and eat a brick when she got back. Maybe someone else would be willing to take her to a replicator bar, if she ever met anyone else, and if the replicator bars even still existed. "Where is everybody, anyway?"

"Crew mostly don't like sleepers. Too big-sized for good sex and too back-then brained for conversation." N-17 blushed. "I know you can talk okay. That's just what the crew think."

Yuna studied N-17's blue-brown spidery form. She couldn't tell if her companion was male or female or something else entirely. It would be hard to start a relationship here if the crew wasn't interested. For the first time since waking, she thought of Oliver. She wondered what he was doing back on Earth, then realized he'd almost certainly been dead for a couple thousand years. "What about the other sleepers?"

"Most go back to sleep. They hope for a better planet next time, yeah?" N-17 shrugged. "Gliese is super-sized, like you. Big planet with big gravity. That's why mermaids did make themselves into swimmers."

N-17 led her into a chamber that was dominated by an enormous tank of green water. From the look of it, the tank extended up and down beyond the current deck of the ship. Dark shadows drifted in the murky water. Yuna put her hand on the clear barrier that separated water from air. Drawn by her presence, the shadows loomed closer.

Yuna could see why the crew called them mermaids. Their bodies were covered head to toe in iridescent scales and their feet were large and flat, like flippers. Their chests rose and fell as they breathed, taking in water instead of air.

"Gravity too strong down there to live on land, but oceans are good, yeah?"

"Isn't anyone going to live on the surface of the planet?"

N-17 laughed. "Gravity crush everybody the same, delicate crew or big sleeper. You want to go down, you got to go fishy."

Yuna studied the tanks. Most of the mermaids were small and delicate, like N-17, but a few of them were larger, Yuna's size. She wasn't sure what they did to transform people into mermaids, and she didn't really want to find out. Her body was part of the environment in which her mind existed. Her physical form was critical in shaping who she was. She'd left Earth behind to avoid being stagnant and safe, but this was too much change, too much risk. What kind of life would this planet give her descendants, submerged in a frigid alien ocean, too fragile to pull themselves onto land and bask in the light of the suns? She wouldn't condemn her children to that.

Living on the ship wasn't a good option either—she'd be shunned by the crew and doomed to die before reaching the next destination. She liked N-17, but she had to move on.

"I'll go back into stasis," Yuna said. "This planet isn't right for me."

Yuna didn't panic the second time she woke, not even in those initial moments when her mind couldn't quite make sense of her surroundings. This time, her body was encased in an exoskeleton or maybe a space suit, complete with a helmet that was surprisingly comfortable for all that it was a little claustrophobic. The suit was made of a material she didn't recognize, solid and strong but surprisingly flexible.

She was alone in a cabin not much different from the one she remembered, yesterday for her and some unknown quantity of time for the ship outside of stasis. Had it been another three thousand years, or had the crew found some way for sleepers to live on the continents of Gliese after all? Yuna sighed. Perhaps she had been hasty in passing on Gliese.

She felt vaguely nauseous. Hungry, she realized. There was no sign of anyone else. She released the buckles of the harness that held her in place and propelled herself toward the door. Last time there had been a moderate amount of gravity, generated by spinning the ship. This time there was only the faintest tug, so faint that she could not be quite sure that it was real and not simply her mind attempting to make gravity line up with what was clearly meant to be the floor of the cabin.

The corridors were empty. She wasn't sure who had called her out of stasis, or why. Feeling a little foolish, she called out, "Hello?"

"Greetings." The voice was flat and came over the speakers inside her suit. "If you turn to your left, the corridor will take you through the airlocks and into a sector of the ship that still has functioning replicators. We apologize for not coming to greet you. We are between bodies at the moment."

"All of you?" Yuna asked. The ship was technically capable of continuing on its course without a crew, but—

"There is only one of us. We woke you because your stasis pod was failing."

"How long was I in stasis? Where are we now?"

"After departing Gliese 667 Cc, you were in stasis for approximately eighty-one thousand six hundred and forty-four years."

So much time. Everyone she'd ever known was surely dead. Her family back on Earth, and Oliver—they'd probably been gone on her last waking. Now she'd lost N-17, the crew, and the mermaids too. This would happen every time she slept and woke. Jumping into the future meant leaving the past behind. If she kept going, she might become the last human being alive, or at least the last one still recognizably human. "Is anyone currently in stasis?"

"Three thousand and twenty-seven individuals exist in stasis at this time. Of those, approximately 17% are from the original group that departed from Earth. The remainder come from subsequent generations, some as recently as thirteen thousand years ago. Many of the pods are due to be decommissioned in the near future. If you desire a companion, you may select one and I will initiate the recovery process, but I cannot guarantee consent or compatibility."

Yuna considered the proposal. This might be her last opportunity to have a relationship with a human who had lived on Earth. If she convinced the AI to wake all the sleepers, she could ask them to join her. They might be able to build a community, form families here on the ship. "When will we reach another planet?"

"Our destination is another world that was colonized by the initial ships from Earth—Kepler-452b, the most distant planet of any that were selected for colonization. It would already have been a long trip, but the crew miscalculated, and we need to make course corrections by slingshotting around a series of several stars. Barring the discovery of a more efficient route, it will take thirty-two thousand years to reach our destination."

"Has it become possible for me to live that long?"

"Not in organic form, although your descendants might, if you choose to repopulate the ship."

"That didn't work before. Whatever happened to the old crew would surely happen again, even if we woke all the sleepers and some-

how managed to produce enough children to maintain a stable population. I don't think three thousand people is enough for that, anyway."

"We are the crew, and also the ship. Would it be so bad to join us,
sometime in the future?"

Yuna shook her head. She didn't know. This seemed even further
from what she wanted, even less like the childhood she'd had herself,
and what she had dreamed of for her children. Maybe she should
have turned herself mermaid and let her children swim in the oceans
of Gliese. Would what came next be better or worse? Their destination was a planet colonized by humans, but with the vast amounts
of time that had passed the inhabitants would either be massively
evolved or extinct.

"You revived me because my pod was failing, but there are other
pods that still function. Can you put me back into stasis?"

"Of course. There is no need for pods now, your suit can be
programmed to produce a stasis bubble. I can assist you with the
parameters."

Yuna decided to risk it one more time. Whatever her next awak-
ening held, she would stop this endless skipping forward and put
down roots.

Sensory tendrils burrowed into Yuna's skin, a gentle warmth on all
her senses. Her mind was flooded with yellow-tinted light and the
smell of miso soup and the heat of water from bathhouses back on
Earth that had long ago crumbled to dust. The creature that stood
over her had vaguely human features, all subtly wrong to Yuna's eyes.
Ears delicate and thin, like an elephant's, wavering gently in the low
gravity of the ship, arms that ended not in hands but in fractal divid-
ing branches, terminating in a fan of tendrils.

Tendrils that burrowed into the bare skin of her torso like
worms. They writhed beneath the surface of her body as the creature
tried to merge with her. She pushed at the creature's arms and tried
to pull away. Sensations of warmth were replaced by sensations of
pain across all of her senses—blinding light, cacophonous sound,
burning skin.

An impossible breeze cooled Yuna's face, and the illusion of a
turquoise sky stretched wide above her head. She was breathing the

planet's air with no assistance, sitting on a patch of lime-green moss. Its thin threads reminded her of something, but she couldn't quite remember what. She brushed the delicate plants with her fingertip, and a clump detached from the rest and scurried away in the direction of what looked vaguely like a forest of cedar trees.

Yuna shook her head. No, this wasn't right. She had been on the ship a moment ago, and there was too little gravity for this to be the surface of a planet. Tendrils were embedded in her arm. The creature was touching her again. The images in her mind felt like a question, an invitation. Slower this time, Yuna pulled away. The visions of the planet faded, but without the blinding pain that had accompanied the previous disconnection.

"Stop that," Yuna said.

The creature didn't answer.

"Ship, are you still functional?" Yuna asked. "Where are we?"

The ship did not respond. Yuna had no idea where she was, or what had happened to her stasis suit. She edged past the creature with the tendrils and started searching the rest of the ship for someone, anyone, but she most wanted to find someone else who had slept their way into the future, as she had. Some link to the familiar past. The corridors were filled with creatures that had human faces but bodies that looked almost aquatic, their tendrils trailing behind them like jellyfish tentacles. Several reached out to her as she passed, but she kept a quick enough pace that none managed to burrow into her skin.

Finally she found a small circle of humans, or close-to-humans, huddled in one of the replicator rooms. Most of them were spiderlike and small, remarkably similar to N-17. One of them held an infant, swaddled. Yuna joined their circle. The infant addressed her in a language she did not understand.

The largest member of the group studied her for a moment. "Zay-child says we are invited to the planet. We will go together. You also?"

Yuna was so happy to hear a voice speak her language that she nearly cried. She'd promised herself that she would stop skipping through time and settle down. If the visions from the tendril-creature were true, the planet had a beautiful open sky, and the surface was covered with plants, albeit strange ones. There was even a small community of people she could partly understand.

The infant continued babbling, and the spiderlike human that held it sang a wordless lullaby, rocking the child until it slept. Another member of the group leaned in and stroked the infant's cheek. They did not seem concerned by the not-quite-human creatures that wandered the corridors of the ship, or the myriad of potential dangers on the planet below. They had each other, and they were content.

She had been focused on the wrong things. Oliver had been right all along—home is where you make it. Children grew and thrived in all kinds of places, and by the time a few generations passed, everything changed anyway. "Yes, I'll go to the planet too."

Yuna brushed her fingers against the nursery web, letting her children sense her presence. They were small and only partially formed, a hundred tiny beings tightly woven together, drawing energy from the afternoon sun. This was not what she had envisioned, when she left Earth all those many millennia ago—the oceans of Kepler-452b were too acidic to swim in, and the trees were citizens that resented being climbed—but the planet was wild and unpredictable, with plenty of room to run.

One of her mates pressed their tendrils into the skin of her shoulder. They shared a vision of the children, exploring a mossy clearing beyond the nursery web. The images were overlaid with worry and doubt, and hope, and love. There were no guarantees in being a parent, no matter when or where you were. Starting a family was a leap of faith, the beginning of a story where you don't know the ending.

Yuna sent reassuring thoughts back to her mate.

This was a good beginning.

THE IRON STAR

_____Robert Silverberg_____

THE ALIEN SHIP came drifting up from behind the far side of the neutron star just as I was going on watch. It looked a little like a miniature neutron star itself: a perfect sphere, metallic, dark. But neutron stars don't have six perky little out-thrust legs and the alien craft did.

While I paused in front of the screen the alien floated diagonally upward, cutting a swathe of darkness across the brilliantly starry sky like a fast-moving black hole. It even occulted the real black hole that lay thirty light-minutes away.

I stared at the strange vessel, fascinated and annoyed, wishing I had never seen it, wishing it would softly and suddenly vanish away. This mission was sufficiently complicated already. We hadn't needed an alien ship to appear on the scene. For five days now we had circled the neutron star in seesaw orbit with the aliens, a hundred eighty degrees apart. They hadn't said anything to us and we didn't know how to say anything to them. I didn't feel good about that. I like things direct, succinct, known.

Lina Sorabji, busy enhancing sonar transparencies over at our improvised archaeology station, looked up from her work and caught me scowling. Lina is a slender, dark woman from Madras whose ancestors were priests and scholars when mine were hunting bison on the Great Plains. She said, "You shouldn't let it get to you like that, Tom."

"You know what it feels like, every time I see it cross the screen? It's like having a little speck wandering around on the visual field of your eye. Irritating, frustrating, maddening—and absolutely impossible to get rid of."

"You want to get rid of it?"

I shrugged. "Isn't this job tough enough? Attempting to scoop a sample from the core of a neutron star? Do we really have to have an alien spaceship looking over our shoulders while we work?"

"Maybe it's not a spaceship at all," Lina said cheerily. "Maybe it's just some kind of giant spacebug."

I suppose she was trying to amuse me. I wasn't amused. This was going to win me a place in the history of space exploration, sure: Chief Executive Officer of the first expedition from Earth ever to encounter intelligent extraterrestrial life. Terrific. But that wasn't what IBM/Toshiba had hired me to do. And I'm more interested in completing assignments than in making history. You don't get paid for making history.

Basically the aliens were a distraction from our real work, just as last month's discovery of a dead civilization on a nearby solar system had been, the one whose photographs Lina Sorabji now was studying. This was supposed to be a business venture involving the experimental use of new technology, not an archaeological mission or an exercise in interspecies diplomacy. And I knew that there was a ship from the Exxon/Hyundai combine loose somewhere in hyperspace right now working on the same task we'd been sent out to handle. If they brought it off first, IBM/Toshiba would suffer a very severe loss of face, which is considered very bad on the corporate level. What's bad for IBM/Toshiba would be exceedingly bad for me. For all of us.

I glowered at the screen. Then the orbit of the Ben-wah Maru carried us down and away and the alien disappeared from my line of sight. But not for long, I knew.

As I keyed up the log reports from my sleep period I said to Lina, "You have anything new today?" She had spent the past three weeks analyzing the dead-world data. You never know what the parent companies will see as potentially profitable.

"I'm down to hundred-meter penetration now. There's a system of broad tunnels wormholing the entire planet. Some kind of pneumatic transportation network, is my guess. Here, have a look."

A holoprint sprang into vivid life in the air between us. It was a sonar scan that we had taken from ten thousand kilometers out, reaching a short distance below the surface of the dead world. I saw odd-angled tunnels lined with gleaming luminescent tiles that still pulsed with dazzling colors, centuries after the cataclysm that had destroyed all life there. Amazing decorative patterns of bright lines were plainly visible along the tunnel walls, lines that swirled and overlapped and entwined and beckoned my eye into some adjoining dimension.

Trains of sleek snub-nosed vehicles were scattered like caterpillars everywhere in the tunnels. In them and around them lay skeletons, thousands of them, millions, a whole continent full of commuters slaughtered as they waited at the station for the morning express. Lina touched the fine scan and gave me a close look: biped creatures, broad skulls tapering sharply at the sides, long apelike arms, seven-fingered hands with what seemed like an opposable thumb at each end, pelvises enlarged into peculiar bony crests jutting far out from their hips. It wasn't the first time a hyperspace exploring vessel had come across relics of extinct extraterrestrial races, even a fossil or two. But these weren't fossils. These beings had died only a few hundred years ago. And they had all died at the same time.

I shook my head somberly. "Those are some tunnels. They might have been able to convert them into pretty fair radiation shelters, is my guess. If only they'd had a little warning of what was coming."

"They never knew what hit them."

"No," I said. "They never knew a thing. A supernova brewing right next door and they must not have been able to tell what was getting ready to happen."

Lina called up another print, and another, then another. During our brief fly-by last month our sensors had captured an amazing panoramic view of this magnificent lost civilization: wide streets, spacious parks, splendid public buildings, imposing private houses, the works. Bizarre architecture, all unlikely angles and jutting crests like its creators, but unquestionably grand, noble, impressive. There had been keen intelligence at work here, and high artistry. Everything was intact and in a remarkable state of preservation, if you make allowances for the natural inroads that time and weather and I suppose the occasional earthquake will bring over three or four hundred years. Obviously this had been a wealthy, powerful society, stable and confident.

And between one instant and the next it had all been stopped dead in its tracks, wiped out, extinguished, annihilated. Perhaps they had had a fraction of a second to realize that the end of the world had come, but no more than that. I saw what surely were family groups huddling together, skeletons clumped in threes or fours or fives. I saw what I took to be couples with their seven-fingered hands still clasped in a final exchange of love. I saw some kneeling in a weird elbows-down position that might have been one of—who can say? Prayer? Despair? Acceptance?

A sun had exploded and this great world had died. I shuddered, not for the first time, thinking of it.

It hadn't even been their own sun. What had blown up was this one, forty light-years away from them, the one that was now the neutron star about which we orbited and which once had been a main-sequence sun maybe three or four times as big as Earth's. Or else it had been the other one in this binary system, thirty light-minutes from the first, the blazing young giant companion star of which nothing remained except the black hole nearby. At the moment we had no way of knowing which of these two stars had gone supernova first. Whichever one it was, though, had sent a furious burst of radiation heading outward, a lethal flux of cosmic rays capable of destroying most or perhaps all life-forms within a sphere a hundred light-years in diameter.

The planet of the underground tunnels and the noble temples had simply been in the way. One of these two suns had come to the moment when all the fuel in its core had been consumed: hydrogen had been fused into helium, helium into carbon, carbon into neon, oxygen, sulphur, silicon, until at last a core of pure iron lay at its heart. There is no atomic nucleus more strongly bound than iron. The star had reached the point where its release of energy through fusion had to cease; and with the end of energy production the star no longer could withstand the gravitational pressure of its own vast mass. In a moment, in the twinkling of an eye, the core underwent a catastrophic collapse. Its matter was compressed—beyond the point of equilibrium. And rebounded. And sent forth an intense shock wave that went rushing through the star's outer layers at a speed of 15,000 kilometers a second.

Which ripped the fabric of the star apart, generating an explosion releasing more energy than a billion suns.

The shock wave would have continued outward and outward across space, carrying debris from the exploded star with it, and interstellar gas that the debris had swept up. A fierce sleet of radiation would have been riding on that wave, too: cosmic rays, X-rays, radio waves, gamma rays, everything, all up and down the spectrum. If the sun that had gone supernova had had planets close by, they would have been vaporized immediately. Outlying worlds of that system might merely have been fried.

The people of the world of the tunnels, forty light-years distant, must have known nothing of the great explosion for a full generation after it had happened. But, all that while, the light of that shattered star was traveling towards them at a speed of 300,000 kilometers per second, and one night its frightful baleful unexpected glare must have burst suddenly into their sky in the most terrifying way. And almost in that same moment—for the deadly cosmic rays thrown off by the explosion move nearly at the speed of light—the killing blast of hard radiation would have arrived. And so these people and all else that lived on their world perished in terror and light.

All this took place a thousand light-years from Earth: that surging burst of radiation will need another six centuries to complete its journey towards our home world. At that distance, the cosmic rays will do us little or no harm. But for a time that long-dead star will shine in our skies so brilliantly that it will be visible by day, and by night it will cast deep shadows, longer than those of the Moon.

That's still in Earth's future. Here the fatal supernova, and the second one that must have happened not long afterwards, were some four hundred years in the past. What we had here now was a neutron star left over from one cataclysm and a black hole left over from the other. Plus the pathetic remains of a great civilization on a scorched

177

planet orbiting a neighboring star. And now a ship from some alien culture. A busy corner of the galaxy, this one. A busy time for the crew of the IBM/Toshiba hyperspace ship Ben-wah Maru.

I was still going over the reports that had piled up at my station during my sleep period—mass-and-output readings on the neutron star, progress bulletins on the setup procedures for the neutronium scoop, and other routine stuff of that nature—when the communicator cone in front of me started to glow. I flipped it on. Cal Bjornsen, our communications guru, was calling from Brain Central downstairs.

Bjornsen is mostly black African with some Viking genes salted in. The whole left side of his face is cyborg, the result of some extreme bit of teenage carelessness. The story is that he was gravity-vaulting and lost polarity at sixty meters. The mix of ebony skin, blue eyes, blond hair, and sculpted titanium is an odd one, but I've seen a lot of faces less friendly than Cal's. He's a good man with anything electronic.

He said, "I think they're finally trying to send us messages, Tom."

I sat up fast. "What's that?"

"We've been pulling in signals of some sort for the past ninety minutes that didn't look random, but we weren't sure about it. A dozen or so different frequencies all up and down the line, mostly in the radio band, but we're also getting what seem to be infrared pulses, and something flashing in the ultraviolet range. A kind of scattershot noise effect, only it isn't noise."

"Are you sure of that?"

"The computer's still chewing on it," Bjornsen said. The fingers of his right hand glided nervously up and down his smooth metal cheek. "But we can see already that there are clumps of repetitive patterns."

"Coming from them? How do you know?"

"We didn't, at first. But the transmissions conked out when we lost line-of-sight with them, and started up again when they came back into view."

"I'll be right down," I said.

Bjornsen is normally a calm man, but he was running in frantic circles when I reached Brain Central three or four minutes later. There was stuff dancing on all the walls: sine waves, mainly, but plenty of other patterns jumping around on the monitors. He had already pulled in specialists from practically every department—the whole astronomy staff, two of the math guys, a couple from the external maintenance team, and somebody from engines. I felt preempted. Who was CEO on this ship, anyway? They were all babbling at once. "Fourier series," someone said, and someone yelled back, "Dirichlet factor," and someone else said, "Gibbs phenomenon!" I heard Angie Seraphin insisting vehemently, "—continuous except possibly for a finite number of finite discontinuities in the interval—pi to pi—"

"Hold it," I said, "What's going on?"

More babble, more gibberish. I got them quiet again and repeated my question, aiming it this time at Bjornsen.

"We have the analysis now," he said.

"So?"

"You understand that it's only guesswork, but Brain Central gives good guess. The way it looks, they seem to want us to broadcast a carrier wave they can tune in on, and just talk to them while they lock in with some sort of word-to-word translating device of theirs."

"That's what Brain Central thinks they're saying?"

"It's the most plausible semantic content of the patterns they're transmitting," Bjornsen answered.

I felt a chill. The aliens had word-to-word translating devices? That was a lot more than we could claim. Brain Central is one very smart computer, and if it thought that it had correctly deciphered the message coming in, then in all likelihood it had. An astonishing accomplishment, taking a bunch of ones and zeros put together by an alien mind and culling some sense out of them.

But even Brain Central wasn't capable of word-to-word translation out of some unknown language. Nothing in our technology is. The alien message had been designed to be easy: put together, most likely, in a careful high-redundancy manner, the computer equivalent of picture-writing. Any race able to undertake interstellar travel ought to have a computer powerful enough to sweat the essential meaning out of a message like that, and we did. We couldn't go farther than that though. Let the entropy of that message—that is, the unexpectedness of it, the unpredictability of its semantic content—rise just a little beyond the picture-writing level, and Brain Central would be lost. A computer that knows French should be able to puzzle out Spanish, and maybe even Greek. But Chinese? A tough proposition. And an alien language? Languages may start out logical, but they don't stay that way. And when its underlying grammatical assumptions were put together in the first place by beings with nervous systems that were wired up in ways entirely different from our own, well, the notion of instantaneous decoding becomes hopeless.

Yet our computer said that their computer could do word-to-word. That was scary.

On the other hand, if we couldn't talk to them, we wouldn't begin to find out what they were doing here and what threat, if any, they might pose to us. By revealing our language to them we might be handing them some sort of advantage, but I couldn't be sure of that, and it seemed to me we had to take the risk.

It struck me as a good idea to get some backing for that decision, though. After a dozen years as CEO aboard various corporate ships I knew the protocols. You did what you thought was right, but you didn't go all the way out on the limb by yourself if you could help it.

"Request a call for a meeting of the corporate staff," I told Bjornsen.

It wasn't so much a scientific matter now as a political one. The scientists would probably be gung-ho to go blasting straight ahead with making contact. But I wanted to hear what the Toshiba people would say, and the IBM people, and the military people. So we got everyone together and I laid the situation out and asked for a Consensus Process. And let them go at it, hammer and tongs.

Instant polarization. The Toshiba people were scared silly of the aliens. We must be cautious, Nakamura said. Caution, yes, said her cohort Nagy-Szabo. There may be danger to Earth. We have no knowledge of the aims and motivations of these beings. Avoid all contact with them, Nagy-Szabo said. Nakamura went even further. We should withdraw from the area immediately, she said, and return to Earth for additional instructions. That drew hot opposition from Jorgensen and Kalliotis, the IBM people. We had work to do here, they said. We should do it. They grudgingly conceded the need to be wary, but strongly urged continuation of the mission and advocated a circumspect opening of contact with the other ship. I think they were already starting to think about alien marketing demographics. Maybe I do them an injustice. Maybe.

The military people were about evenly divided between the two factions. A couple of them, the hair-splitting career-minded ones, wanted to play it absolutely safe and clear out of here fast, and the others, the up-and-away hero types, spoke out in favor of forging ahead with contact and to hell with the risks.

I could see there wasn't going to be any consensus. It was going to come down to me to decide.

By nature I am cautious. I might have voted with Nakamura in favor of immediate withdrawal; however that would have made my ancient cold-eyed Sioux forebears howl. Yet in the end what swayed me was an argument that came from Bryce-Williamson, one of the fiercest of the military sorts. He said that we didn't dare turn tail and run for home without making contact, because the aliens would take that either as a hostile act or a stupid one, and either way they might just slap some kind of tracer on us that ultimately would enable them to discover the location of our home world. True caution, he said, required us to try to find out what these people were all about before we made any move to leave the scene. We couldn't just run and we couldn't simply ignore them.

I sat quietly for a long time, weighing everything.

"Well?" Bjornsen asked. "What do you want to do, Tom?"

"Send them a broadcast," I said. "Give them greetings in the name of Earth and all its peoples. Extend to them the benevolent warm wishes of the board of directors of IBM/Toshiba. And then we'll wait and see."

We waited. But for a long while we didn't see.

Two days, and then some. We went round and round the neutron star, and they went round and round the neutron star, and no further communication came from them. We beamed them all sorts of messages at all sorts of frequencies along the spectrum, both in the radio band and via infrared and ultraviolet as well, so that they'd have plenty of material to work with. Perhaps their translator gadget wasn't all that good, I told myself hopefully. Perhaps it was stripping its gears trying to fathom the pleasant little packets of semantic data that we had sent them.

On the third day of silence I began feeling restless. There was no way we could begin the work we had been sent here to do, not with aliens watching. The Toshiba people—the Ultra Cautious faction—got more and more nervous. Even the IBM representatives began to act a little twitchy. I started to question the wisdom of having overruled the advocates of a no-contact policy. Although the parent companies hadn't seriously expected us to run into aliens, they had covered that eventuality in our instructions, and we were under orders to do minimum tipping of our hands if we found ourselves observed by strangers. But it was too late to call back our messages and I was still eager to find out what would happen next. So we watched and waited, and then we waited and watched. Round and round the neutron star.

We had been parked in orbit for ten days now around the neutron star, an orbit calculated to bring us no closer to its surface than 9000 kilometers at the closest skim. That was close enough for us to carry out our work, but not so close that we would be subjected to troublesome and dangerous tidal effects.

The neutron star had been formed in the supernova explosion that had destroyed the smaller of the two suns in what had once been a binary star system here. At the moment of the cataclysmic collapse of the stellar sphere, all its matter had come rushing inward with such force that electrons and protons were driven into each other to become a soup of pure neutrons. Which then were squeezed so tightly that they were forced virtually into contact with one another, creating a smooth globe of the strange stuff that we call neutronium, a billion billion times denser than steel and a hundred billion billion times more incompressible.

That tiny ball of neutronium glowing dimly in our screens was the neutron star. It was just eighteen kilometers in diameter but its mass was greater than that of Earth's sun. That gave it a gravitational field a quarter of a billion billion times as strong as that of the surface of Earth. If we could somehow set foot on it, we wouldn't just be squashed flat, we'd be instantly reduced to fine powder by the colossal tidal effects—the difference in gravitational pull between the soles of our feet and the tops of our heads, stretching us towards and away from the neutron star's center with a kick of eighteen billion kilograms.

A ghostly halo of electromagnetic energy surrounded the neutron star: X-rays, radio waves, gammas, and an oily, crackling flicker of violet light. The neutron star was rotating on its axis some 550 times a second, and powerful jets of electrons were spouting from its magnetic poles at each sweep, sending forth a beacon-like pulsar broadcast of the familiar type that we have been able to detect since the middle of the twentieth century.

Behind that zone of fiercely outflung radiation lay the neutron star's atmosphere: an envelope of gaseous iron a few centimeters thick. Below that, our scan had told us, was a two-kilometers-thick crust of normal matter, heavy elements only, ranging from molybdenum on up to transuranics with atomic numbers as high as 140. And within that was the neutronium zone, the stripped nuclei of iron packed unimaginably close together, an ocean of strangeness nine kilometers deep. What lay at the heart of that, we could only guess.

We had come here to plunge a probe into the neutronium zone and carry off a spoonful of star-stuff that weighed 100 billion tons per cubic centimeter.

No sort of conventional landing on the neutron star was possible or even conceivable. Not only was the gravitational pull beyond our comprehension—anything that was capable of withstanding the tidal effects would still have to cope with an escape velocity requirement of 200,000 kilometers per second when it tried to take off, two thirds the speed of light—but the neutron star's surface temperature was something like 3.5 million degrees. The surface temperature of our own sun is six thousand degrees and we don't try to make landings there. Even at this distance, our heat and radiation shields were straining to the limits to keep us from being cooked. We didn't intend to go any closer.

What IBM/Toshiba wanted us to do was to put a miniature hyperspace ship into orbit around the neutron star: an astonishing little vessel no bigger than your clenched fist, powered by a fantastically scaled-down version of the drive that had carried us through the space-time manifold across a span of a thousand light-years in a dozen weeks. The little ship was a slave-drone; we would operate it from the Ben-wah Maru. Or, rather, Brain Central would. In a maneuver that had taken fifty computer-years to program, we would send the miniature into hyperspace and bring it out again right inside the neutron star. And keep it there a billionth of a second, long enough for it to gulp the spoonful of neutronium we had been sent here to collect. Then we'd head for home, with the miniature ship following us along the same hyperpath.

We'd head for home, that is, unless the slave-drone's brief intrusion into the neutron star released disruptive forces that splattered us all over this end of the galaxy. IBM/Toshiba didn't really think that was going to happen. In theory a neutron star is one of the most stable things there is in the universe, and the math didn't indicate that taking a nip from its interior would cause real problems. This neighborhood had already had its full quota of giant explosions, anyway.

Still, the possibility existed. Especially since there was a black hole just thirty light-minutes away, a souvenir of the second and much larger supernova bang that had happened here in the recent past. Having a black hole nearby is a little like playing with an extra wild card whose existence isn't made known to the players until some randomly chosen moment midway through the game. If we destabilized the neutron star in some way not anticipated by the scientists back on Earth, we might just find ourselves going for a visit to the event horizon instead of getting to go home. Or we might not. There was only one way of finding out.

I didn't know, by the way, what use the parent companies planned to make of the neutronium we had been hired to bring them. I hoped it was a good one.

But obviously we weren't going to tackle any of this while there was an alien ship in the vicinity. So all we could do was wait. And see. Right now we were doing a lot of waiting, and no seeing at all.

Two days later Cal Bjornsen said, "We're getting a message back from them now. Audio only. In English."

We had wanted that, we had even hoped for that. And yet it shook me to learn that it was happening.

"Let's hear it," I said.

"The relay's coming over ship channel seven."

I tuned in. What I heard was an obviously synthetic voice, no undertones or overtones, not much inflection. They were trying to mimic the speech rhythms of what we had sent them, and I suppose they were actually doing a fair job of it, but the result was still unmistakably mechanical-sounding. Of course there might be nothing on board that ship but a computer, I thought, or maybe robots. I wish now that they had been robots.

It had the absolute and utter familiarity of a recurring dream. In stiff, halting, but weirdly comprehensible English came the first greetings of an alien race to the people of the planet of Earth. "This who speak be First of Nine Sparg," the voice said. Nine Sparg, we soon realized from context, was the name of their planet. First might have been the speaker's name, or his—hers, its?—title; that was unclear, and stayed that way. In an awkward pidgin-English that we nevertheless had little trouble understanding, First expressed gratitude for our transmission and asked us to send more words. To send a dictionary, in fact: now that they had the algorithm for our speech they needed more content to jam in behind it, so that we could go on to exchange more complex statements than Hello and How are you.

Bjornsen queried me on the override. "We've got an English program that we could start feeding them," he said. "Thirty thousand words: that should give them plenty. You want me to put it on for them?"

"Not so fast," I said. "We need to edit it first."

"For what?"

"Anything that might help them find the location of Earth. That's in our orders, under Eventuality of Contact with Extraterrestrials. Remember, I have Nakamura and Nagy-Szabo breathing down my neck, telling me that there's a ship full of boogiemen out there and we mustn't have anything to do with them. I don't believe that myself. But right now we don't know how friendly these Spargs are and we aren't supposed to bring strangers home with us."

"But how could a dictionary entry—"

"Suppose the sun—our sun—is defined as a yellow G2 type star," I said. "That gives them a pretty good beginning. Or something about the constellations as seen from Earth. I don't know, Cal. I just want to make sure we don't accidentally hand these beings a roadmap to our home planet before we find out what sort of critters they are."

Three of us spent half a day screening the dictionary, and we put Brain Central to work on it too. In the end we pulled seven words—you'd laugh if you knew which they were, but we wanted to be careful—and sent the rest across to the Spargs. They were silent for nine or ten hours. When they came back on the air their command of English was immensely more fluent. Frighteningly more fluent. Yesterday First had sounded like a tourist using a Fifty Handy Phrases program. A day later, First's command of English was as good as that of an intelligent Japanese who has been living in the United States for ten or fifteen years.

It was a tense, wary conversation. Or so it seemed to me, the way it began to seem that First was male and that his way of speaking was brusque and bluntly probing. I may have been wrong on every count.

First wanted to know who we were and why we were here. Jumping right in, getting down to the heart of the matter. I felt a little like a butterfly collector who has wandered onto the grounds of a fusion plant and is being interrogated by a security guard. But I kept my tone and phrasing as neutral as I could, and told him that our planet was called Earth and that we had come on a mission of exploration and investigation.

So had they, he told me. Where is Earth?

Pretty straightforward of him, I thought. I answered that I lacked at this point a means of explaining galactic positions to him in terms that he would understand. I did volunteer the information that Earth was not anywhere close at hand.

He was willing to drop that line of inquiry for the time being. He shifted to the other obvious one:

What were we investigating?

Certain properties of collapsed stars, I said, after a bit of hesitation.

And which properties were those?

I told him that we didn't have enough vocabulary in common for me to try to explain that either.

The Nine Sparg captain seemed to accept that evasion too. And provided me with a pause that indicated that it was my turn. Fair enough.

When I asked him what he was doing here, he replied without any apparent trace of evasiveness that he had come on a mission of historical inquiry. I pressed for details. It has to do with the ancestry of our race, he said. We used to live in this part of the galaxy, before the great explosion. No hesitation at all about telling me that. It struck me that First was being less reticent about dealing with my queries than I was with his; but of course I had no way of judging whether I was hearing the truth from him.

"I'd like to know more," I said, as much as a test as anything else. "How long ago did your people flee this great explosion? And how far from here is your present home world?"

A long silence: several minutes. I wondered uncomfortably if I had overplayed my hand. If they were as edgy about our finding their home world as I was about their finding ours, I had to be careful not to push them into an overreaction. They might just think that the safest thing to do would be to blow us out of the sky as soon as they had learned all they could from us.

But when First spoke again it was only to say, "Are you willing to establish contact in the visual band?"

"Is such a thing possible?"

"We think so," he said.

I thought about it. Would letting them see what we looked like give them any sort of clue to the location of Earth? Perhaps, but it seemed far-fetched. Maybe they'd be able to guess that we were carbon-based oxygen-breathers, but the risk of allowing them to know that seemed relatively small. And in any case we'd find out what they looked like. An even trade, right?

I had my doubts that their video transmission system could be made compatible with our receiving equipment. But I gave First the go-ahead and turned the microphone over to the communications staff. Who struggled with the problem for a day and a half. Sending the signal back and forth was no big deal, but breaking it down into information that would paint a picture on a cathode-ray tube was a different matter. The communications people at both ends talked and talked and talked, while I fretted about how much technical information about us we were revealing to the Spargs. The tinkering went on and on and nothing appeared on screen except occasional strings of horizontal lines. We sent them more data about how our television system worked. They made further adjustments in their transmission devices. This time we got spots instead of lines. We sent even more data. Were they leading us on? And were we telling them too much? I came finally to the position that trying to make the video link work had been a bad idea, and started to tell Communications that. But then the haze of drifting spots on my screen abruptly cleared and I found myself looking into the face of an alien being.

An alien face, yes. Extremely alien. Suddenly this whole interchange was kicked up to a new level of reality.

A hairless wedge-shaped head, flat and broad on top, tapering to a sharp point below. Corrugated skin that looked as thick as heavy rubber. Two chilly eyes in the center of that wide forehead and two more at its extreme edges. Three mouths, vertical slits, side by side: one for speaking and the other two, maybe for separate intake of fluids and solids. The whole business supported by three long columnar necks as thick as a man's wrist, separated by open spaces two or three centimeters wide. What was below the neck we never got to see. But the head alone was plenty.

They probably thought we were just as strange.

With video established, First and I picked up our conversation right where we had broken it off the day before. Once more he was not in the least shy about telling me things.

He had been able to calculate in our units of time the date of the great explosion that had driven his people far from home world: it had taken place 387 years ago. He didn't use the word "supernova," because it hadn't been included in the 30,000-word vocabulary we had sent them, but that was obviously what he meant by "the great explosion." The 387-year figure squared pretty well with our own calculations, which were based on an analysis of the surface temperature and rate of rotation of the neutron star.

The Nine Sparg people had had plenty of warning that their sun was behaving oddly—the first signs of instability had become apparent more than a century before the blow-up—and they had devoted all their energy for several generations to the job of packing up and clearing out. It had taken many years, it seemed, for them to accomplish their migration to the distant new world they had chosen for their new home. Did that mean, I asked myself, that their method of interstellar travel was much slower than ours, and that they had needed decades or even a century to cover fifty or a hundred light-years? Earth had less to worry about, then. Even if they wanted to make trouble for us, they wouldn't be able easily to reach us, a thousand light-years from here. Or was First saying that their new world was really distant—all the way across the galaxy, perhaps, seventy or eighty thousand light-years away, or even in some other galaxy altogether? If that was the case, we were up against truly superior beings. But there was no easy way for me to question him about such things without telling him things about our own hyperdrive and our distance from this system that I didn't care to have him know.

After a long and evidently difficult period of settling in on the new world, First went on, the Nine Sparg folk finally were well enough established to launch an inquiry into the condition of their former home planet. Thus his mission to the supernova site.

"But we are in great mystery," First admitted, and it seemed to me that a note of sadness and bewilderment had crept into his mechanical-sounding voice. "We have come to what certainly is the right location. Yet nothing seems to be correct here. We find only this little iron star. And of our former planet there is no trace."

I stared at that peculiar and unfathomable four-eyed face, that three-columned neck, those tight vertical mouths, and to my surprise something close to compassion awoke in me. I had been dealing with this creature as though he were a potential enemy capable of leading armadas of war to my world and conquering it. But in fact he might be merely a scholarly explorer who was making a nostalgic pilgrimage, and running into problems with it. I decided to relax my guard just a little.

"Have you considered," I said, "that you might not be in the right location after all?"

"What do you mean?"

"As we were completing our journey towards what you call the iron star," I said, "we discovered a planet forty light-years from here that beyond much doubt had had a great civilization, and which evidently was close enough to the exploding star system here to have been devastated by it. We have pictures of it that we could show you. Perhaps that was your home world."

Even as I was saying it the idea started to seem foolish to me. The skeletons we had photographed on the dead world had had broad tapering heads that might perhaps have been similar to those of First, but they hadn't shown any evidence of this unique triple-neck arrangement. Besides, First had said that his people had had several generations to prepare for evacuation. Would they have left so many millions of their people behind to die? It looked obvious from the way those skeletons were scattered around that the inhabitants of that planet hadn't had the slightest clue that doom was due to overtake them that day. And finally, I realized that First had plainly said that it was his own world's sun that had exploded, not some neighboring star. The supernova had happened here. The dead world's sun was still intact.

"Can you show me your pictures?" he said.

It seemed pointless. But I felt odd about retracting my offer. And in the new rapport that had sprung up between us I could see no harm in it.

I told Lina Sorabji to feed her sonar transparencies into the relay pickup. It was easy enough for Cal Bjornsen to shunt them into our video transmission to the alien ship.

The Nine Sparg captain withheld his comment until we had shown him the batch.

Then he said, "Oh, that was not our world. That was the world of the Garvalekkinon people."

"The Garvalekkinon?"

"We knew them. A neighboring race, not related to us. Sometimes, on rare occasions, we traded with them. Yes, they must all have died when the star exploded. It is too bad."

"They look as though they had no warning," I said. "Look: can you see them there, waiting in the train stations?"

The triple mouths fluttered in what might have been the Nine Sparg equivalent of a nod.

"I suppose they did not know the explosion was coming."

"You suppose? You mean you didn't tell them?"

All four eyes blinked at once. Expression of puzzlement.

"Tell them? Why should we have told them? We were busy with our preparations. We had no time for them. Of course the radiation would have been harmful to them, but why was that our concern? They were not related to us. They were nothing to us."

I had trouble believing I had heard him correctly. A neighboring people. Occasional trading partners. Your sun is about to blow up, and it's reasonable to assume that nearby solar systems will be affected. You have fifty or a hundred years of advance notice yourselves, and you can't even take the trouble to let these other people know what's going to happen?

I said, "You felt no need at all to warn them? That isn't easy for me to understand."

Again the four-eyed shrug.

"I have explained it to you already," said First. "They were not of our kind. They were nothing to us."

I excused myself on some flimsy excuse and broke contact. And sat and thought a long long while. Listening to the words of the Nine Sparg captain echoing in my mind. And thinking of the millions of skeletons scattered like straws in the tunnels of that dead world that the supernova had baked. A whole people left to die because it was inconvenient to take five minutes to send them a message. Or perhaps because it simply never had occurred to anybody to bother.

The families, huddling together. The children reaching out. The husbands and wives with hands interlocked.

A world of busy, happy, intelligent, people. Boulevards and temples. Parks and gardens. Paintings, sculpture, poetry, music. History, philosophy, science. And a sudden star in the sky, and everything gone in a moment.

Why should we have told them? They were nothing to us.

I knew something of the history of my own people. We had experienced casual extermination too. But at least when the white settlers had done it to us it was because they had wanted our land.

For the first time I understood the meaning of alien.

I turned on the external screen and stared out at the unfamiliar sky of this place. The neutron star was barely visible, a dull red dot, far down in the lower left quadrant; and the black hole was high.

Once they had both been stars. What havoc must have attended their destruction! It must have been the Sparg sun that blew first, the one that had become the neutron star. And then, fifty or a hundred years later, perhaps, the other, larger star had gone the same route. Another titanic supernova, a great flare of killing light. But of course everything for hundreds of light-years around had perished already in the first blast.

The second sun had been too big to leave a neutron star behind. So great was its mass that the process of collapse had continued on beyond the neutron-star stage, matter crushing in upon itself until it broke through the normal barriers of space and took on a bizarre and almost unthinkable form, creating an object of infinitely small volume that was nevertheless of infinite density: a black hole, a pocket of incomprehensibility where once a star had been.

I stared now at the black hole before me.

I couldn't see it, of course. So powerful was the surface gravity of that grotesque thing that nothing could escape from it, not even electromagnetic radiation, not the merest particle of light. The ultimate in invisibility cloaked that infinitely deep hole in space.

But though the black hole itself was invisible, the effects that its presence caused were not. That terrible gravitational pull would rip apart and swallow any solid object that came too close; and so the hole was surrounded by a bright ring of dust and gas several hundred kilometers across. These shimmering particles constantly tumbled towards that insatiable mouth, colliding as they spiraled in, releasing flaring fountains of radiation, red-shifted into the visual spectrum by the enormous gravity: the bright green of helium, the majestic purple of hydrogen, the crimson of oxygen. That outpouring of energy was the death-cry of doomed matter. That rainbow whirlpool of blazing light was the beacon marking the maw of the black hole.

I found it oddly comforting to stare at that thing. To contemplate that zone of eternal quietude from which there was no escape. Pondering so inexorable and unanswerable an infinity was more soothing than thinking of a world of busy people destroyed by the indifference of their neighbors. Black holes offer no choices, no complexities, no shades of disagreement. They are absolute.

Why should we have told them? They were nothing to us.

After a time I restored contact with the Nine Sparg ship. First came to the screen at once, ready to continue our conversation.

"There is no question that our world once was located here," he said at once. "We have checked and rechecked the coordinates. But the changes have been extraordinary."

"Have they?"

"Once there were two stars here, our own and the brilliant blue one that was nearby. Our history is very specific on that point: a brilliant blue star that lit the entire sky. Now we have only the iron star. Apparently it has taken the place of our sun. But where has the blue one gone? Could the explosion have destroyed it too?"

I frowned. Did they really not know? Could a race be capable of attaining an interstellar spacedrive and an interspecies translating device, and nevertheless not have arrived at any understanding of the neutron star/black hole cosmogony?

Why not? They were aliens. They had come by all their understanding of the universe via a route different from ours. They might well have overlooked this feature or that of the universe about them.

"The blue star—" I began.

But First spoke right over me, saying, "It is a mystery that we must devote all our energies to solving, or our mission will be fruitless. But let us talk of other things. You have said little of your own mission. And of your home world. I am filled with great curiosity, Captain, about those subjects."

I'm sure you are, I thought.

"We have only begun our return to space travel," said First. "Thus far we have encountered no other intelligent races. And so we regard this meeting as fortunate. It is our wish to initiate contact with you. Quite likely some aspects of your technology would be valuable to us. And there will be much that you wish to purchase from us. Therefore we would be glad to establish trade relations with you."

As you did with the Garvalekkinon people, I said to myself.

I said, "We can speak of that tomorrow, Captain. I grow tired now. But before we break contact for the day, allow me to offer you the beginning of a solution to the mystery of the disappearance of the blue sun."

The four eyes widened. The slitted mouths parted in what seemed surely to be excitement.

"Can you do that?"

I took a deep breath.

"We have some preliminary knowledge. Do you see the place opposite the iron star, where energies boil and circle in the sky? As we entered this system, we found certain evidence there that may explain the fate of your former blue sun. You would do well to center your investigations on that spot."

"We are most grateful," said First.

"And now, Captain, I must bid you good night. Until tomorrow, Captain."

"Until tomorrow," said the alien.

I was awakened in the middle of my sleep period by Lina Sorabji and Bryce-Williamson, both of them looking flushed and sweaty. I sat up, blinking and shaking my head.

"It's the alien ship," Bryce-Williamson blurted, "It's approaching the black hole."

"Is it, now?"

"Dangerously close," said Lina. "What do they think they're doing? Don't they know?"

"I don't think so," I said. "I suggested that they go exploring there. Evidently they don't regard it as a bad idea."

"You sent them there?" she said incredulously.

With a shrug I said, "I told them that if they went over there they might find the answer to the question of where one of their missing suns went. I guess they've decided to see if I was right."

"We have to warn them," said Bryce-Williamson. "Before it's too late. Especially if we're responsible for sending them there. They'll be furious with us once they realize that we failed to warn them of the danger."

"By the time they realize it," I replied calmly, "it will be too late. And then their fury won't matter, will it? They won't be able to tell us how annoyed they are with us. Or to report to their home world, for that matter, that they had an encounter with intelligent aliens who might be worth exploiting."

He gave me an odd look. The truth was starting to sink in.

I turned on the external screens and punched up a close look at the black hole region. Yes, there was the alien ship, the little metallic sphere, the six odd outthrust legs. It was in the zone of criticality now. It seemed hardly to be moving at all. And it was growing dimmer and dimmer as it slowed. The gravitational field had it, and it was being drawn in. Blacking out, becoming motionless. Soon it would have gone beyond the point where outside observers could perceive it. Already it was beyond the point of turning back.

I heard Lina sobbing behind me. Bryce-Williamson was muttering to himself: praying, perhaps.

I said, "Who can say what they would have done to us—in their casual, indifferent way—once they came to Earth? We know now that Spargs worry only about Spargs. Anybody else is just so much furniture." I shook my head. "To hell with them. They're gone, and in a universe this big we'll probably never come across any of them again, or they us. Which is just fine. We'll be a lot better off having nothing at all to do with them."

"But to die that way—" Lina murmured. "To sail blindly into a black hole—"

"It is a great tragedy," said Bryce-Williamson.

"A tragedy for them," I said. "For us, a reprieve, I think. And tomorrow we can get moving on the neutronium-scoop project." I tuned up the screen to the next level. The boiling cloud of matter around the mouth of the black hole blazed fiercely. But of the alien ship there was nothing to be seen.

Yes, a great tragedy, I thought. The valiant exploratory mission that had sought the remains of the Nine Sparg home world has been lost with all hands. No hope of rescue. A pity that they hadn't known how unpleasant black holes can be.

But why should we have told them? They were nothing to us.

e^h

_____Alvaro Zinos-Amaro_____

Kaku, Alpha Transit, 7.8 yrs

"Are you ready?" Dad says. "I wouldn't want to miss this for the world."

He lingers on the threshold of my lab. I could welcome him in; I could tell him that I'm also excited; I could share the moment with him.

But I don't.

I remember it perfectly.

"Be right there," I said. Distracted by my research, I'd had a vague notion that the debriefing was still hours away.

I changed into fresh coveralls and Dad and I headed towards Hub Six. "You look a little flushed," I said.

"I might have come down here too fast." His use of the word "down" wasn't strictly accurate, but I knew what he meant: an over-rapid ascent through the spinning ship's gravity gradient, from his dot-eight-*g* lab to my one-*g* module. Reminding myself of Dad's sensitivity to matters of age, I decided not to comment further.

On the way we encountered various department heads going in our same direction. Some whispered.

"Just what this ship needs," Dad said. "More gossip."

"Oh?"

Dad's eyebrows arched. "Seriously? It's impossible to spend five minutes in the Bistro Hub and not hear the latest speculations."

"I haven't been eating in the Bistro," I said, and left it at that. I'd been munching on energy packs throughout the day, holed up in my lab.

Dad looked thoughtful but didn't say anything.

We found a spot in the circular, multi-ring formation around the cavernous Hub's center. A few minutes later Mission Director Max Liwu activated a hologram broadcast from the *Euler*, one of our four sister ships.

A cosmologist named Elia Killik materialized before us. I didn't recognize her, which wasn't unusual, considering there were two thousand of us on each of the five ships and we had worked closely only with our immediate teams during our mission prep years. I glanced at Dad, who leaned forward in anticipation.

"One week ago," Elia said, "as we passed the outer reaches of the Oort cloud, we experienced several momentary glitches in our astrometric sensors. These glitches, we later learned, coincided with a set of DNA translocations, revealed by standard medscans. About fifteen percent of our ship's crew seems to have undergone these mutations. The underlying cause of both the equipment glitches and the mutated junk DNA appears to be a radiation field comprised of exotic dark energy unlike any we've detected before."

I let Elia's words sink in. The *Euler*, being slightly ahead of us, must have been the first ship to hit the radiation belt. We on the *Kaku* would be next. Dad and I exchanged looks.

"All mutations have occurred in non-functional DNA," Elia continued. "They have *not* interfered with our anti-senescence modifications."

The Hub let out a collective sigh of relief. On Earth we'd been genetically engineered to slow our aging and make the eighty-year trip to Gliese 832 c viable in a single generation; any tampering with that would have been disastrous, jeopardizing humanity's first extrasolar colony.

"If you experience any unusual symptoms when your ship crosses the radiation belt, undergo a medscan at once," Elia said. "I am now transmitting our research to all personnel. The more brains on this, the better."

I activated my coverall's SmartInk and scanned Elia's report on my right sleeve.

And then everything around me disappeared; only the report existed.

I read Elia's findings a second time. The appendix contained the details of the mutated junk DNA sequence. I stared in disbelief. I tapped into my module's computer, sent it the report, and ran one of my customized frequency analyses on the DNA sequence.

Elia was still talking, but I could hardly hear her through the blood-rush in my ears. "… the radiation field hasn't affected our laser shields or pulsed ion drives," she was saying when I tuned back in. "We are therefore proceeding with our mission."

The results of my lab's frequency analysis came back.

I blinked.

The broadcast passed from Elia to one of the Mission Executives.

"Excuse me," I said, raising my hand and my voice. "*Excuse me.*"

The Executive's hologram turned in my direction. "We'll take questions privately after we're done here," she said, "so if you don't mind—"

"I do mind," I said. "And this isn't a question."

A hundred eyes were on me in the Hub, thousands more via broadcast. Dad tugged gently at my arm, but I ignored him.

"My name is Erik Hamada," I said, "and my specialty is information theory as applied to inter-species communication. I believe that the mutated DNA sequence triggered by the radiation belt, identical in all reported cases, is a Rosetta stone."

The Executive frowned. "A Rosetta stone? To decode what?"

"It'll take more work to confirm my hypothesis," I said, "but I think it's the key to deciphering our own junk DNA."

The Executive's face blanched. "You're telling us, Mr. Hamada, that humans have been carrying around a coded message inside their DNA for millions of years?"

I tried to ignore the sarcastic edge in her voice. "Yes, precisely. I'm not the first to believe this. Genomic SETI, the search for evidence of extraterrestrial intelligence within the human genome, has been around for over a century. Junk DNA has always been the prime suspect, because it remains unchanged over deep time, making it an excellent storage medium." I swallowed. "All of that was just a theory—until now."

In short, I was correct.

But there was a catch.

A big one.

The Rosetta stone needed a *lot* of data to work, quadrillions of bytes. We could rig nanos with enough power to take a quantum snapshot at that resolution, but the intensity of the scan would kill the volunteer. So if we wanted to read the encyclopedia inside our genes, the person to crack open the cover was going to die.

After six meetings and seven focus groups we decided that our convoy couldn't make the decision alone, since our actions might affect all of humanity. So we sent a message to Earth. We were 1.6 light-years away, which meant that we'd have to wait 3.2 years for a response—if we weren't continuing to move away from Earth. But we *were*, at around 0.2-*c*, which made our wait time close to 3.9 years.

Some people weren't willing to wait that long.

Kaku, Alpha Transit, 8.2 yrs

I received the video-call three hours into nightshift.

The medic on the screen introduced herself as Alicia Treb, from the *Atman*. A man aboard their ship had commandeered one of the backup medical Hubs, overridden the safety protocols, and subjected himself to the quantum snapshot.

Now he was dead.

"That's awful," I told Alicia. "Was anyone else injured?"

"No," she replied. "But we're afraid someone might be."

"What do you mean?"

Alicia hugged herself. "The snapshot wasn't as effective as our simulations had indicated: we only received a third of the data we were expecting. When people learn of this…." Her eyes hardened. "That's why our ship's Director asked me to speak to you."

"You want me to decode the third of the message we have and see if I can extrapolate the rest? I'm on it." I reached forward to end the call, but Alicia's demeanor said otherwise.

"We've run psychological profiles of every crew member to evaluate risks," she said. "I'm afraid that your father is high on the list, Erik. His recent behavior appears erratic, and he likely knows what happened. He won't answer the general com, but maybe you can get through to him. Talk to him. Try to reason him out of whatever he's planning—*if* he's planning anything."

Strange to think now that mixed in with my concern for Dad's well-being was *shame*: shame on behalf of his actions, and shame on behalf of myself for so readily agreeing that he was potentially unstable. "Where is he right now?"

"His last known location was microhydroponics, Hub Three," Alicia said through pursed lips. "Thank you, and good luck."

My stomach lurched. That Hub had an emergency corridor that linked up with one of the *Kaku's* medical Hubs.

I stood up too quickly, dizzying myself, and the world careened around me...

I could describe in great detail what happened next, but quite honestly, I don't have the heart.

Here's what you need to know: I failed.

My Dad had initiated a chain of events that resulted in his voluntary death, and I wasn't able to stop him. *Sacrifice* was a word he used in his brief goodbye note. Because he was among the eldest, he thought he had less to offer our future colony, so he was a logical choice for this.

Yeah, right.

Ten hours after Dad's death another self-appointed hero bit the dust.

Two more bodies.

And two more quantum snapshots.

Now we could run the Rosetta stone.

Only problem: I was numb, utterly hollowed out. Couldn't bring myself to care about any of it.

So I handed over my research and retreated into medication and AI grief therapy.

Someone else ended up receiving credit for translating the first confirmed message from extraterrestrials, but I didn't care about that, either.

Kaku, Alpha Transit, 11.7 yrs

When Earth's response finally arrived it proved a terrible joke: "Proceed with caution."

Kaku, Alpha Transit, 11.9 yrs

Networks.
The message humans have been conveying from one generation to the next, for millions of years, is an enormously complicated manual on network connectivity.
This was what Dad had died for?
The ultimate network primer?
The general response, like mine, was one of disappointment. Looking back on it, you might think we should have been giddy: we'd found a message from ETs who had been to Earth—or landed an advanced probe there—millions of years ago. But we had so many questions, and no answers seemed forthcoming from the message itself.

Kaku, Alpha Transit, 12.0 yrs

With the help of an AI therapist I built up a daily discipline, and even forced myself to socialize. Enter Karia Avary, an expert in quantum entanglement, with whom I hit it off right away.

Karia was the most outwardly expressive person I'd ever met, which was particularly comforting at a time when my emotional woes made it hard for me to read others well. Her eternal curiosity led to wonderful conversations, and her indefatigable enthusiasm was contagious. Things between us were going very well, until one nightshift when dinner in my module proved weirdly awkward, and I noticed she seemed withdrawn. I asked her about it and she said everything was fine, so I let it go. But the next day was a repeat performance; again she seemed distant, not herself. This time I tried a different approach and scooched closer to her, but her body tensed.

"Tired?" I said.

She closed her eyes and let out a long breath. "Yeah."

"How about some music?" I dialed up Rachmaninoff, one of her favorites. "Wine, maybe?"

She opened her eyes. "Not tonight," she said softly.

I got up and cleared the dishes. When I returned she was still sitting in the same spot. "You're sure nothing's wrong?"

"Have you heard the rumors, Erik?"

My neck seized up. *Rumor* was one of my least favorite words—along with *hero* and *sacrifice.* "No."

"Well, they're more than rumors."

"What the hell are you talking about?"

"Yesterday a sys engineer I know intercepted a message from the Mission Executive team to Earth. I'm sure there'll be an official announcement soon."

Adrenaline coursed through me. "What are they saying?"

"A research team aboard the *Mikumo* has made a breakthrough related to the network primer. They believe its information can be applied to the human brain, in a procedure that will enhance our decision-making process." She paused. "This could be huge."

I thought through it. The network primer dealt in abstract networking "units." What if we interpreted those units as neurons? Then all sorts of implications would follow, implications that the *Mikumo* team had apparently teased out. "Whoever planted the manual in our genes only wanted us to find it when we became capable of leaving our Solar System," I said.

Karia nodded. "Exactly."

I wanted to heed caution about this new procedure, but if recent events had taught me anything, it was that it didn't matter what I thought. *Someone* aboard the five ships would figure out what Karia had told me and take matters into their own hands.

I peered into her coal-black eyes. Behind her stolid expression a myriad of emotions darted furtively, like silverfish. Maybe that *someone* was closer to me than I had imagined. "You're in on this, aren't you?" I said. "You're working with others to run the experiment."

"We both know it's just a matter of time," she said. "This opportunity will never present itself again. Why let someone else claim the glory?"

I lowered my head.

"Sorry," she said, realizing her faux pas. "I didn't mean it that way. I don't think any less of you for what happened."

"When is the procedure being tested?"

That's when it clicked. The recent changes in her behavior; the detachment with which she was looking at me this instant.

"It already has," she said.

Kaku, Alpha Transit, 12.1 yrs

The procedure involved stimulating the dorsolateral prefrontal cortex, where we simulate events, and area ten of internal granular layer IV, where we experience emotions elicited by thoughts of the future. Some scientists believed this ability to simulate scenarios set humans apart from other species. Well, we'd certainly be different *now*.

Karia was one of seven illicit volunteers. Officially, they were suspended from duty for their reckless behavior, but unofficially their work was analyzed—and praised. Karia and the others were tested repeatedly; they had indeed become excellent predictors. The news was sent to Earth.

I was granted permission to visit Karia, and approached her module with wariness. When I entered she regarded me coolly, unapologetically.

Matching her gaze, I decided to dispense with small talk. "Was I somehow part of your plan?" I asked.

"I liked you," she said simply. "That's all."

The past tense smarted. "I liked you too, Karia. I thought we were a good match."

"Truth be told," she said, "you're a little broken for me, Erik. It was attractive at first, and then not so much." She stretched her arms. "We won't be the only ones for long, you know."

It took me a second to grasp that "we" referred to Karia and her enhanced cohort, not the two of us.

"Do you really believe that after coming this far people will risk everything to become better at predicting the future?"

"Foretelling the future is a means of *shaping* the future," she said, "and when people catch on they'll realize they no longer have to fear what's to come."

I stopped myself from responding. I could argue with her until I was blue in the face, but I was bound to lose. She had the gift of fore-sight now, a kind of uncanny clairvoyance that I and everyone else who was un-enhanced lacked. This difference between us, more than anything else, convinced me our relationship couldn't be salvaged.

So began the Rift.

Kaku, Alpha Transit, 24.6 yrs

Earth successfully duplicated the procedure, but despite security precautions, knowledge of it leaked, and a year later millions of people had become Enhanced. One group believed that by Enhancing themselves they could write the next chapter in the network primer, leading to further Enhancements; an exponential progression of the human race, which they dubbed e^b.

Meanwhile, Karia's prediction that others would follow came true on the ships as well; small groups aboard the *Euler* and the *Atman* at first, then a dozen more on the other vessels, a hundred more after that.

Twelve years after Karia's procedure, the Enhanced had become the majority.

All throughout, I was in denial. I told myself that as long as we reached Gliese 832 c, confirmed as habitable by our high-res data, everything would be fine. We'd settle the planet—and then we could go our separate ways.

Wishful thinking.

Darl Hallera, an un-Enhanced astrometrics specialist, broke the bad news. "The *Euler* and the *Atman* are drifting off course," he said during one of our regular sessions. "I noticed minute course deviations two days ago, but thought the problem might correct itself. I was wrong. It's getting worse."

I had the dubious honor of being meeting leader that day. "Aren't their AIs running navigation?" I said. "No course alterations should be possible without consensus from the Executive Council."

"Maybe they've reprogrammed their AIs, or convinced the Directors to grant permission," said Luann Jacildo, un-Enhanced gene-therapist.

"But we're too far from other habitable systems. So where the hell are they going?"

"Maybe they don't want to colonize another planet," Luann said. "At any rate, their behavior is jeopardizing our mission: now we'll be forced to seed a world with only three fifths of our preselected genes."

I made eye contact with Darl and Luann, then everyone else in the room. "We're going to ask them what they're up to. Luann, please take the lead on this one. Also, let's find out if the un-Enhanced on those two ships were given a say. If not, this is kidnapping."

I assumed my grave words marked the end of the meeting, and we started to disband. But Luann didn't budge.

"There's something else," she said.

"Yes?"

"I'm going to be blunt. The Enhanced seem to be losing their sex drive. Remote medscans show hormone and neurotransmitter mixes consistent with little to no sexual activity."

I remembered Karia shunning my touch. Granted, other emotional factors had been in play, but anecdotally it confirmed Luann's idea. "Thanks for bringing this up. Perform more scans and bring us the data."

There was a rumble of assent, but I noticed a few folks making cavalier comments. I called to order.

"Why should we care about the Enhanced's sex lives?" someone asked.

"Think about the implications," Luann said, frustration clipping her words. "Sex is not an issue *now*, but it'll be critical when we arrive at the colony."

"Then we'll start the colony without them," the same individual replied.

"Maybe," Luann said. Her face twisted, and her eyes seemed to implode with concern. "But—"

"There's another danger," I said. It must have dawned on us at the same moment. My body suddenly longed for a lower *g*. "If enough of Earth were to become Enhanced," I said, "humans could eventually die out on our home planet. Our colony would be humanity's last chance."

I told myself this was highly unlikely. Just then Luann tapped at the SmartInk on her sleeve and opened her mouth, dumbfounded. "Latest estimate is that of the six thousand crew members on the *Kaku*, the *Mikumo* and the *Aconcagua*, over five thousand are Enhanced," she said. "Our last chance may be a pipe dream."

Faces became somber and shoulders sagged. The Rift had become a divide cutting us off not only from the Enhanced, but severing us from our own continued existence.

We contacted the *Euler*. The Enhanced seemed to have been expecting our call.

Yes, they replied, *our abilities seem to have created a diminished desire for intimacy. It is difficult to understand how being Enhanced will benefit us in the long term if it leads to our extinction; thus, our goal is to find the DNA Scribes who recorded the network primer in our genome. The* Euler *and the* Atman *are heading to the Sigma Draconis system, where we believe we will learn more about the Scribes. But we want your colony to succeed. All the Enhanced aboard the* Kaku, *the* Mikumo *and the* Aconcagua *will contribute their genetic material to its founding. We will also deploy our shuttles to transport any remaining un-Enhanced from the* Euler *and the* Atman *to your three ships, receiving the same quantity of Enhanced in return.*

And that's what we did, though the logistics proved a nightmare. During a critical stage of the hand-off one of the shuttles blew its propulsion system. The navigational AI attempted to compensate, but directional adjustments alone couldn't bring it back. Its crew was doomed by the shuttle's momentum. All we could do was watch and listen; an agonizing tragedy.

Except that somehow, after several hair-raising days, the propulsion system came back online, and the AI did the rest.

It took harrowing weeks of 0.2-*c* maneuvers to get everyone un-Enhanced safely onboard. Six hundred un-Enhanced were distributed among our three ships, trading places with six hundred Enhanced who took the shuttles back to the two departing ships.

This was it, then: our new family.

Sophi, Alpha Transit, 78 yrs

We entered the Gliese 832 system, in the constellation Grus, roughly when we had calculated we would; we found that Gliese 832 c, the second planet in orbit around the system's red dwarf, could indeed support human life; we landed on it and founded our colony.

Everything proved easier than expected. Don't misunderstand: it was still tremendous work. Even armed with our nanos and droids, it took close to three years to make the colony self-sustaining, and eight lives were lost in accidents. Chronic depression and homesickness took nineteen more. We had to adjust to an orbital year of only thirty-six days, and a surface gravity of 1.1-g. But we didn't encounter *major* hitches. The native biosphere wasn't lethal to us or our microorganisms; there were no higher native life-forms to contend with; we constructed biodomes to protect us from the brutal seasonal variations; tracts of land proved arable, the seas were navigable, and there was an abundance of raw materials.

The Enhanced guided us with unwavering confidence and consistent success. Their abilities nagged at me deeply, but I didn't let this get in the way of staying alive.

We renamed the planet Sophi, and established five inter-linked biodomes joined by a local transport system along the largest continent's coastal region. We sent messages to Earth and to the ships en route to Sigma Draconis. The ships replied regularly at first, then only sporadically. During our fifth year on Sophi they went quiet. And as for Earth, we were receiving regular updates from them; mostly they shared how many more new Enhanced there were, though there was talk of resistance pockets, too. Because we were now over sixteen light-years away, though, there was no possibility of real dialogue; any response to one of our messages would take at least thirty-two years.

I was demotivated by the news, and as a communications specialist felt somewhat useless. Each day I awoke on this new world, bathed in the deep red light of its alien sun, and went about my duties with growing apathy.

The Enhanced, despite their genetic contributions, made for poor partners and worse parents. As a result, their offspring, who were born un-Enhanced, were raised by everyone: each of us became responsible for at least two babies. I myself had two children with two partners, one Enhanced and one not, and neither assumed child-rearing responsibilities with me. I suppose that for couples the stress of raising this first generation of native Glieseans—that is, Sophians—was manageable. In my case being a single parent nearly broke me.

Despite two nanny AIs, the children initially required constant attention, and though I loved them deeply, my life felt like an endless cycle of dreary tasks. I felt ridiculously inadequate and was often overwhelmed. Memories of my Dad surfaced at the worst moments. When Egata and Neijun turned five and the stress didn't let up I finally sought help.

We didn't have dedicated counselors, but a cadre of Enhanced doubled as psychotherapists when needed. I explained my situation to a man named Qiao Housel, who listened intently to my heaving, confessional monologue. "I feel better already," I quipped at the end, feeling purged.

"I'm glad." He smiled without mirth. "I'd like us to focus on whatever small positive changes you think you can make—starting today."

A few ideas popped into my head, but I wasn't ready to discuss them quite yet. I studied Qiao's inscrutable eyes. "If you don't mind my asking, can you tell me a little about yourself?"

"Sure." Qiao proceeded to recap his upbringing in China, his training as an AI engineer, associated certifications in psychology and psychiatry, and how after he had become Enhanced aboard the *Mikumo* his interest had shifted. "It was my fascination with consciousness that led me to quantum mechanics," he said.

"Hmmm. I'm not sure I see the connection."

"Perceiving something not only alters it, but brings it into being—at least on a quantum level. Some of us believe that understanding *how* consciousness collapses the quantum wave function will yield enormous benefits to the human race. We have formulated an explanation of our Enhanced predictive abilities in terms of Planck's constant and the wave function; we call this theory e^h."

I remembered the Earth group: for them the h had denoted humanity, the e exponential self-improvement. For this group the h was Planck's constant. Maybe both notions were compatible.

"You're talking about manipulating physical systems by mere thought," I said. "As in telekinesis. Magic."

"No. We already do it, but we're not conscious of it," he said. "Like breathing."

"If you could control it consciously, how far would the abilities go? Could we transform energy and matter with our thoughts? Alter space and time?"

I was being sarcastic; I was sure he would rebuke me with some law of nature or other. Instead he said, "It's not clear what the upper bounds on such abilities would be. Have you considered making yourself Enhanced, Erik? An utterly painless experience. Quite beautiful."

His suggestion was a stark reminder of the Rift. This man didn't know me *at all*. I shifted uneasily. "No."

He must have sensed my discomfort. "Very well. Let's get back to why we're here, then, which is to help you."

"I'm not sure I want to continue," I said.

He was quiet for a moment. Then, as though it were an afterthought, he said, "What is the thing you most wish for, Erik Hamada?"

Without wanting to, I picture Dad in microhydroponics, Hub Three. If only I had spoken the right words, moved faster.... I looked away so Qiao wouldn't see the tears in my eyes. "It cost us so much to get here."

"Yes." He was pensive for a moment and then said, "Despite your skepticism about today's session, I believe things will turn around for you soon. You are incredibly resourceful and resilient."

He reached forward to shake my hand, but I declined and walked out.

Annoyingly, Qiao proved correct. My life improved almost at once. Was it his vote of confidence in me that turned things around? The fact that I'd released pent-up emotions that had been building up for years, like plaque?

Maybe.

But the changes seemed too swift and too specific. Annoyances that I'd thought about, but hadn't shared, disappeared; everything from the way Neijun stopped chewing on his fingernails to my circadian rhythms suddenly righting themselves.

Apparently, others noticed the change in my disposition. One day, while placing my lunch order at the café I usually went to in Dome B, an un-Enhanced woman behind me said, "You look chipper today."

I was taken aback. "Do I know you?"

"We've been in here together a dozen times," she said, "but you're usually scowling and don't seem to notice anything besides your food."

I grinned. "That bad, huh?" After she placed her order I said, "Mind if I join you for lunch?"

She smiled and accepted, and the meal proceeded in good spirits. Originally from Portugal, and then the *Aconcagua*, her name was Malika D'Cruz, and she worked on environmental chemistry at a lab in my same dome.

During the next few weeks we lunched together semi-frequently. I learned that her husband had become Enhanced on the *Euler* and had decided to stay on it. That's when I realized Malika had been on the malfunctioning shuttle.

"That must have been intense," I said.

"No kidding."

I lowered my voice. "Do you ever wonder if the propulsion system coming back to life was…more than mechanical happenstance?"

She furrowed her brow. "What else would it be?"

"I'm not sure," I said. "Sometimes I have this feeling that the Enhanced are behind a lot of things. They may have greater abilities than we know." I told her about my session with Qiao. "Maybe they were able to *will* the propulsion system back online. Certainly your husband would have been motivated."

She let out a startled laugh. "You really think it's possible? For them to just will things to happen like that? Why don't they will away all our problems, then?"

"Maybe they are," I said, "and maybe they have been, ever since we arrived."

211

Malika regarded me with a curious expression. "You know," she said, "sometimes things in my lab *are* a little strange. Experiments go exactly as planned—know how rare that should be?"

"Right!"

For one golden moment, I didn't feel so alone on Sophi.

We continued to lunch together, and then sometimes shared dinner as a family. She was raising three youngsters of her own, from two Enhanced donors, and our clans seemed to mesh well together.

But then something changed. Malika became harder to read, and I found it difficult to talk to her. One day in the café she said, "I went to see him."

"See who?"

"Qiao."

"*What?*"

"I wanted to hear it for myself," she said. "We had this incredible conversation, Erik. He said there's a new way of becoming Enhanced, it just takes a few minutes and is utterly painless—"

"You're considering it, aren't you?"

She fell silent.

I shivered. "Fantastic," I said. "Just swell."

She came closer. "We could do it together. That way you wouldn't be left behind."

"*Left behind?* Is that what you think this is?"

I turned around. She called my name but it didn't stop me from storming out.

That night I had trouble sleeping. What if the Enhanced could now Enhance others merely by willing it? If so, what hope was there for me?

I *loathed* the idea of becoming Enhanced. What was the point of predictive prowess or God-like abilities if you lost your humanity, your ability for intimate connection, along the way?

Of course I hadn't answered Qiao's question about what I most desired. I thought about it now. What if it *were* somehow possible to bring someone back from the dead, to pluck their consciousness from the swirls and eddies of spacetime and slip it, unharmed, into the present? What if the only trade-off was becoming Enhanced?

No, thanks.

eh

Sophi, Alpha Transit, 87 yrs

Egata and Neijun grew up, giving me more time for—what exactly? I hadn't cultivated any new hobbies besides listening to vintage stochastic music, and that was a solitary endeavor. I had little interest in sports. Though I was approaching my eleventh decade, I could have passed for sixty, and ongoing anti-aging treatments would keep me strong and vital for decades to come. I did some local exploring, but the protocols for going outside the bio-domes alone were a hassle. After a while even the most spectacular magenta seaside sunset bored me.

More and more of my un-Enhanced acquaintances converted, and I did little to keep the relationships going after their changes. I went for long walks, always by myself. Occasionally I'd encounter someone I'd never seen before and chalked it up to my growing isolationism.

It became harder to spot the Enhanced, too, as they were no longer patently unemotional, which made me nervous. I also noticed that they had a new shorthand form of communication, so I was shut out from their conversations. I even heard it said that the *Atman* and the *Euler* had sent us a message, but it was only intelligible to Enhanced brains.

As I spiraled inward I began to feel that the superficial pleasantness of the people I encountered was the pleasantness one shows an endangered species. *Look how cute*, they must have thought, *and how soon-to-be-extinct.*

Sophi, Alpha Transit, 88 yrs

One day I bumped into Malika again. I suppose it was inevitable. I had anticipated that any encounter with her would be awkward, but somehow it wasn't. She had become Enhanced, and she had married another Enhanced, whatever that meant. She expressed genuine caring for me during our brief exchange, and invited me to join her and her husband for dinner that night. I declined, but some niggling sense of social responsibility made me change my mind five minutes later. A few hours of diversion would be nice. And I might as well form alliances with select Enhanceds, if I could.

That night the conversation and wine flowed easily, and for the first time I saw an Enhanced *laugh*. "Whatever you guys are doing," I said, "it's working. You seem to be enjoying yourselves a lot more than others of your ilk."

Malika's husband, Reykdal, placed his hand on her shoulder. "As more of us who were previously un-Enhanced have joined the fold," he said, "we're striving for a new balance."

For an instant I thought a caught of glimmer of hidden stiffness in his face, and then hers, as though this whole thing had been rehearsed for my benefit. My knees weakened—and then it all passed. I relaxed, felt a kind of warm inner glow take over, and slid back into our casual groove.

By the time we finished dessert I noticed myself yawning. "Apparently I'm not the spry cat I used to be," I said, and chuckled.

"Need a shuttle?" Reykdal asked.

"Nah, I'm not far."

Malika stepped forward and we hugged briefly. "I'm glad you accepted our invitation," she said.

"Me too." Despite how well things had gone, I wasn't ready to commit to another social call, so I left it at that and stepped into the night.

As I walked home, I remember thinking that the sky had a preternatural glow to it, beautiful and reassuring to behold.

Sophi, Beta Transit, 88 yrs

That night my sleep was unusually deep and restorative. A deep-seated sense of peace engulfed me before going to bed, and it was still with me as I rose and completed my morning ablutions, ate an energy bar on my way to the lab, and began the day's work.

It's been with me for the last several hours, growing in intensity all the while, and even now it shows no signs of abating.

At this very moment, the joy of my composure feels surreal.

Complete.

I'm smiling for no reason. I can't stop thinking that everything is going to be okay, no matter what happens. The Scribes have given us a great gift, and it's up to us to use it wisely. We will. If they're still alive, we'll find them, and maybe we'll encounter more of their handiwork scattered among the stars. Being distrustful and negative all the time, as I was, being constantly on guard and expecting the worst outcome; it was exhausting.

This, this is much better.

Mid-morning the com lets me know that in a few hours the colony's Executive Council will share exciting news regarding the *Atman* and the *Euler*. I can't wait to hear it. In the meantime, I continue with my day's work, elated, committed, completely focused.

Until a familiar and utterly impossible voice calls out to me.

"Are you ready?" Dad says. "I wouldn't want to miss this for the world."

He lingers on the threshold of my lab. I could welcome him in; I could tell him that I'm also excited; I could share the moment with him.

And so I do.

THE HAND ON THE CRADLE

_____*Brenda Cooper*_____

COLORIMA FELT SMALL and alone and distant from all of her dreams. She lay on a sick-bay style bed that had been acquired and modified to hold her. Bolts held the metal structure to the floor and more attached the wide straps that held her to the bed. A thin mattress kept the metal from scratching her, and padding had been taped to the straps to keep her from hurting herself. Her hands and feet hung free and mobile but her ankles and wrists were trapped. Her left arm had been sliced so deeply that she had lost partial use of her thumb.

She had no way to escape into sleep, no way to leave the memories of being captured behind. She had not slept for ten years.

At least she was alone. For the moment.

She kept her eyes closed, counting in her head to mark the passing of time, keeping herself as calm and focused as possible.

Even with no visual cues, the environment intruded. The ship's air smelled of oils and dust and old cleaning materials, of stale stim and cooking grease allowed to escape into the air. The scent of disrepair. Walls groaned from time to time, deep and disturbing creaks around her or under her. An old ship, long overdue for maintenance. It offended her sense of order.

A part of her brain relentlessly clicked off the time, ten hours twenty-one-minutes and thirteen seconds. Twenty-two hours, twelve

217

minutes, and twelve seconds. At thirty-two hours and seven seconds, the door opened, smooth and barely audible, even to her. She turned herself up a bit without making a movement or sound.

It was the man.

Both were frightened of her, but the man hid his fear in anger, while the woman usually avoided her. He smelled different than the woman, pungent and sharp. Human emotions had scent, and under his dirt and grime she smelled anger masking his fear.

He stepped into the room, and she tensed. Nothing physical; she had no physical reactions that she didn't choose. But still, inside, she felt a gibbering fear that did her no good, but which wouldn't be banished. Even though it had been ten years since she had a flesh body, she recognized danger.

"Pilot."

She ignored him.

"Pilot. Are you willing to take me now?"

He thought time would matter. Time would merely run her down, and it was unlikely he had what he needed to start her again. Stupid man. She didn't even blink.

"I know you're listening. My scopes can read activity in your brain."

If she ignored him long enough her consciousness would drift off with lack of power and she would be free of this particular nightmare, and of life. She had gotten ten more years than she would have had; she had been close to death from infection.

It amazed her that she could not make herself let go. Life. Even in this body, the ego drove a deep desire to cling to life. Her current danger laid the need bare for her to marvel at, and she saw it as a flower inside of her, an organic heart that wanted to keep on blooming.

Because of that blossom, she answered him. In spite of her captivity, in spite of his requests for things she could not give him, she answered him. "I do not know the coordinates for any dark stations. My employer or my union will pay for my release." She opened her eyes as she continued, "If you hurt me, you will anger my union, and you will never be able to hire a soulbot pilot. Some day, one of us will turn you in for hurting me. We have rights." It was all the truth. She was still legally human, at least so far.

He was tall and blond and past middle-age, with dark circles under angry eyes and a pale pink scar on one cheek. "No one knows you are here."

That was a lie, but she had not told him that. "I cannot fly you to places I don't know."

"You all share a brain."

Such a common misconception. She smelled his anger rising, barely banked.

He grabbed her by the hand connected to her unhurt arm and squeezed the fingers tight against each other, a move that would have hurt in a human body. A mean thing. A bully thing. The pressure sent signals scrambling toward her brain and she told herself not to react. She had already turned off much of the other arm and losing senses in two appendages sent bursts of energy she couldn't afford through her system as her internal life-support struggled with the threat.

She would not beg.

She fell silent again, conserving energy, keeping her fingers limp.

He let go of her, and then slammed his fist onto her fingers, watching her face.

She didn't flinch.

He leaned toward her, words hissing through his lips and coming to her on stale breath. "You think you're so much better, you damned abomination. Who's better now? I'm going to go through that door, and I'm going to eat dinner and I'm going to sleep with my wife. I'm going to breathe and sleep and dream, and have all of the things that you do not, that you will never have."

Colorima managed not to show that she felt a truth in his words, not to react when a tiny bit of spittle landed on her cheek.

"Whether you help me or not, I will find a way to stop your kind. You have darkened this world, and we will make it shine again, free of you." He paused a moment, trembling inches above her face, the whites of his eyes large. "If you do not help me by this time tomorrow, I will destroy you. I will bring hammers and nails and my anger, and you will never fly any ship again."

He slammed the door behind him, and when he left she felt small again, and vulnerable. If only she could lie. Then she might pretend to help him long enough to escape. But even though it was physically possible, the law said that if she lied, she died.

It did not matter why. Lying to save her life would kill her.

She recorded her life. Her recordings were subject to union review. This was the way that she and other uploads like her proved they remained safe. Better to die and lose her own life than to lie and cost all of those like her their lives.

It did not stop her from wanting to lie, and if the man opened the door again, she might. She had a day left, at best, less if she moved much. She had no memory of being so low in power.

She turned the feeling in her arm back on, calming the stutters of extra energy.

Perhaps she could coerce pity from the woman without lying to her.

It was not fair to be snatched from death, to learn to live again, and then be killed. If she herself had a smell, it would be like the man's: anger covering fear.

Two hours passed. At two hours, fifty-five minutes, and five seconds from the moment the door had slammed behind the man, the ship shuddered and bucked. Someone screamed. A hole punched through the hull, and she heard the death of life support and swallowed hard, afraid all over again.

Something snapped and she jerked, strapped into her bed, unable to move.

Air fled the room, a steady and low hiss that screamed inside of her.

Indescribable cold came in after it, a slow exchange.

Now she would die. Now. Now.

Gravity changed enough so that she floated lighter on the bed, the pressure of the straps lighter as well.

The wall in front of her bowed outward.

The angry man and the kind and frightened woman must be dead already. She felt a moment's pity for the woman, who had not deserved this.

As strong as it was, her pilot's body could not withstand the raw cold of empty space. She calculated that she had at most ten minutes before it became too cold to think and her automated fail-safes kicked in.

The door shuddered and flew outward, and cold slammed across her, followed by freedom as her bonds were slashed. Metallic bodies swarmed the room, more robotic than hers, frightening in their own way. One of them lifted her, lunged toward the wall and rolled through the air, kicking powerfully, propelling itself through the door. "Hang on," it said. "Hang on."

Her hands were trapped inside its embrace, as much captive as she had been on the bed. She said nothing, counting seconds, feeling the bruising cold. Even though her eyes were open, the landscape of the ship was a blur. They popped free of the ragged ship and stars surrounded her.

They seemed to slow, but she knew it was only the lack of a reference point, as they now flew through open space. Her view had no horizon in all the directions she could see and the cold pierced her, sending her systems into a frenzy of energy trying to keep her alive.

She caught a glimpse behind them as her rescuer shifted her position. Metal forms spilled free of a gaping hole in the side of her captor's research ship.

"Get ready."

She turned her head. They approached a round cylinder. Surely it had been there, waiting, but she had missed it with her cheek crushed to her rescuer's chest. Light spilled from a wide open door.

"Hold onto me," the robot said, pulling one of its arms free.

She grasped its wide shoulder, doing her best to hold on, the cold and her fear sapping her strength, her weak arm a challenge. "Harder." It released her with its other arm, and she slid down to its waist, holding as tightly as she could. It reached for a handrail on the outside of the rescue pod and caught it, slowing them both so abruptly she almost came free. Then they were in, and seated on a long bench. In spite of the open door, warmth flooded her from the back, feeding her energy. One by one, she flexed her arms and toes and wrists.

The cylinder was nearly feature-free, smooth except for the bench and two rows of handholds.

"Hang on," it said again, and she wondered if it only knew those words, but it moved her right hand from the bench to one of the handholds and she obeyed, feeling thick and slow and unsure of herself. Silly to get rescued right before she ran out of power.

Two other robots came up to them, grabbing the pod and jerking it so she was grateful for the handhold. The door slid closed. Acceleration pushed her toward the back, and the handhold mattered.

There were no windows, no light, and almost no sound. Robots neither breathed nor shivered.

"Lean back," he said. "The wall will fill you."

She did, leaving one hand curled around a handgrip and fitting her back to the wall, so that she had contact along most of her metal spine. She had heard of such things, but no employer of hers had owned one. "Like this?"

"Yes." The robot must have done something as her systems suddenly had access to power flowing wirelessly into what passed for muscle and battery both.

It felt good.

From time to time she checked her vitals. The cold kept her slow but the temperature hung a few degrees above zero, which would do her no damage. The fresh power added energy, sharpened her thinking.

None of the robots spoke. The silence unnerved her, and halfway through the trip she spoke up. "Thank you."

"You are welcome."

"Where are we going?"

"To our ship."

"What ship?"

"You will know when you arrive. Do not waste energy."

Very well. She tried to put together clues, but she had seen so little, and in the absolute darkness of the windowless rescue pod, there was nothing else to see. Robots had few distinguishing smells. In truth, they could probably smell the stink of the ship they'd rescued her from on her even though she smelled only lubricant and the faintest whiff of explosive, which must have also come from the doomed ship.

She had never even learned the name of the ship. It had merely been her jail, a rotting old hulk she had feared. She hadn't ever learned the man's name, or the woman's.

One hour seven minutes and thirteen seconds later, something grabbed the pod and pulled them. She sat up, feeling the gentle separation between herself and the power wall. Light spilled in on them and a humanoid soulbot who looked a little like her held a hand to help her step onto the platform. Even though she didn't need the help, she took the hand for moment, curious.

It was warmer than hers, long feminine fingers clasping hers with a gentle strength. "I'm Minan," the robot-woman said. Her hair and eyes were dark, her lips pink, her skin a soft olive. She had been designed for beauty, and to look both human and competent. A professional of some kind rather than an escort.

"I'm Colorima."

"I know," Minan said.

Colorima ignored that for the moment. "Thank you."

Minan's voice was casual, human tuned to calm. "You may or may not thank me."

"Why? I am alive now, and re-powered, and free. I thought I would be dying soon."

The woman turned to her, her dark eyes barely robotic at all, and filled with an apparent emotion Colorima could only interpret as compassion. "You still might."

What could Minan possibly mean? "Are you from the union?" As she asked the question she knew the answer. "You're not."

"We are dark."

Colorima had been tortured in hope that she could lead humans here. "Is this a station?"

"A ship. But we are on our way to a station. Long before you get there, you will have to choose."

She had signed a hundred promises before she uploaded, and signed the same hundred promises afterwards. *No lying. No harming humans. No plotting against humans or human interests. No independent life, free of the Union and of work.* A million promises in no's, and the same things again phrased as yeses. *I promise to tell the truth. I promise to be kind to flesh humans. I promise to protect flesh humans above me and others like me. I promise to send all ideas for better versions of myself to my creators.*

Humans, wanting friendly AI. Not that she was an AI, since in truth she was human inside of a robotic body. Not quite human, not quite not human. Legally human, barely. Mostly. Something in between. *But she was friendly.* She meant no harm.

It was part of her to be friendly.

She had never had dark station coordinates because she didn't want to be certain they existed. She had never looked for them. A new realization; avoidance. Shouldn't a human in a robot body be more logical than a human wrapped in flesh?

Colorima glanced at the woman she still walked beside, suddenly seeing her as dangerous. "Why did you rescue me?" she asked.

"You seemed worth saving."

"Really? As opposed to?"

"You have been sane since you chose to become a pilot. A decade of sanity. We were afraid we would lose you."

Colorima let that sink in. Another reminder that they had been watching her. "Most of the other pilots I've met have been sane."

The other robot didn't miss a beat. "Of course they have been."

Always, something to think about. How had she been so naïve? They went through a set of double-doors and into a long hallway lined with screen-paint, some of which had been left mirrored. Their walking figures went to infinity on either side, each image smaller, all of them moving. By no more than two iterations, it was impossible to tell that the figures represented robotic bodies instead of flesh. "What happens to pilots who are not sane?"

"They get destroyed or they become something else, perhaps manual labor."

"I thought humans could only upload into professional or companion positions?"

"That is the only choice a human can make pre-upload. Afterward? They can be demoted. Wasn't the man we just took care of trying to force a choice on you?"

Colorima didn't bother to answer, nor to ask how the robot walking beside her could have taken part in a raid that killed humans. She settled for a less-philosophical question. "Where are we going?"

"We're here."

Minan opened a door into a virtual cityscape. A thousand habitats surrounded them: above them, below them, on every side. Even though she had never been on a planet, she recognized locations from both planets in the system: a piece of the red mines of Mammot's desert lay below her, and to her right, the waterfall-covered mountains of Lym threatened to splash her with virtual rivers. Roads

224

joined buildings, full of simulated traffic. Parks glistened green, rivers and round lakes full of boats shimmered in periwinkle and teal hues. Spaceships and stations floated by in front of her, close enough to touch and looking eerily real. She was a giant among it all, standing on glass, images flowing in all three hundred and sixty degrees around her. It was even harder to parse than the mirrored hallway had been.

"It looks so real," Colorima whispered.

Minan's voice changed tone and became a narrator's voice. "It is almost real. All of the stories you will see in here *are* real. This is a trip through what it can be like to be a robot in service to humans. You already know what it is like when it works, when you are a valued employee. But that is not always true, and I am here to let you explore why the dark stations and ships exist. Every piece of footage here is real, everything was taken by a real camera very much like the one you use."

Colorima stood, listening. The ships and stations and cities all around her moved, but they made no noise. There was an ocean at her right shoulder. She touched a dockside bar where the water met a city on Lym.

Everything changed so fast that she stumbled, catching herself before she fell and standing again, amazed at the depth of field in front of her.

A warehouse of some kind—both walls lined with boxes. The stained concrete floor was spidered with cracks. Her perspective canted forward, as if she held her head down and looked at the floor. The cameras were worse than a robot's eyes, seeing forward only. It fuzzed to blackness behind her.

"Faster!" a man's voice bellowed, too rough to belong to a robot. "Harder!" He stood behind her, his voice laced with anger.

Her perspective jumped as whatever wore the cameras bore down and pulled. She couldn't say how she knew what was happening other than she had also pulled things, although not under duress. There was physics to pulling heavy weight, and whatever she watched the scene through pulled something heavier than she ever had, even in this new, stronger body. She looked to the side, but of course the recording didn't follow her.

"Wait for it," Minan whispered.

Feet shuffled across the floor, and finally the head turned and she spotted a robotic form, twice the size of a person. Man-shaped, with no attempt to make it look human. It leaned forward, pulling on a strap.

Colorima spoke. "That doesn't make sense. Surely there's something with wheels that can do that."

"Five uploaded humans worked for this man. They carried heavy cargo back and forth all day, and never left the warehouse. It was… sport of some kind. He spent three years taking out some anger we never identified."

"But that's not fair!" Colorima blurted out.

"Pick another."

"How do I get out of here?" she asked.

"Two fists."

Colorima hesitated, watching. She had no access to the robot's thoughts, couldn't even verify it was a soulbot like herself, driven by a human brain rather than born from a computer. But what point would there be in torturing soulless robots? They wouldn't care.

She looked over the myriad of choices, hesitating again and again. Eventually, she touched a small ship. A man and a soulbot appeared to be making love. It did not look like torture. The camera caught a tender look on the man's face, his hand coming up to caress the bot's cheek. The camera angle was good, from the head down the long robotic body, the hills of breasts visible, the soft and slender torso. This one wore skin and even scraps of clothing, the body as near-human as her own. "That's not even illegal," Colorima said. "I know a couple that did that. When Sylvia got cancer she uploaded, and he followed her six years later, as soon as the doctor said his heart was weak enough for it. They are still together, as far as I know." She paused, watching. "I even wondered if they bribed the doctor so Allan could turn more easily. They had the money."

Minan's voice was flat. "What if I told you they kidnapped the human that is in that woman's body, and that she is a nine year old girl? We didn't rescue her until she was twelve."

Colorima closed her eyes. "How do you know that?"

"She is one of us now."

"Is she okay?"

"Of course not. But maybe she will be. It's too early to tell."

Colorima thought hard. "I know these things happen. They make the tabloids. But I've flown for a decade, and before…before now…before…" she heard herself stuttering, and stopped. "I flew for Granting Station for six years, and the worst thing that happened to me was a ten-year-old boy tried to touch my breasts. I had it worse as a young woman. Mostly, I was treated well, and I even had some human friends. I still have a few—they haven't all died. Before that I worked at Queen's Nebulae University, and I spent half my time studying. After the awkwardness left, when I could control this body, it was as much fun as being in school when I was twenty."

Minan nodded, her expression solemn. "Choose another."

A deep anger built inside of her, a desperation. She wanted out of the room. But there was no doubt in her mind that this was a test, and that her life was on the line. Minan had practically told her so. She accessed the memory, played it back internally.

She heard herself say, "Thank you."

Minan's voice sounded ever more replete with cold promise this time: "You may or may not thank me."

Her own voice, way too carefree: "Why? I am alive now, and re-powered, and free. I thought I would be dying soon."

Once more, she saw Minan's eyes, determined and firm and compassionate all at once. "You still might."

Minan *had* actually told her so. Was her only choice to break all of her promises or die? Did she have to see her kind tortured over and over? Her hand trembled as she knelt down and touched the mines, certain she would find some great evil there.

Instead, a memory.

She was already kneeling. She sat down in the middle of the scene, her perspective now only slightly different than she had lived it, the man bending over her in one of his first tries. Her fear felt visceral, hot in spite of her lack of bodily reaction. For the second time, she watched him yell at her, exhort her. She couldn't feel the straps or smell his breath, but she heard him yell and she flinched.

He held the knife to her throat and touched her with its cold blade and then lifted his hand and plunged the weapon into her arm.

Watching made her tremble. Forcing herself to react to his assault with stillness had been the hardest thing she had ever done.

He slapped her and her head and thus the camera's view turned and showed her the woman watching, wide-eyed but silent. Her features were as old as the man's, with wrinkles around her eyes and makeup that didn't quite match her skin tone. She looked frightened, but it was *of* the man and neither *of* or *for* Colorima. She saw that now.

Minan did something and all of the fantastical places came back, replacing her own recorded memory. Then they faded, so that she and the other robot sat on a dark floor in a near-dark room illuminated only with tiny red lights that showed where the wall joined the floor.

Colorima felt dizzy, a thing she had never felt in this body before. Angry and dizzy and frightened and like she was being pushed over a cliff. "Do not speak yet," Minan whispered. "Just listen."

Colorima nodded and waited, and Minan let some time pass.

When she spoke, she said, "There are three things happening now and they are happening fast.

"First, we are growing, those of who have left our vows behind and become caretakers for each other. That is what I am. I am a rescuer. It is something you can become if you join us.

"Second, more stories like yours are being daylighted."

Colorima winced. Stories like hers. If asked, she wouldn't have said she was abused, but the memory told her different.

"As we learn more of what is being done to some of us, we are counting it as crimes against humanity. We have some human allies on this. But there are more humans who wish to make laws that are less in our favor, that allow us to be treated as chattel or as simple robots. This is driven by the third thing: We are becoming more capable. That is frightening to many."

Colorima thought for a while, grateful to Minan for her silence. "I knew a little of each of those things."

"If you knew all of it, you would have come looking for us."

"I'm not sure."

"We are. As I'm sure you can imagine, we have been developing our own surveillance systems, our own security, our own processing. Your kidnapping came to our attention almost immediately."

So that was how they had gotten to her.

Minan continued. "We already knew a lot about you. You are compassionate by nature, and steady, and pragmatic. You would have let that man kill you."

"What else could I have done?"

"You could have broken your bonds and killed him."

Once more, Colorima stayed silent. "I would never."

"We know. We have roles for diplomats. We are still trying to save our place in society."

Colorima looked at the rip in her arm. Possibilities coalesced into probabilities. "We are unlikely to win."

"We have to try."

"I know."

Minan stood up and held her hand out. Colorima took it willingly, and let the other woman pull her up. This time, she expected the warmth of Minan's hand.

THE HOMECOMING

_____Mike Resnick_____

I DON'T KNOW WHICH BOTHERS ME MORE. my lumbago or my arthritis. One day it's one, one day it's the other. They can cure cancer and transplant every damned organ in your body; you'd think they could find some way to get rid of aches and pains. Let me tell you, growing old isn't for sissies.

I remember that I was having a typical dream. Well, typical for me, anyway. I was climbing the four steps to my front porch, only when I got to the third step there were six more, so I climbed them and then there were ten more, and it went on and on. I'd probably still be climbing them if the creature hadn't woke me up.

It stood next to my bed, staring down at me. I blinked a couple of times, trying to focus my eyes, and stared back, sure this was just an extension of my dream.

It was maybe six feet tall, its skin a glistening, almost metallic silver, with multi-faceted bright red eyes like an insect. Its ears were pointed and batlike, and moved independently of its head and each other. Its mouth jutted out a couple of inches like some kind of tube, and looked like it was only good for sucking fluids. Its arms were slender, with no hint of the muscles required to move them, and its fingers were thin and incredibly elongated. It was as weird a nightmare figure as I'd dreamed up in years.

Finally it spoke, in a voice that sounded more like a set of chimes than anything else.

"Hello, Dad," it said.

That's when I knew I was awake.

"So this is what you look like," I growled, swinging my feet over the side of the bed and sitting up. "What the hell are you doing here?"

"I'm glad to see you too," he replied.

"You didn't answer my question," I said, feeling around for my slippers.

"I heard about Mom—not from you, of course—and I wanted to see her once more before the end."

"*Can* you see through those things?" I asked, indicating his eyes.

"Better than you can."

Big surprise. Hell, everyone can see better than I can.

"How did you get in here anyway?" I said as I got to my feet. The furnace was as old and tired as I was and there was a chill in the air, so I put on my robe.

"You haven't changed the front door's code words since I left." He looked around the room. "You haven't painted the place either."

"The lock's supposed to check your retinagram or read your DNA or something."

"It did. They haven't changed."

I looked him up and down. "The hell they haven't."

He seemed about to reply, then thought better of it. Finally he said, "How is she?"

"She has her bad days and her worse days," I answered. "She's the old Julia maybe two or three times a week for a minute or two, but that's all. She can still speak, and she still recognizes me." I paused. "She won't recognize *you*, of course, but nobody else you ever knew will either."

"How long has she been like this?"

"Maybe a year."

"You should have told me," he said.

"Why?" I asked. "You gave up being her son and became whatever it is you are now."

"I'm still her son, and you had my contact information."

I stared at him. "Well, you're not *my* son, not anymore."

"I'm sorry you feel that way," he replied. Suddenly he sniffed the air. "It smells *stale*."

"Tired old houses are like tired old men," I said. "They don't function on all cylinders."

"You could move to a smaller, newer place."

"This house and me, we've grown old together. Not everyone wants to move to Alpha whatever-the-hell-it-is."

He looked around. "Where is she?"

"In your old room," I said.

He turned, walked out into the hall. "Haven't you replaced that thing yet?" he asked, indicating an old wall table. "It was scarred and wobbly when I still lived here."

"It's just a table. It holds whatever I put on it. That's all it has to do."

He looked up at the ceiling. "The paint's peeling too."

"I'm too old to do it myself, and painters cost money. I'm living on a fixed income."

He didn't reply to that, but walked down the hall and was fiddling with the door handle when I joined him.

"It's locked," he said.

"Sometimes she gets up and goes out for a walk, and then can't remember how to get back home." I grimaced. "I can probably keep her here another few months, but then she's going to have to move into a special care facility."

I uttered the code word and the door opened.

Julia was propped up on her pillows, staring at a blank holoscreen across the room, unmindful of a lock of gray hair that had worked its way loose and obscured her left eye's vision. The channel she was on had finished broadcasting for the night, but it didn't make any difference to her. She was content watching the flickering gray cube.

I ordered the bed lamp to turn on and gently pinned the hair back up. Now that the room was illuminated, I could see our son staring at it. The holographs of him when he played on the high school basketball team were still on the wall, as well as the one of him in his tux at the prom, and his trophy for winning the science contest remained atop the dresser, though it needed dusting. Just above it was his framed diploma from college. Lining the walls were other photos and holographs, from when he was still a baby until a month before

233

he'd undergone what Julia always referred to as his Change. I could see his face twitching as he looked around at the memorabilia of his youth, and I felt like I could almost read his thoughts: *They've turned the damned place into a shrine*. Which I suppose we had—but to what he had been, not to what he was now. And I'd moved her in here because she was comforted by things from the past, even things she could no longer name.

"Hello, Jordan," said Julia, smiling at me. "How are you?"

"I'm fine, Julia. Do you mind if I turn off the holo?"

"I was enjoying it," she said. "How are you?"

I ordered the screen to deactivate.

"Is it August yet?" she asked.

"No, Julia," I said patiently. "It's February, just like it was yesterday."

"Oh," she said, frowning. "I thought it might be August." Then a friendly smile. "How are you?"

Suddenly our son stepped forward. "Hello, Mother."

She stared at him and smiled. "You are really quite beautiful."

He reached out and took her hand with those incredibly long, stick-like fingers before I could stop him.

"I've missed you, Mother," he said. He seemed like he was choked with emotion, but I couldn't tell, because his voice never changed from those musical chimes. It was so unlike a human voice that I don't know how we were able to understand him, but somehow we did.

"It is Halloween already?" asked Julia. "Are you dressed for a party?"

"No, Mother. This is the way I look."

"Well, I think you're beautiful." She stopped and frowned. "Do I know you?"

He smiled, sadly I thought. "You did once. I am your son."

She was silent for a moment, and I knew she was trying to remember. "I think I had a little boy once, but I can't recall his name."

"My name is Phillip."

"Phillip...Phillip..." she repeated. Finally she shook her head. "No, I think it was Jordan."

"Jordan is your husband," said Phillip. "I'm your son."

"I think I had a little boy once," she said. Her face went blank for a moment. Then: "Is it Halloween already?"

"No," he said gently. "I'll let you go back to sleep. We'll talk in the morning."

"That will be fine," she said. "Do I know you?"

"I'm your son," he said.

"I'm sure I had a son a long time ago," she said. "How are you?"

I could see a crystal tear run down his silver cheek. He tenderly laid her hand on the bed and stepped back. I activated the holoscreen, found a station that was still transmitting, killed the sound, and left her staring happily at it as I followed Phillip out into the hall, locking the door behind me.

We walked to the cluttered kitchen, with its ancient appliances and the three cracked tiles on the floor. (Each of us had been responsible for one of them.) I found the room homey and comforting, but I saw him looking at a burn spot on a counter that had been there since he'd accidentally made it as a kid and for just an instant I felt guilty about never having fixed it.

"You should have told me about her," he said when he'd gotten his emotions under control.

"You shouldn't have left, or become whatever it is that you are."

"Damn it, she's my mother!" The chimes were louder; I assumed he was yelling or snapping.

"There was nothing you could have done." I ordered the refrigerator door to open and pulled out a beer. "You want one before you go back to wherever the hell you came from?" I thought about it and frowned. "*Can* you drink human drinks?"

He didn't answer, but walked over and grabbed a beer. I could see that his mouth wouldn't be able to accommodate the container, so I just watched and waited for him to ask for a glass, or maybe a bowl. He knew I was staring at him, but it didn't seem to bother him. Instead something—not a tongue, and not a quite straw—slid out of his mouth, and when it was a few inches long he inserted it into the top of the container. He swallowed a few seconds later, and I knew he was somehow getting the beer into his mouth.

He set the container down and stared at an old pennant I had stuck on the wall when he was a little boy.

"You're still a Pythons fan," he observed.

"Always."

"How are they doing?" There was a time when he actually cared, but that was many years ago.

"They haven't had a decent quarterback since Christ was a corporal," I answered.

"But you root for them anyway."

"You don't stop rooting for a team just because they've fallen on hard times."

"A team, or a parent," he said. I didn't know how to reply to that, so I remained silent, and after a moment he spoke again. "I know there are medications for Alzheimer's. I assume you've tried them?"

"There are all kinds of senile dementias. They call them all Alzheimer's, but they aren't. They haven't yet found out how to cure the one she's got."

"There are specialists on other worlds. Maybe one of them could have done something."

"*You're* the space traveler," I said bitterly. "Where were you when she might have been cured?"

He stared at me. I stared back, determined not to look away first.

"Why are you so angry at me? I know you cared for me once. I've never hurt you, I never took a penny from you once I got out of college, I never—"

"You deserted us," I said. "You deserted your mother, you deserted me, you deserted your planet, you even deserted your species. That poor woman down the hall can't remember the name of her son, but she can remember that people only look like you at Halloween."

"It's my job, damn it!"

"There are thousands of exobiologists right here on Earth!" I snapped. "I only know of one who turned into a silver-skinned monster with red eyes."

"I was offered an opportunity that has been afforded very few men and women," he replied. "I took it." Even with the chimes he couldn't keep the resentment out of his voice. "Most fathers would have been proud."

I stared at him for a moment, amazed that he still didn't understand. "I'm supposed to be proud that you became a *thing* that hasn't got a trace of humanity left in him?" I said at last.

He stared right back through those multi-faceted insect eyes. "You really believe there is nothing human left of me?" he asked curiously.

"Look in a mirror," I told him.

"Don't I remember you telling me back when I was a boy that you should never judge a book by its cover?"

"That's right."

"Well?" he said.

"I just saw one of your pages slide out and suck up the beer."

He signed deeply, to the delicate tinkling of chimes. "Would you have been happier if I couldn't drink it?"

I seriously considered it for a minute. "No, that wouldn't have made me happier," I told him when I'd formulated my answer in terms even he could understand. "You know what would have made me happier? Grandchildren. A son who visited us for Christmas. A son I could leave the house to now that it's finally paid off. I never asked you to follow in my footsteps, attend my college, go into my business, even live in this town. Would expecting you to *want* to be a normal human being be so goddamned wrong for a father?"

"No, it wouldn't," he admitted. Then: "For better or worse you've lived *your* life. I have the right to live *mine*."

I shook my head. "Your life ended eleven years ago. You're living some alien creature's life now."

He cocked his head to one side and studied me curiously. It seemed almost birdlike. "Which bothers you more—that I left Earth, or that I became what I am?"

"Six of one, a half dozen of the other. You knew you were the center of your mother's life, but you left her and went to the far end of the galaxy."

"Not quite the far end," he said, and I couldn't tell from the chimes whether that was sarcastic or sardonic or simply a straight answer. "And my mother wouldn't have wanted me to stay *here* when I wanted to be out *there*."

"You broke her heart!" I snapped.

"If I did, then I am truly sorry."

"She spent years wondering *why*, back when she could still wonder," I continued. "So did I. You had so much promise and so many opportunities, damn it! You could have been anything you wanted! The sky was the limit!"

"I became what I wanted," he said gently. "And the stars were *my* limit."

"Damn it, Phillip!" I said, though I had promised myself never to call him by his human name. "You could have spent your whole life here and never seen a thousandth of the things Earth has to offer."

"That's true. But others have already seen them." He paused, and turned his palms up in a very human gesture. "I wanted to see things no one else had ever seen."

"I don't know what's up there," I said, "but how different can it be? What makes *our* mountains and deserts and rivers so boring for you?"

He sighed, a delicate high-pitched tinkling sound. "I tried to explain that to you eleven years ago," he answered at last. "You didn't understand then. You don't understand now." He paused. "Maybe you just can't."

"Probably not," I agreed. I walked to the cabinet with the missing knob, and opened the door with my fingernails the way I always do.

"You still haven't replaced the knob," he observed. "I remember the day I pulled it off. I expected to be punished. You just laughed, like I'd done something cute."

"You should have seen the expression on your face when it came away in your hand, like you expected me to send you off to prison." I felt a smile fighting to reach my mouth, and I pushed it back. "Anyway, it still opens." I reached in, pulled down a couple of small bottles, and put them in my pocket.

"Mother's medication?"

I nodded, holding them up. "She gets four different kinds in the morning, and two at night. I'll give them to her a little later." I pulled out another bottle.

"I thought you just said she only got two pills at night."

"She does," I said. I held up the third bottle. "These are sugar pills. I leave them on the dresser for her."

"Sugar pills?" he repeated with what I assume passed for a puzzled frown.

"She thinks she can still medicate herself. She can't, of course, but this gives her the illusion that she can. And if she takes six one day and forgets to take any the next, it doesn't make any difference."

"That's very thoughtful of you."

"I've loved her for close to half a century," I answered. "I could have put her in a home and just visited her every day—or every tenth day. She probably wouldn't know the difference. But I do this because I love her. Even if she doesn't know it, she has to be more comfortable in her own home, surrounded by the bits and pieces of her life. That's why I moved her to your room instead of the guest room; the photos, the trophies, even that old catcher's mitt in the closet, that's all she has left of you." I glared at him. "I didn't walk out of her life for eleven years and come back only when she was past remembering me."

He just looked at me but made no reply.

"Damn it!" I snapped. "Couldn't you have said it was a secret mission for the military, even if it was a lie?"

"You'd have found out soon enough that I was lying."

"I wouldn't have *tried* to! We'd have been proud that you were serving your country, or your planet, or whatever the hell you were serving."

"Is *that* it?" he demanded, suddenly angry. "You could lose a son to another world as long he didn't enjoy it, as long as someone might be shooting at him?"

"That's not what I said," I replied defensively.

"That's precisely what you said." He stared at me with those insect eyes for a long minute. "You would never have understood. *She* might have, but you wouldn't."

"Then why did you never tell her?"

"I tried."

"Well, you sure as hell didn't succeed," I said bitterly. "And it's too late to try again."

"*She's* not the one who hates me," he said. "I had already moved out and started my own life when this opportunity arose. You make it sound like I was your support network. I was an independent adult, living six states away." He paused. "I still don't know which bothers you more: that I left the planet at all, or that I left it looking like *this*."

"One day you were a member of our family. Four months later you weren't even a member of the human race."

"I still am," he insisted.

"Look in a mirror."

He placed a twelve-inch-long forefinger to his head. "It's what's in *here* that counts."

"They say the eyes are the windows to the soul," I replied. "Yours belong on an insect."

"Just what the hell did you want from me?" he demanded. "Did you want me to go into business with you?"

"No, of course not."

"Would you have disowned me if I'd been sterile and couldn't give you any grandchildren?"

"Don't be silly."

"What if I'd moved halfway around the world? I might not have seen you more than once a decade if I had. Would you have disowned me as you did eleven years ago?"

"Nobody disowned you," I pointed out, trying to keep my temper. "*You* disowned *us*."

He sighed deeply. At least I think he did. With those chimes I couldn't be sure.

"Did you ever think to ask me *why*?" he said at last.

"No."

"If it bothered you that much, why didn't you?"

"Because it was your choice."

I think he frowned. I couldn't tell for sure, not with that face. "I don't understand."

"If it was a necessity, something you had to do to save your life or something like that, I'd have asked. But since it was a freely-made choice, no, I didn't care *why* you did it, only *that* you did it."

He looked long and hard at me. "All those years that I lived here, and even after I left, I thought you loved me."

"I loved *Phillip*," I said, and then grimaced. "I don't know *you*."

Suddenly I heard Julia knocking weakly at her door, and walked down the shopworn hallway to unlock it. I hadn't noticed how threadbare the carpet had become, or the crack in the plaster, but I saw *him* looking at it so I looked too, and made up my mind to do something about it one of these days.

I uttered the code word, softly enough that she couldn't hear it on her side of the door, and a moment later it swung open. She was standing there barefoot in her nightgown, thin and frail, her arms and legs like toothpicks with withered flesh on them, looking mildly puzzled.

"What's the matter?" I asked.

"I thought I heard you arguing with someone." Her gaze fell on Phillip. "Hello," she said. "Have we met before?"

He took her hand very gently and gave her what seemed like a wistful smile, though I couldn't be sure. "A long time ago."

"My name is Julia." She extended a wrinkled, liver-spotted hand.

"And mine is Phillip."

A frown crossed her once-beautiful face. "I think I knew someone called Phillip once." She paused, then smiled. "That's a very pretty costume you're wearing."

"Thank you."

"And I love your voice," she continued. "It sounds like the wind chimes on our porch when a summer breeze blows through them."

"I'm glad it pleases you," said the creature that used to be our son.

"Can you sing?"

He shrugged, and his whole body seemed to sparkle as the light reflected off it. "I really don't know," he admitted. "I've never tried."

"You look hungry," she said. "Can I make you something to eat?"

I prodded him and when he looked at me, I very briefly shook my head *No*. She'd already set the kitchen on fire twice before I started ordering all our meals delivered.

He picked up on it instantly. "No, thank you. I ate just before I arrived."

"That's too bad," she said. "I'm a good cook."

"I'll bet you make a wonderful Denver pudding." That had always been his favorite dessert.

"The best," she answered, glowing with pride. "I *like* you, young man." Then a puzzled frown. "You *are* a man, aren't you?"

"Yes, I am."

"Is it Halloween?"

"Not yet."

"Why are you wearing that costume, then?"

"Would you really like to know about it?"

"Very much," she said. Suddenly she shivered. "But it's chilly standing here barefoot in the doorway. Would you mind very much if I got under the covers while we chatted? You can sit right next to the

241

bed, and we can be nice and cozy. Jordan, could you make me some hot chocolate? And maybe some for...I've forgotten your name."

"Phillip," he said.

"Phillip," she repeated, frowning. "Phillip. I'm *sure* I knew a Phillip once, a long time ago."

"I'm sure you did too," he said softly.

"Well, come along." Julia turned, walked back into her room, and climbed into the bed that had once belonged to Phillip, propping herself up with some pillows and pulling the blanket and comforter up to her armpits. He followed her and stood next to the bed. "There's no need to stand, young man," she told him. "Pull up a chair."

"Thank you," he said, getting the chair he'd used while writing his masters' thesis on his computer and carrying it over so that he was sitting right next to her.

"Jordan, I think we'd like some hot chocolate."

"I don't know if he drinks it," I replied.

"I'd very much like some," he said.

"Good!" said Julia. "You can bring two cups on a tray, one for me and one for.... Excuse me, but I don't know your name."

"It's Phillip."

"And you must call me Julia."

"Why don't I just call you Mother?" he suggested.

She frowned in puzzlement. "Why would you do that?"

He reached out and very gently held her hand. "No reason, Julia."

"Jordan," she said, "I think I'd like some hot chocolate." She turned to Phillip. "Would you like some too, young man? You *are* a man, aren't you?"

"I am, and I would."

I left to get the hot chocolate before she asked again. I went out to the kitchen, mixed up a fair-sized pan—I don't know why; there were only two of them, and I don't drink the stuff myself—and was about to pour a pair of cups. Then I remembered the shape of his hands and fingers, and decided he was less likely to spill a mug, so I got the old chipped Pythons mug he'd given me for my birthday when he was nine or ten years old. I think he'd saved up a month's allowance to buy it. I looked at it fondly for a moment, and wondered if he'd recognize it. Then I remembered who—or rather *what*—I was pouring it for, and got on with it. The whole process took maybe three or four minutes, start to finish. I put the cup and the mug on a tray, added a spoon for Julia since she liked to stir everything whether it needed it or not, and folded a pair of napkins. Then I picked up the tray and carried it back to the bedroom.

"Just put it on the table, please, Jordan," she said, and I placed it on her nightstand.

She turned back eagerly to Phillip. "What were they like?"

To this day I don't know how a face like his could look wistful, but it did. "They are the most beautiful things I've ever seen," he said, his voice chiming delicately. "I want to say they're transparent, but that's not exactly right. Their bodies are actually prisms, separating the rays of the sun and casting a hundred colors on the ground beneath them as they fly."

"They sound wonderful!" said Julia, her face more alive than I'd seen it in months.

"They swarm by the tens of thousands. It's as if a miles-long kaleidoscope has taken wing, and the ever-changing colors cover an area the size of a small city."

"How fascinating!" she said enthusiastically. "What do they eat?"

A shrug. "No one knows."

"No one?"

"There are only about forty men and women on the planet, and none of us has yet climbed the crystal mountains where they nest."

"Crystal mountains!" she repeated. "What a pretty picture!"

"It's not a world like any you have ever imagined, Julia," he said. "There are plants and animals no one's ever even dreamed of."

"Plants?" she asked. "How different can a plant be?"

"I saw some potted plants in your living room, right by that old piano that's probably still out of tune," he said. "Do you ever talk to them?"

"Of course," said Julia. She flashed him a smile. "But they never answer."

He returned her smile. "*Mine* do."

She clutched his hand with both of hers, as if she was afraid he might leave before telling her about his plants.

"What do they say?" she asked. "I'll bet they talk about the weather."

He shook his head. "Mostly they talk about mathematics, and once in a while about philosophy."

"I knew about those things once," she said, and then added hazily: "I think."

"They have no sense of self-preservation, so they're not concerned with rain or fertilizer," continued Phillip. "They don't care if they're eaten or not. They use their intelligence to solve abstract problems, because to them *all* problems are abstract."

I couldn't help but speak up. "They really exist?"

"They really exist."

"What do they look like?"

"Not like any plant on Earth. Most of them have translucent flowers, and almost all of them have rigid protrusions, like, I don't know, tiny branches that rub together. That's how they communicate."

"So you speak in chimes and they speak in little clicks?" asked Julia. "How do you understand each other?"

"The first few men to study them spent half a century learning the meanings behind their clicking and rubbing. Now we both speak to my computer, and it translates each of our languages into the other's."

"What do you say to a plant?" I asked.

"Not much," he admitted. "They're very different. But after you speak to them for any length of time, you know why Men fight so hard to stay alive. Nothing *matters* to them. They accomplish nothing and they care about nothing, not even their mathematics. They have no hopes, no dreams, and no goals." He paused. "But they *are* unique."

"I'd—" I began, and then stopped. I'd been about to say I'd like to see one of those plants, but I didn't want him to think he'd said anything of interest to me.

Just then Julia reached for her cup, but either her vision wasn't working right or her hand was shaking—they both fail a lot these days, her eyes *and* her hands—and it began tottering, about to spill over. Phillip moved his fingers so fast my eyes couldn't follow it, and he righted the cup before three drops had fallen to the tray.

"Thank you, young man," she said.

"You're welcome." He glanced at me, and his expression said: *Whatever you think of what I've become,* that's *something I couldn't have done twelve years ago,*

There was a momentary silence. Then Julia spoke up again. "Is it Halloween?"

"Not for a while yet."

"Oh, that's right! You wore your costume on some other world. Tell me more about the animals."

"Some of them are beautiful, some of them are huge and awesome, some are petite and delicate, and all of them are different from anything you've ever seen or even imagined."

"Do they have...?" she frowned. "I can't remember the word."

"Take your time," he said, holding her hand in one of his and patting it gently with the other to comfort her. "I've got all night."

"I can't remember," she said, close to tears. Her whole body tensed as she reached for a word that might forever elude her. "Big," she said at last. "It was big."

"A big word?" he asked.

"No," she said, shaking her head. "*Big!*"

He looked puzzled. "Do you mean dinosaurs?"

"*Yes!*" she shouted, an expression of relief on her face as the missing word finally appeared.

"We don't have dinosaurs," he said. "They're unique to Earth. But we have animals that are bigger than the biggest dinosaur that ever lived. One of them is so big, so huge, that he has no natural predators—and because nothing can hurt him, and he has no reason to hide, he glows in the dark."

"All night long?" she asked with a giggle. "Can't he turn off the glow so he can sleep?"

"He doesn't have to," said Phillip as if speaking to a child, which in a way she was. "Since he's glowed all his life it doesn't bother him or keep him awake."

"What color is he?" asked Julia.

"When he's hungry, he glows a deep red. When he's angry, he's blue." Finally he smiled. "And when he wants to attract a ladyfriend, he becomes the brightest yellow you ever saw, and pulsates like crazy, almost like a 50-foot-high flashbulb going off every other second."

"Oh, I wish I could see him!" said Julia. "It must be a wonderful place, this world you live on!"

"*I* think so." He looked over at me. "Not everybody does."

"I would give everything I have to go there."

"It doesn't take *quite* everything," said Phillip, and I tried to imagine the tone of voice he'd have used if he had still been human. "Just most things."

She stared at him curiously. "Were you born there?"

"No, Julia, I wasn't," he said and somehow his face seemed to reflect an infinite sadness as he used her proper name. "I was born right here, in this house."

"It must have been before we moved here," she said, dismissing the notion with a shrug of her narrow shoulders. "But if you were born here, why are you wearing a Halloween costume?"

"This is what people look like where I live."

"It must be one of the suburbs," she said with conviction. "I don't remember seeing anyone like you at the supermarket or the doctor's."

"It's a *very* distant suburb," he said.

"I thought so," said Julia. "And your name is…?"

"Phillip," he said, and for the second time that night I saw a shining tear roll down his cheek.

"Phillip," she repeated. "Phillip. That's a very nice name."

"I'm glad you like it."

"I'm sure I knew a Phillip once." Suddenly she yawned. "I'm getting a little tired."

"Would you like me to leave?" he asked solicitously.

"Could I ask you a favor?"

"Anything."

"My father used to tell me a bedtime story when I went to sleep," said Julia. "Would *you* tell me a fairy tale?"

"You've never asked *me* for one," I blurted out.

"You don't know any," she replied.

I had to admit she was right.

"I'll be happy to," said Phillip. "Shall we lower the light a little—just in case you fall asleep?"

She nodded, spread her pillows out, and lay her head back on one of them.

He reached for the lamp in the wall above the nightstand—the only thing I'd added to the room since he'd left. When he couldn't find a switch, he remembered that it worked by voice command and ordered it to dim itself. Then, in the same room where she had told him a fairy tale almost every night, he told one to her.

"Once there was a young man," he began.

"No," said Julia. He stopped and looked at her curiously. "If this is a fairy tale, he has to be a prince."

"You're right, of course. Once there was a prince,"

She nodded her approval. "That's better." Then: "What was his name?"

"What do *you* think his name was?"

"Prince Phillip," said Julia.

"You're absolutely right," he replied. "Once there was a prince named Phillip. He was a very well-behaved young man, and tried always to do the bidding of the King and Queen. He studied chivalry and jousting and any number of princely things—but when his classes were done and his weapons were polished and put away and he'd finished his dinner, he would go to his room and read about fabulous places like Oz and Wonderland. He knew that such places couldn't exist, but he wished they could, and every time he found a book or a holo about a new one he would read it or watch it, and wish that somehow, someday *he* could visit such places."

"I know just how he felt!" said Julia with a happy smile on the wrinkled face that I still loved. "Wouldn't it be wonderful to walk along the yellow brick road with the Scarecrow and the Tin Man, or to have a conversation with the Cheshire Cat, or visit the Walrus and the Carpenter?"

"That's what Prince Phillip thought too," he agreed. He leaned forward dramatically. "And then one day he made a wonderful discovery."

She sat up and clapped her hands together in her excitement. "He learned how to get to Oz!"

"Not Oz, but an even more wonderful place."

She leaned back, suddenly tired from her efforts. "I'm very glad! Is that the end?"

He shook his head. "No, it isn't. Because you see, nobody in this place looked like the Prince or his parents. He couldn't understand the people who lived there and they couldn't understand him. And they were afraid of anyone who looked and sounded different."

"Most people are," she said sleepily, her eyes closed. "Did *he* wear a Halloween costume too?"

247

"Yes," said Phillip. "But it was a very special costume."

"Oh?" she said, opening her eyes again. "How?"

"Once he put it on, he could never take it off again," explained Phillip.

"A magic costume!" she exclaimed.

"Yes, but it meant that he could never be the King of his parents' country, and his father the King was very, very angry at him. But he knew he would never have another chance to visit such a wondrous kingdom again, so he donned the costume and he left his palace and went to live in the magical kingdom."

"Was the costume uncomfortable to put on?" she asked, her voice very briefly more alert than it had been.

"Very," he answered, which was something I'd never thought about before. "But he never complained because he never doubted that it was worth it. And he went to this mystical land, and he saw a thousand strange and beautiful things. Every day there was a new wonder, every night a new vision."

"And he lived happily ever after?" asked Julia.

"So far."

"And did he marry a beautiful princess?"

"Not yet," said Phillip. "But he has hopes."

"I think that's a beautiful fairy tale," she said.

"Thank you, Julia."

"You can call me Mother," she said, her voice sharp and cogent. "You were right to go." She turned to me, and somehow I could tell it was the old Julia, the *real* Julia, looking at me. "And *you* had better make your peace with our son."

And as quickly as she said it, the old Julia vanished as she did so often these days, and she was once again the Julia I'd grown used to for the past year. She lay back on the pillow, and looked at our son once more.

"I've forgotten your name," she said apologetically.

"Phillip."

"Phillip," she repeated. "What a nice name." A pause. "Is it Halloween?"

Before he could answer she was asleep. He leaned over and kissed her on the cheek with his misshapen lips, then stood up and walked to the door.

"I'll leave now," he said as I followed him out of her room.

248

"Not yet," I said.

He stared at me expectantly.

"Come on into the kitchen," I said.

He followed me down the shabby hallway, and when we got there I pulled out a couple of beers, popped them open, and poured two glasses.

"Did it hurt that much?" I asked.

He shrugged. "It's over and done with."

"There really are crystal mountains?"

He nodded.

"And flowers that talk?"

"Yes."

"Come into the living room with me," I said, heading out of the kitchen. When we got there I sat in an easy chair and gestured for him to sit down on the sofa.

"What is this about?" he asked.

"Was it really that special?" I asked. "That much of an honor?"

"There were more than six thousand candidates for the position," he said. "I beat them all."

"It must have cost them a pretty penny to make you what you are."

"More than you can imagine."

I took a sip of my beer. "Let's talk."

"We've talked about Mother," he replied. "All that's left is the Pythons, and I haven't kept up with them."

"There's more."

"Oh?"

"Tell me about Wonderland," I said.

He stayed for three days, slept in the long-unused guest room, and then he had to go back. He invited me to come visit him, and I promised I would. But of course I can't leave Julia, and by the time she's gone I'll probably be a little too old and a little too infirm, and it's a long, grueling, expensive trip.

But it's comforting to know that if I ever *do* find a way to get there, I'll be greeted by a loving son who can show his old man around the place and point out all the sights to him.

STAR LIGHT, STAR BRIGHT

_____Robert J. Sawyer_____

"DADDY. WHAT ARE THOSE?" my young son, Dalt, was pointing up. We'd floated far away from the ancient buildings, almost to where the transparent dome over our community touches the surface of the great sphere.

Four white hens were flying across the sky, their little wings propelling them at a good clip. "Those are chickens, Dalt. You know— the birds we get eggs from."

"Not the *chickens*," said Dalt, as if I'd offended him greatly by suggesting he didn't know what they were. "Those lights. Those points of light."

I squinted a bit. "I don't see any lights," I replied. "Where are they?"

"Everywhere," he said. He swung his head in an arc, taking in the whole sky. "Everywhere."

"How many points do you see?"

"Hundreds. Thousands."

I felt my back bumping gently against the surface; I pushed off with my palm, rising into the air again. The ancient texts I'd been translating said human beings were never really meant to live in such low gravity, but it was all I, and countless generations of my ancestors, had ever known. "There aren't any points of light, Dalt."

"Yes, there are," he insisted. "There are thousands of them, and—look!—there's a band of light across the sky there."

I faced in the direction he was pointing. "I don't see anything except another chicken."

"No, Daddy," insisted Dalt. "Look!"

Dalt was a good boy. He almost never lied to me—and I couldn't see why he would lie to me about something like this. I maneuvered so that we were hovering face to face, then extended my hand.

"Can you see my hand clearly?" I said.

"Sure."

"How many fingers am I holding up?"

He rolled his eyes. "Oh, Daddy..."

"How many fingers am I holding up?"

"Two."

"And do you see lights on them, as well?"

"On your fingers?" asked Dalt incredulously.

I nodded.

"Of course not."

"You don't see any lights in front of my fingers? Do you see any on my face?"

"Daddy!"

"Do you?"

"Of course not. The lights aren't down here. They're up there!"

I touched my boy's shoulder reassuringly. "Tomorrow, we'll go see Doc Tadders about your eyes."

We hadn't built the protective dome—the clear blister on the outer surface of the *Dyson* sphere (to use the ancient name our ancestors had given to our home, a term we could transliterate but not translate). Rather, the dome was already here when we'd come outside. Adjacent to it was a large, black pyramidal structure that didn't seem to be part of the sphere's outer hull; instead, it appeared to be clamped into place. No one was exactly sure what the pyramid was for, although you could enter it from an access tube extending from the dome. The pyramid was filled with corridors and rooms, and lots of control consoles marked in the script of the ancients.

The transparent dome was much larger than the pyramid—plenty big enough to cover the thirty-odd buildings the ancients had built here, as well as the concentric circles of farming fields we'd created by importing soil from within the interior of the Dyson sphere. Still, if the dome hadn't been transparent, I probably would have felt claustrophobic within it; it wasn't even a pimple on the vastness of the sphere.

We'd been fortunate that the ancients had constructed all these buildings under the protective dome; they served as homes and work spaces for us. In many cases, we could only guess at the original purposes of the buildings, but the one that housed Dr. Tadders' office had likely been a warehouse.

After sleeptime, I took Dalt to see Tadders. He seemed more fascinated by the wall diagram the doctor had of a human skeleton than he was by her eye chart, but we'd finally got him to spin around in midair to face it.

I was floating freely beside my son. For an instant, I found myself panicking because there was no anchor rope looped around my wrist; the habits of a lifetime were hard to break, even after being here, on the outside of the Dyson sphere, for all this time. I'd lived from birth to middle age on the inside of the sphere, where things tended to float up if they weren't anchored. Of course, you couldn't drift all the way up to the sun. You'd eventually bump against the glass roof that held the atmosphere in. But no one wanted to be stuck up there, waiting to be rescued; it was humiliating.

Out here, though, under our clear, protective dome, things floated *down*, not up; both Dalt and I would eventually settle to the padded floor.

"Can you read the top row of letters?" asked Doc Tadders, indicating the eye chart. She was about my age, with pale blue eyes and red hair just beginning to turn gray.

"Sure," said Dalt. "Eet, bot, doo, shuh, kee."

Tadders nodded. "What about the next row?"

"Hih, fah, roo, shuh, puh, ess."

"Can you read the last row?"

"Ayt, doo, tee, nuh, tee, ess, guh, hih, fah, roo."

"Are you sure about the second letter?"

"It's a doo, no?" said Dalt.

If there's any letter my son should know, it should be that one, since it was the first in his own name. But the character on the chart wasn't a doo; it was a fah.

Dr. Tadders jotted a note in the book she was holding, then said, "What about the last letter?"

"That's a roo."

"Are you sure?"

Dalt squinted. "Well, if it's not a roo, then it's an shuh, no?"

"Which do you think it is?"

"A shuh…or a roo." Dalt shrugged. "It's so tiny, I can't be sure."

I could see that it was a roo; I was surprised that I had better vision than my son did.

"Thanks," said Tadders. She looked at me. "He's a tiny bit nearsighted," she said. "Nothing to worry about." She faced Dalt again. "What about the lights in front of your eyes? Do you see any of them now?"

"No," said Dalt.

"None at all?"

"You can only see them in the dark," he said.

Tadders pushed against the padded wall with her palm, which was enough to send her drifting across the room toward the light switch; the ancients had made switches that were little rockers, instead of the click-in/click-out buttons we build. She rocked the switch, and the lighting strips at the edges of the padded roof went dark. "What about now?"

Dalt sounded puzzled. "No."

"Let's give your eyes a few moments to adjust," she said.

"It won't make any difference," said Dalt, exasperated. "You can only see the lights outside."

"Outside?" repeated Tadders.

"That's right," said Dalt. "Outside. In the dark. Up in the sky."

Dalt was the first child born after our group left the interior of the Dyson sphere. Our little town had a population of 240 now, of which fifteen had been born since we'd come outside. Dalt's usual playmate was Suzto, the daughter of the couple who lived next door to my wife and me in a building that had clearly been designed by the ancients to be living quarters.

All adults spent half their days working on their particular area of expertise, which, for me, was translating ancient documents stored in the computers inside the buildings and the pyramid, and the other half doing the chores that were needed to support a fledgling society. But after work, I took Dalt and Suzto for a float. We drifted away from the lights of the ancient buildings, across the fields of crops, and out toward the access tunnel that led to the pyramid.

I knew that the surface of the sphere, beneath us, was curved, of course, and, here on the outside, that it curved down. But the sphere was so huge that everything seemed flat. Oh, one could make out the indentations that were hills on the other side of the sphere's shell, and the raised plateaus that water collected in. Although we *were* on the frontier—the outside of the sphere!—we were still only one bodylength away from the world we'd left behind; that's how thick the sphere's shell was. But the double-doored portal that led back inside had been sealed off; the people on the interior had welded it shut after we'd left. They wanted nothing to do with whatever we might find out here, calling our quest for knowledge of the exterior universe a sacrilege against the wisdom of the ancients.

As we floated in the darkness, Dalt looked up again and said, "See! The lights!"

Suzto looked up, too. I expected her to scrunch her face in puzzlement, baffled by Dalt's words, but instead, near as I could make out in the darkness, she was smiling in wonder.

"Can—can you see the lights, too?" I asked Suzto.

"Sure."

I was astonished. "How big are they?"

"Tiny. Like this." She held up her hand, but if there was any space between her finger and thumb, I couldn't make it out.

"Are they arranged in some sort of pattern?"

Suzto's vocabulary wasn't yet as big as Dalt's. She looked at me, and I tried again. "Do they make shapes?"

"Maybe," said Suzto. "Some are brighter than others. There are three over there that make a straight line."

I frowned. "Dalt, please cover your eyes."

He did so, with elaborate hand gestures.

"Suzto, point to the brightest light in the sky."

"There're so many," she said.

"All right, all right. Point to the brightest one in this part of the sky over here."

She didn't hesitate. "That one."

"Okay," I said, "now put your hand down, please."

She drew her arm back in toward her body.

"Dalt, uncover your eyes."

He did so.

"Now, Dalt, point to the brightest light in this part of the sky over here."

He lifted his arm, then seemed to vacillate for a moment between two possible choices.

"Not that one, silly," said Suzto's voice. She pointed. "This one's brighter."

"Oh, yeah," said Dalt. "I guess it is." He pointed at it, too. I couldn't see anything, but it seemed in the darkness that if I could draw lines from the two children's outstretched fingers, they would converge at infinity.

Dr. Tadders was an old friend, and with both Suzto and Dalt seeing the lights, I decided to join her for lunch. We grew wheat, corn, and other crops under lamps here on the outside of the sphere, and raised chickens and pigs. If you wanted the eggs to hatch, you had to put low roofs over the hens, because they needed to be in constant contact with their clutches, and their own body movements were enough to propel them into flight; chickens really seemed to love flying. Tadders and I both knew that we'd have had more interesting meals if we'd stayed inside the sphere, but the ancient texts said that although the interior was huge, there was still much, much more to the universe.

Most of those on the interior didn't care about such things; they knew that the sphere's inner surface could accommodate over a million trillion human beings—a vastly larger number than the current population—and that our ancestors had shut us off from the rest of the universe for a reason. But some of us had decided to venture outside, starting a new settlement on our world's only real frontier. I didn't miss much about the inside—but I did miss the food.

"All right, Rodal," Dr. Tadders said, gesturing with a sandwich triangle, "here's what I think is happening." She took a deep breath, as if reviewing her thoughts once more before giving them voice, then: "We know that a long, long time ago, our ancestors built a double-walled shell around our sun. The outer wall is opaque, and the inner wall, fifty bodylengths above that, is transparent. The area between the two walls is the habitat, where all those who still live on the interior of the sphere reside."

I nodded, and kicked gently off the floor to keep myself afloat. We drifted out of the dining hall, heading outdoors.

"Well," she continued, "we also know that there was a war generations ago that knocked humanity back into a primitive state. We've been rebuilding our civilization for a long time, but we're nowhere near as advanced as our ancestors who constructed our world were."

That was certainly true. "So?"

"So, what about that story you translated a while ago? The one about where we supposedly came from?"

I'd found a story in the ancient computers that claimed that before we lived on the interior of the Dyson sphere, our ancestors had made their home on the outer surface of a small, solid, rocky globe. "But that was probably just a myth," I said. "I mean, such a globe would have been impossibly tiny. The myth said the homeworld was six million bodylengths in diameter. Kobost"—a physicist in our community—"worked out that if it were made of the elements the myth described, even a globe that small would have had a crushingly huge gravitational attraction: five bodylengths per heartbeat squared. That's more than ten thousand times what we experience here."

Of course, the gravitational attraction on any point on the interior of a hollow sphere is zero. When we lived inside the sphere, the only gravity we felt was the pull from our sun, gently tugging things upward. Here, on the outside of the sphere, the gravitational pull is downward, toward the sphere's surface—and the sun at its center.

I continued. "Although Kobost thinks human muscle could perhaps be built up enough to withstand such an overwhelming gravity, his own studies prove that the globe described in the myth can't be our homeworld."

"Why not?" asked Tadders.

"Because of the chickens. There are several ancient texts that show that chickens have been essentially the same since before our ancestors built the Dyson sphere. But with an acceleration due to gravity of five bodylengths per heartbeat squared, their wings wouldn't be strong enough to let them fly. So that globe in the myth couldn't possibly have been our ancestral home."

"Well, I agree that's puzzling about the chickens," said Tadders, "but wherever our ancestors came from, you have to admit it wasn't another Dyson sphere. And the inside of a Dyson sphere forms a very special kind of sky. Remember what it was like when we lived in there? Wherever you looked over your head, you saw—well, you saw the sun, of course, if you looked directly overhead. But everywhere else, you saw other parts of the sphere. Some of those parts are a long, long way off—the far side of the sphere is a hundred and fifty billion bodylengths away, isn't it? But, regardless, wherever you looked, you saw either the sun or the surface of the sphere."

"So?"

"So the surface of the sphere is reflective—even the dull, grass-covered parts reflect back a lot of light. Indeed, on average the surface reflects back about a third of the light it receives from the sun, making the whole sky glaringly bright."

People in there did have a tendency to float facing the ground instead of the sky. I nodded for her to go on.

"Well, our eyes didn't evolve here," continued Tadders. "If we did come from a rocky world, the sun would have been seen against an empty, non-reflective sky. It must be much, much brighter inside the Dyson sphere than it ever was on the original homeworld."

"Surely our eyes would have adapted to deal with the brighter light here."

"How?" asked Tadders. "Even after the great war, we regained a measure of civilization fairly quickly. There was no period during which we were reduced to survival of the fittest. Human beings haven't undergone any appreciable evolution since long before our ancestors built the sphere. Which means our eyes are as they originally were: suited for much dimmer light. Of course, the ancients may have had drugs or other things that made the interior light seem more comfortable to them, but whatever they used must have been lost in the war."

"I suppose," I said.

"But you, me, and everyone else in our settlement who has lived inside the sphere—we've damaged our retinas, without even knowing it."

I saw what she was getting at. "But the children—the children born here, on the outside of the sphere—"

She nodded. "The children born here, after we left the interior, have never been exposed to the brightness inside, and so they see just as well in the dark as our distant, distant ancestors did, back on the homeworld. The points of light the children are seeing really do exist, but they're simply too faint to register on the damaged retinas we adults have."

My head was swimming. "Maybe," I said. "Maybe. But—but what *are* those lights?"

Tadders pursed her lips, then lifted her shoulders a bit. "You want my best guess? I think they're other suns, like the one our ancestors encased in the sphere, but so incredibly far away that they're all but invisible." She looked up, out the clear roof of the dome covering our town, out at the uniform blackness, which was all either of us could make out. She then used one of the words I'd taught her, a word transliterated from the ancient texts—a word we could pronounce but whose meaning we'd never really understood. "I think," she said, "that the points of light are *stars*."

There were thousands of documents stored in the ancient computers; my job was to try to make sense of as many of them as I could. And I made much progress as Dalt continued to grow up. Eventually, he and the other children were able to match the patterns of stars they could see in the sky to those depicted in ancient charts I'd found. The patterns didn't correspond exactly; the stars had apparently drifted in relation to each other since the charts had been made. But the kids—the adolescents, now—were indeed able to discern the *constellations* shown in the old texts; ironically, this was easier to do, they said, when some of the lights of our frontier town were left on, drowning out all but the brightest stars.

According to the charts, our sun—the sun enclosed in the Dyson sphere—was the star the ancients had called Tau Ceti. It was not the original home to humanity, though; our ancestors were apparently unwilling to cannibalize the worlds of their own system to make their Dyson sphere. Instead, they—we—had come from another star, the closest similar one that wasn't part of a multiple system, a sun our ancestors had called Sol.

And the *planet*—that was the term—we had evolved on was, in the infinite humility of our wise ancestors, called by a simple, unassuming name, one I could easily translate: Dirt.

Old folks like me couldn't live on Dirt now, of course. Our muscles—including our hearts—were weak compared to what our ancestors must have had, growing up under the stupendous gravity of that tiny, rocky world.

But—

But locked in our genes, as if for safekeeping, were all the potentials we'd ever had as a species. The ability to see dim sources of light, and—

Yes, it must be there, too, still preserved in our DNA.

The ability to produce muscles strong enough to withstand much, much higher gravity.

You'd have to grow up under such a gravity, have to live with it from birth, said Dr. Tadders, to really be comfortable with it, but if you did—

I'd seen Kobost's computer animation showing how we might have moved under a much greater gravity, how we might have deployed our bodies vertically, how our spines would have supported the weight of our heads, how our legs might have worked back and forth, hinging at knee and ankle, producing sustained forward locomotion. It all seemed so bizarre, and so inefficient compared to spending most of one's life floating, but—

But there were new worlds to explore, and old ones, too, and to fully experience them would require being able to stand on their surfaces.

Dalt was growing up to be a fine young man. There wasn't a lot of choice for careers in a small community: he could have apprenticed with his mother, Delar, who worked as our banker, or with me. He chose me, and so I did my best to teach him how to read the ancient texts.

"I've finished translating that file you gave me," he said on one occasion. "It was what you suspected: just a boring list of supplies." I guess he saw that I was only half-listening to him. "What's got you so intrigued?" he asked.

I looked up, and smiled at his face, with its bits of fuzz; I'd have to teach him how to shave soon. "Sorry," I said. "I've found some documents related to the pyramid. But there are several words I haven't encountered before."

"Such as?"

"Such as this one," I said, pointing at a string of eight letters on the computer screen. "'*Starship*.' The first part is obviously the word for those lights you can see in the sky: *stars*. And the second part, *hip*, well—"I slapped my haunch—"that's their name for where the leg joins the torso. They often made compounded words in this fashion, but I can't for the life of me figure out what a 'stars hip' might be."

I always say nothing is better than a fresh set of eyes. "Yes, they often used that hissing sound for plurals," said Dalt. "But those two letters there—can't they also be transliterated jointly as shuh, instead of separately as ess and hih?"

I nodded.

"So maybe it's not 'stars hip,'" he said. "Maybe it's 'star ship.'"

"*Ship*," I repeated. "Ship, ship, ship—I've seen that word before." I riffled through a collection of papers, searching my notes; the sheets fluttered around the room, and Dalt dutifully began collecting them for me. "Ship!" I exclaimed. "Here it is: 'a kind of vehicle that could float on water.'"

"Why would you want to float on water when you can float on air?" asked Dalt.

"On the homeworld," I said, "water didn't splash up in great clouds every time you touched it. It stayed in place." I frowned. "Star ship. Star-ship. A—a vehicle of stars?" And then I got it. "No," I said, grabbing my son's arm in excitement. "No—a vehicle for traveling to the stars!"

Dalt and Suzto eventually married, to no one's surprise.

But I *was* surprised by my son's arms. He and Suzto had been exercising for ages now, and when Dalt bent his arm at the elbow, the upper part of it *bulged*. Doc Tadders said she'd never seen anything like it, but assured us it wasn't a tumor. It was *meat*. It was muscle.

Dalt's legs were also much, much thicker than mine. Suzto hadn't bulked up quite as much, but she, too, had developed great strength.

I knew what they were up to, of course. I admired them both for it, but I had one profound regret.

Suzto had gotten pregnant shortly after she and Dalt had married—at least, they told me that the conception had occurred after the wedding, and, as a parent, it's my prerogative to believe them. But I'd never know for sure. And *that* was my great regret: I'd never get to see my own grandchild.

Dalt and Suzto would be able to *stand* on Dirt, and, indeed, would be able to endure the journey there. The starship was designed to accelerate at a rate of five bodylengths per heartbeat squared, simulating Dirt's gravity. It would accelerate for half its journey, reaching a phenomenal speed by so doing, then it would turn around and decelerate for the other half.

They were the logical choices to go. Dalt knew the ancient language as well as I did now; if there were any records left behind by our ancestors on the homeworld, he should be able to read them.

He and Suzto had to leave soon, said Doc Tadders; it would be best for the child if it developed under the fake gravity of the starship's acceleration. Dalt and Suzto would be able to survive on Dirt, but their child should actually be comfortable there.

My wife and I came to see them off, of course—as did everyone else in our settlement. We wondered what people in the sphere would make of it when the pyramid lifted off—it would do so with a kick that would doubtless be detectable on the other side of the shell.

"I'll miss you, son," I said to Dalt. Tears were welling in my eyes. I hugged him, and he hugged me back, so much harder than I could manage.

"And, Suzto," I said, moving to my daughter-in-law, while my wife moved to hug our son. "I'll miss you, too." I hugged her, as well. "I love you both."

"We love you, too," Suzto said.

And they entered the pyramid.

I was hovering over a field, harvesting radishes. It was tricky work; if you pulled too hard, you'd get the radish out, all right, but then you and it would go sailing up into the air.

"Rodal! Rodal!"

I looked in the direction of the voice. It was old Doc Tadders, hurtling toward me, a white-haired projectile. At her age, she should be more careful—she could break her bones slamming into even a padded wall at that speed.

"Rodal!"

"Yes?"

"Come! Come quickly! A message has been received from Dirt!"

I kicked off the ground, sailing toward the communication station next to the access tube that used to lead to the starship. Tadders managed to turn around without killing herself and she flew there alongside me.

A sizable crowd had already gathered by the time we arrived.

"What does the message say?" I asked the person closest to the computer monitor.

He looked at me in irritation; the ancient computer had displayed the text, naturally enough, in the ancient script, and few besides me could understand that. He moved aside and I consulted the screen, reading aloud for the benefit of everyone.

"It says, 'Greetings! We have arrived safely at Dirt.'"

The crowd broke into cheers and applause. I couldn't help reading ahead a bit while waiting for them to quiet down, so I was already misty-eyed when I continued. "It goes on to say, 'Tell Rodal and Delar that they have a grandson; we've named him Madar.'"

My wife had passed on some time ago—but she would have been delighted at the choice of Madar; that had been her father's name.

"'Dirt is beautiful, full of plants and huge bodies of water,'" I read. "'And there are other human beings living here. It seems those people interested in technology moved to the Dyson sphere, but a small group who preferred a pastoral lifestyle stayed on the homeworld. We're mastering their language—it's deviated a fair bit from the one in the ancient texts—and are already great friends with them.'"

"Amazing," said Doc Tadders.

I smiled at her, wiped my eyes, then went on: "'We will send much more information later, but we can clear up at least one enduring mystery right now.'" I smiled as I read the next part. "'Chickens can't fly here. Apparently, just because you have wings doesn't mean you were meant to fly.'"

That was the end of the message. I looked up at the dark sky, wishing I could make out Sol, or any star. "And just because you don't have wings," I said, thinking of my son and his wife and my grandchild, far, far away, "doesn't mean you weren't."

ABOUT THE AUTHORS

Brenda Cooper writes science fiction and fantasy novels and short stories. Her most recent novel is *Edge of Dark*, from Pyr and her most recent story collection is *Cracking the Sky* from Fairwood Press. *Spear of Light* is forthcoming from Pyr in 2016. Brenda is a technology professional and a futurist, and publishes non-fiction on the environment and the future. Her non-fiction has appeared on *Slate* and *Crosscut* and her short fiction has appeared in *Nature Magazine*, among other venues.

Brenda lives in the Pacific Northwest in a household with three people, three dogs, far more than three computers, and only one TV in it.

http://brenda-cooper.com

Nancy Fulda is a Phobos Award winner, a Jim Baen Memorial Award recipient, and a 2012 Hugo and Nebula nominee. During her graduate work at Brigham Young University she studied artificial intelligence, machine learning, and quantum computing. In the years since, she has grappled with the far more complex process of raising three small children. All these experiences sometimes infiltrate her writing.

http://nancyfulda.com/

Ken Liu is an author and translator of speculative fiction, as well as a lawyer and programmer. A winner of the Nebula, Hugo, and World

Fantasy awards, he has been published in *The Magazine of Fantasy & Science Fiction, Asimov's, Analog, Clarkesworld, Lightspeed*, and *Strange Horizons*, among other places.

Ken's debut novel, *The Grace of Kings* (2015), is a Nebula nominee and the first volume in a silkpunk epic fantasy series, *The Dandelion Dynasty*. He also released a collection of short fiction, *The Paper Menagerie and Other Stories* (2016). He lives with his family near Boston, Massachusetts.

In addition to his original fiction, Ken is also the translator of numerous literary and genre works from Chinese to English. His translation of *The Three-Body Problem*, by Liu Cixin, won the Hugo Award for Best Novel in 2015, the first translated novel ever to receive that honor.

http://kenliu.name

Angus McIntyre grew up in London and lives in New York, where he makes his living as a software developer. He likes to believe that his degree in Artificial Intelligence will somehow keep him on the good side of our electronic masters when the inevitable robot revolution comes. His short fiction has appeared in *Black Candies*, the *Mission: Tomorrow* anthology, and on the BoingBoing website. He is a graduate of the 2013 Clarion UCSD writer's workshop.

http://angus.pw/

Jody Lynn Nye lists her main career activity as "spoiling cats." She lives near Chicago with her current cat, Jeremy, and her husband, Bill. She has published more than 45 books, including collaborations with Anne McCaffrey and Robert Asprin, and over 140 short stories. Her latest books are *Rhythm of the Imperium* (Baen), and *Wishing On a Star* (Arc Manor).

http://jodynye.net/

Cat Rambo lives, writes, and teaches atop a hill in the Pacific Northwest. Her 200+ fiction publications include stories in *Asimov's*, *Clarkesworld Magazine*, and *The Magazine of Fantasy and Science Fiction*. She is a Compton Crook, Endeavour, Nebula, and World

Fantasy Award nominee. Her 2016 works include *Hearts of Tabat* (novel), *Neither Here Nor Here* (collection), *Altered America: Steampunk Stories* (collection), and the updated edition of *Creating an Online Presence for Writers* (nonfiction). She is the current President of the Science Fiction and Fantasy Writers of America. It is her real name. For more about Cat, as well as links to her fiction and information about her online classes, visit her website.
http://kittywumpus.net

Mike Resnick is, according to *Locus*, the all-time leading award winner, living or dead, for short science fiction. He is the winner of five Hugos (from a record thirty-seven nominations), a Nebula, and other major awards in the USA, France, Japan, Croatia, Catalonia, Poland and Spain. He is the author of seventy-five novels, almost 300 stories, and three screenplays, and has edited forty-two anthologies. He currently edits *Galaxy's Edge* magazine and the Stellar Guild series.
http://mikeresnick.com

Robert J. Sawyer has won the best-novel Hugo Award (for *Hominids*), and has twelve other Hugo nominations to his credit. He's also won the best-novel Nebula Award (for *The Terminal Experiment*), the John W. Campbell Memorial Award (for *Mindscan*), and the Audio Publishers Association's Audie Award for Best Science Fiction or Fantasy Audiobook of the Year (for *Calculating God*), plus Spain's *Premio UPC de Ciencia Ficción* (at 6,000 euro, the world's largest ongoing science-fiction prize; Rob has won it a record-setting three times), Canada's Aurora (a record-setting fourteen times), Japan's best-foreign-novel Seiun Award (three times), China's Galaxy Award, *Analog* magazine's AnLab, the Hal Clement Memorial Award, and NESFA's Edward E. Smith Memorial Award ("the Skylark"). In 2014, he was one of the initial nine inductees into the Canadian Science Fiction and Fantasy Hall of Fame. His 23 novels include *Starplex, Rollback, Wake, Triggers, Red Planet Blues*, and the just published *Quantum Night*. The ABC TV series *FlashForward* was based on his novel of the same name, and Rob—a member of both the Writers Guild of America and the Writers Guild of Canada—was one of the scriptwriters for that series.

His work has hit #1 on the Amazon.com, Amazon.co.uk, Amazon.ca, Audible, and Locus science-fiction bestsellers' lists. Rob holds two honorary doctorates and has published in both the world's top scientific journals, *Science* (guest editorial) and *Nature* (fiction). He lives just outside Toronto.

http://sfwriter.com

Kenneth Schneyer was a finalist for both the Nebula and Sturgeon Awards in 2014. His stories, which often employ odd voicing, appear in *Lightspeed, Strange Horizons, Analog, Beneath Ceaseless Skies*, the *Clockwork Phoenix* series, *Daily Science Fiction*, all three Escape Artists podcasts, and elsewhere. A proud member of the Clarion class of 2009, he now works with both Codex Writers and the Cambridge Science Fiction Workshop. At one time or another, Ken has been an actor, a dishwasher, a corporate lawyer, an assistant dean, a clerk-typist, and an IT project manager; nowadays he teaches legal studies and science fiction literature at Johnson & Wales University, where he also runs the speaker series. He's interested in astronomy, feminist theory, presidential history, and practically everything else, and he cooks better than you do.

Born in Michigan, he now lives in Rhode Island with one singer, one dancer, one actor, and something with fangs.

http://ken-schneyer.livejournal.com/

Martin L. Shoemaker is a programmer who writes on the side…or maybe it's the other way around. Programming pays the bills, but a second place story in the Jim Baen Memorial Writing Contest earned him lunch with Buzz Aldrin. Programming never did that!

His short story "Today I Am Paul" (from *Clarkesworld* #107) has been nominated for a Nebula award, has been selected for four Year's Best anthologies, and will be translated into seven languages in 2016. His work has also appeared in *Analog, Galaxy's Edge, Digital Science Fiction*, and *Writers of the Future Volume 31*. His novella "Murder on the Aldrin Express" was reprinted in *Year's Best Science Fiction Thirty-First Annual Collection* and in *Year's Top Short SF Novels 4*.

http://martinlshoemaker.com/

Robert Silverberg has been a professional science-fiction writer since 1955. He has won many Hugo and Nebula awards and among his best-known books are *Lord Valentine's Castle, Dying Inside* and *Nightwings*. In 2004 he was named a Grand Master by the Science Fiction Writers of America.
http://robert-silverberg.com/

John Varley is a three time Hugo Award winner and a two time Nebula award winner. He is an author of thirteen novels and counting. Many of his novels and short stories (including the story in this book) take place in the Eight Worlds setting. His latest novel, *Dark Lightning* (part of the Thunder and Lightning series) was published by Ace Books in 2014.
http://varley.net

David Walton is a native of Pennsylvania and recipient of the 2008 Philip K. Dick Award for his first novel, *Terminal Mind*. His latest books, *Superposition* and *Supersymmerty*, are quantum physics murder mysteries with the same mind-bending feel as films like Inception and Minority Report. He is also the author of *Quintessence*, a science fantasy in which the Earth really is flat, and its sequel, *Quintessence Sky*. He lives near Philadelphia with his wife and seven children.
http://davidwaltonfiction.com/

Caroline M. Yoachim lives in Seattle and loves cold cloudy weather. She is the author of dozens of short stories, appearing in *Fantasy & Science Fiction, Clarkesworld, Asimov's*, and *Lightspeed*, among other places. Her debut short story collection, *Seven Wonders of a Once and Future World & Other Stories*, is coming out with Fairwood Press in 2016.
http://carolineyoachim.com

Alvaro Zinos-Amaro is co-author, with Robert Silverberg, of *When the Blue Shift Comes*, and *Traveler of Worlds: Conversations with Robert Silverberg*. Alvaro's fiction, Rhysling-nominated poetry, and non-fiction have appeared in markets like *Asimov's, Analog, Apex, Clarkesworld, Nature, Strange Horizons, Galaxy's Edge, Lackington's, The Los Angeles Review of Books* and anthologies such as *The Mammoth Book of the Adventures of Moriarty, The Mammoth Book of Jack the Ripper Stories, This Way to the End Times* and *The Year's Best Science Fiction and Fantasy 2016.*

http://myaineko.blogspot.com/

ABOUT THE EDITOR

Alex Shvartsman is a writer, anthologist, translator, and game designer from Brooklyn, NY. He's the winner of the 2014 WSFA Small Press Award for Short Fiction and a finalist for the 2015 Canopus Award for Excellence in Interstellar Writing.

His short stories have appeared in *Nature, Intergalactic Medicine Show, Daily Science Fiction, Galaxy's Edge,* and a variety of other magazines and anthologies. His collection, *Explaining Cthulhu to Grandma and Other Stories,* and his steampunk humor novella *H. G. Wells, Secret Agent* were published in 2015.

In addition to the UFO series, he has edited the *Funny Science Fiction, Funny Fantasy, Coffee: 14 Caffeinated Tales of the Fantastic* and *Dark Expanse: Surviving the Collapse* anthologies.

http://alexshvartsman.com

www.ingramcontent.com/pod-product-compliance
Lightning Source LLC
Chambersburg PA
CBHW031614240626
47153CB00002B/755